THE HUNGER

CHARLES BEAUMONT was born Charles Leroy Nutt in Chicago in 1929. He dropped out of high school in the tenth grade and worked at a number of jobs before selling his first story to *Amazing Stories* in 1950. In 1954 his "Black Country" became the first work of short fiction to appear in *Playboy*, and his classic tale "The Crooked Man" was featured in the same magazine the following year. Beaumont published numerous other short stories in the 1950s, both in mainstream periodicals like *Playboy* and *Esquire* and in science fiction and fantasy magazines.

His first story collection, *The Hunger and Other Stories*, was published in 1957 to immediate acclaim and was followed by two further collections, *Yonder* (1958) and *Night Ride and Other Journeys* (1960). He also published two novels, *Run from the Hunter* (1957, pseudonymously, with John E. Tomerlin), and *The Intruder* (1959).

Beaumont is perhaps best remembered for his work in television, particularly his screenplays for *The Twilight Zone*, for which he wrote several of the most famous episodes. His other screenwriting credits include the scripts for films such as *The Premature Burial* (1962), *Burn, Witch, Burn* (1962), *The Haunted Palace* (1963), and *The Masque of the Red Death* (1964).

When Beaumont was 34, he began to suffer from ill health and developed a baffling and still unexplained condition that caused him to age at a greatly increased rate, such that at the time of his death at age 38 in 1967, he had the physical appearance of a 95-year-old man. Beaumont was survived by his wife Helen, two daughters, and two sons, one of whom, Christopher, is also a writer.

Beaumont's work was much respected by his colleagues, and he counted Ray Bradbury, Harlan Ellison, Richard Matheson, Robert Bloch, and Roger Corman among his friends and admirers. His work is in the process of being rediscovered with three new editions recently appearing from Centipede Press and this new edition of *The Hunger* from Valancourt Books.

BERNICE M. MURPHY is Lecturer in Popular Literature at Trinity College Dublin. She is the author of *The Suburban Gothic in American Popular Culture* (Palgrave Macmillan, 2009), the editor of *Shirley Jackson: Essays on the Literary Legacy* (McFarland, 2005), and co-founder of the *Irish Journal of Gothic and Horror Studies*, which she edited from 2006 to 2012.

THE HUNGER
and other stories

by

CHARLES BEAUMONT

with a new introduction by
Bernice M. Murphy

VALANCOURT BOOKS
Kansas City, Missouri
2013

The Hunger and Other Stories by Charles Beaumont
First published New York: G. P. Putnam's Sons, 1957
First Valancourt Books edition 2013

Published by Valancourt Books, Kansas City, Missouri
Publisher & Editor: JAMES D. JENKINS
20th Century Series Editor: SIMON STERN, University of Toronto
http://www.valancourtbooks.com

Library of Congress Cataloging-in-Publication Data

Beaumont, Charles, 1929-1967.
[Short stories. Selections]
The hunger and other stories / by Charles Beaumont, with a new
introduction by Bernice M. Murphy. – First Valancourt Books edition.
pages cm
ISBN 978-1-939140-42-5 (*acid free paper*)
I. Murphy, Bernice M. II. Title.
PS3552.E2316H86 2013
813'.54–dc23
2013009349

Cover by Trent Roach
Set in Dante MT 11/13.5

INTRODUCTION

CHARLES BEAUMONT (1929-1967) is one of the most important American horror writers of the 1950s, and yet his reputation has long been unfairly overshadowed by that of contemporaries such as Shirley Jackson, Richard Matheson, Ray Bradbury, and Robert Bloch. Part of the reason why he has often been neglected is because Beaumont died tragically young (at the age of 38) having contracted a rare form of early-onset Alzheimer's that blighted the final years of his life. However, despite the relatively short duration of his writing career, he published dozens of short stories, two novels, *Run from the Hunter* (1957) and *The Intruder* (1959), and wrote numerous screenplays that were produced for television (many of them were adaptations of his own stories for *The Twilight Zone*). He was also a film screenwriter whose credits included *Burn, Witch, Burn* (1962), *The Premature Burial* (1962) and *The Masque of the Red Death* (1964). Had he lived, Beaumont would most likely have had as productive and high-profile a career as Richard Matheson, with whom his own professional trajectory had much in common.

As it is, while Beaumont's name is certainly held in high esteem by genre aficionados, his fiction has yet to receive the academic attention it richly deserves. It is to be hoped that this reprint of his first collection, *The Hunger and Other Stories* (1957) helps to remedy this state of affairs. As the stories contained in this volume demonstrate, Beaumont is often a more accomplished prose stylist than either Matheson or Bloch, capable of lyrical, impressionistic turns of phrase that inspire in the reader both melancholy and terror. Consider, for instance, this extract from the collection's chilling title story:

> Now, with the sun almost gone, the sky looked wounded—as if a gigantic razor had been drawn across it, slicing deep. It bled richly. And the wind, which came down from High Mountain, cool as

rain, sounded a little like children crying: a soft unhappy kind of sound, rising and falling.

Or the intriguing opening of his eerie paean to jazz, "Black Country":

Spoof Collins blew his brains out all right—right on out through the top of his head. But I don't mean with a gun—I mean with a horn. Every night, slow and easy, eight to one. And that's how he died. Climbing with that horn, climbing up high.

Or this evocation of the obsessive joy felt by a little boy who is obsessed with train travel:

"Listen, Neely! Listen, to the big sharp wind now, how it screams all around you! And see into the night, into the million fear-filled shadows, the cold and lifeless night. Feel the strong iron wheels bump and pound, carrying you through it all. And most important—he went to the railing and put his small hands around the metal—most important, Neely, let it come true. Let it come true!" ("The Train")

Yet as some of the tales contained in *The Hunger and Other Stories* amply illustrate, Beaumont was also capable of sketching scenes of nauseating horror, as in "Open House," which begins as a henpecked husband (a butcher by trade) surveys the crime scene moments after he has murdered his wife:

Mr. Pierce rose and looked at the bathtub. At the water that was not water any longer, but, instead, bright red ink, burning red against the glistening white porcelain sides. At the pale things floating in the bright red water, the pale soft things, floating, drifting, turning, like pieces of lamb in a simmering stew.

It is typical of Beaumont that he should make it clear that Pierce has dismembered his wife, without directly saying so, and that his description of the bathtub captures the sense of shocked detachment being experienced by the murderer, who has transformed his victim into nothing more than meat to be disposed of (an extra element of disgust strikes the reader when we are told that Pierce plans to parcel out his wife to customers at his shop). Beaumont always knows exactly which information to provide to the reader, and what to withhold, in order to create maximum disquiet.

This facility for quickly and carefully establishing deeply disturbing scenarios can also be seen in one of his best-known stories, "Miss Gentilbelle," which, with its depiction of monstrous motherhood and gender confusion, anticipates Bloch's *Psycho* by several years. As in several of the stories contained in this collection, the innocence of a vulnerable youngster (in this case a boy named Robert who is being raised as a girl by his insane mother) is corrupted by the adults around him. Miss Gentilbelle uses little Robert's love of animals against him:

> The parakeet screamed for a considerable time before Miss Gentilbelle pressed the life from it. When it was silent, at last, the white fingers that clutched it were stained with a dark, thin fluid. Miss Gentilbelle put down the butcher knife, and took Robert's hand.
>
> "Here is Margaret," she said. "Take her. Yes. Now: Shall we mend Margaret?"
>
> Robert did not answer.
>
> "Shall we put her together again, glue back her pretty little wing?"
>
> "No, Mother. Nothing can be mended."
>
> "Very good. Perhaps you will learn." Miss Gentilbelle smiled. "Now take the bird and throw it in the stove."

A recurrent theme in these stories is that of the powerful hold that fantasy can have over the imagination of the disturbed, alienated, or lonely individual. In "Miss Gentilbelle," the title character has become so detached from reality that she punishes her child for his very existence by making him act in every respect like her idealized version of a little girl. Ultimately, although the boy's father attempts to save him from this nightmarish existence, help comes too late. After enduring one final act of cruelty, the boy gives in to the vivid and violent delusions that have been plaguing him, and kills his monstrous tormentor, in the process losing whatever remains of himself.

Miss Maple, the deeply repressed protagonist of "The Dark Music," believes that fantasy has no place in her life, and yet finds herself caught up in a lurid sexual relationship with a mythological creature that may or may not be real. Sexual and romantic frustration also finds an unlikely outlet in "Fair Lady," in which an elderly spinster becomes completely besotted with a bus driver with whom she has only ever exchanged a few words. Unbeknownst to the unlikely object of her affections, Miss Elouise finds a deep fulfillment in their entirely one-sided "relationship": "No wife in bed with her husband had ever known one tenth this intimacy; no youngsters in the country under August stars had ever come near to the romance that was hers; nor had ever a woman known such felicity, unspoken, so richly there." Though the awareness that she is in fact deeply deluded flitters around the edges of her consciousness, she prefers the consolations of fantasy to the loneliness of a life lived without love.

As Beaumont appears to suggest in "Fair Lady," there are times therefore when fantasy can ultimately be a positive outlet for the lonely individual. This is certainly true in the charming story "The Vanishing American," which is as evocative a portrait of alienated white collar masculinity as anything found in Matheson or John Cheever. Mr. Minchell, a disenchanted middle-aged office clerk in a "cheap sharkskin suit" suddenly realizes that he is deeply unhappy. As his sense of personal crisis mounts, even the crowds on the street take on a deeply sinister aspect: "They all had furtive appearances, it seemed to him suddenly, even the children, as if each was fleeing from some hideous crime."

Minchell's crisis manifests itself in a very literal way: he finds that no one—not his co-workers, not his wife and children, can see him—even the mirror refuses to reflect his image. Whereas in "Open House" this kind of alienation results in murder, here, a much more benign resolution is reached. Mr. Minchell happens upon a magnificent stone lion at the entrance to the public library and rediscovers the imaginative impulses and sense of playfulness he had reluctantly left behind in childhood. Upon sitting on the lion and being cheered on by an appreciative crowd, he suddenly "reappears": "Mr. Minchell grinned. Somehow, he realized, in some mysterious way he had been given a second chance. And this time he knew what to do with it."

In stories such as "Fair Lady" and "The Vanishing American" the 1950s writer whom Beaumont most resembles is Shirley Jackson, whose work shares with his a recurrent fascination with the devastating effects of loneliness and the empowering and yet dangerous allure of fantasy. As in Jackson's oeuvre, there is also a recurrent sense that his protagonists have drifted into acute unhappiness without realizing quite how this state of affairs came to be.

One of the most characteristic preoccupations of 1950s horror fiction was the post-World War II awareness that the evils perpetrated by human beings themselves were much more terrifying than horrors perpetrated by any of the traditional bogeymen. The result was a trend towards more realistic, and psychologically based, horror fiction rooted in the mundane and the everyday. Though the supernatural is certainly alluded to in *The Hunger and Other Stories* (as in "Tears of the Madonna," "The Black Country," "Free Dirt," and "The Dark Music") *overt* supernaturalism doesn't really feature all that often. The terror here most often comes from the wrongs perpetrated by individuals who believe that their own grievances and twisted mindsets given them the right to inflict pain and suffering upon others, as in "Miss Gentilbelle," "Open House," "A Point of Honor," and "Nursery Rhyme."

A nice twist on this premise comes in "The Murderers," which, like many of Beaumont's tales, opens with a memorable line: "The pale young man in the bright red vest leaned back, sucked reflectively at a Russian candy pellet—the kind with real Jamaican rum inside—and said, yawning, 'Let's kill somebody tonight.'" In "The Murderers," a Leopold-and-Loeb style duo of young men decide to prove their superiority, inviting a homeless man, "Mr. Fogarty," to their apartment and killing him. However, their victim proves more much canny than they have anticipated, and they wake up the next day to find that he has robbed the apartment of all of its priceless paintings, as well as "Mother's silver."

"Free Dirt" and "The Infernal Bouillabaisse" also feature protagonists whose self-absorption rebounds upon them in a fiendishly ironic fashion. "Free Dirt" is an effective and grimly humorous Suburban Gothic tale in which the "heroically miserly" and greedy protagonist "Mr. Aorta" (names often suggest much in Beaumont) decides to fertilize his vegetable garden with dirt stolen from the local cemetery. In a dénouement that evokes the morbid wit of E.C. horror comics such as *Tales from the Crypt*, the glutton is found dead at the dinner table, his stomach packed with "many pounds of dirt."

The protagonist of the "The Infernal Bouillabaisse," a member of an exclusive gourmet dining club, becomes so fixated upon discovering the secret recipe behind the delicious dish mentioned in the title that he murders the rival who refuses to give it to him. The pretension and self-absorption of both men is perfectly anticipated by the story's opening lines: "I like to think of our stomachs," Mr. Frenchaboy said, in conclusion, "as small but select museums, to which a new treasure should be added at least once a day."

The relationship between what society deems "normal" and what is considered "abnormal" is another common theme of 1950s horror fiction and is an obvious response to what was often perceived to be the restrictive conformity and intense focus upon conventional domesticity that characterized the post-war era. Beaumont's fiction often draws upon the violent ruptures that occur when these pressures become too much to cope with. Marriage and family life do not bring happiness for any of the men depicted in the stories featured here: instead, as is vividly evoked in "Open House" and "The Vanishing American," the transformation into husband and father necessitates letting go of the dreams and fancies of youth.

His most striking critique of the decade's culture of conformity comes in "The Crooked Man," which is set in a dystopian society in which homosexuality has become compulsory, and heterosexuality is strictly prohibited. The story exhibits a characteristic sympathy for society's outsiders (the male protagonist, who has fallen in love with a woman, tries to persuade her that, "We're not the unnatural ones, no matter what they say"), but by the end of the story, the forces of repressive authority have triumphed, and the story's "deviant" hero has been arrested and carted off for "treatment." "It'll make a new man of you," one of the leering police officers smugly predicts. Whilst the rather simple inversion of existing societal taboo could perhaps be seen today as a little pat, the story is nevertheless a daring and ambitious one, and like his melancholy tale "Last Night the Rain" (another story of misfits who briefly find solace in each other's company) further illustrates Beaumont's strong interest in those who have, either by dint of their sexuality, their sensitivity, or their insanity, been excluded from "mainstream" society.

Those reading this collection may also notice, however, that Beaumont's stories often display a problematic attitude towards female sexuality and physicality. During "Open House," we are told that the henpecked murderer Mr. Pierce married a pretty Southern Belle, but ended up bound for life to "a fat, candy-eating, movie-magazine-reading dirty-bathrobe-wearing *wife* with a million nauseating habits." Mr. Minchell's unhappiness in "The Vanishing American" similarly has much to do with a controlling wife who is notable for her "vicious, unending complaints."

Beaumont's often negative depiction of female characters can most notably be found in the four stories here about repressed, sexually frustrated, and deluded spinsters—"Miss Gentilbelle," "Fair Lady," "The Dark Music," and "The Hunger." "Fair Lady" admittedly presents its protagonist as a fairly benign (if obsessive) character, but whilst the wives here are nagging harridans, unmarried women are, at best, to be pitied, and, at worst, are depicted as actively horrific, as in "Miss Gentilbelle." In both "The Hunger" and "Dark Music," for instance, repressed sexual urges drive frustrated women in their late thirties to engage in dangerous and self-destructive behavior.

Miss Maple, the protagonist of "The Dark Music," is a 37-year-old teacher of biology so repulsed by the thought of anything to do with reproduction or sexuality that she even refuses to teach classes in Sex Education. She also engages in blackmail in order to safeguard her position. Miss Maple regards sexual knowledge as an affront to "goodness" and "innocence" and sees herself as a heroic defender of "traditional" values. As she gazes upon a patch of the countryside that appears never to have been sullied by a human presence, we are told that she views herself in similar terms: "She believed in purity, and had her own definition of the word." Nevertheless, as her name suggests, Miss Maple cannot deny nature forever: ". . . she fought her body and her face every morning, but she was not victorious. In spite of it all, and to her eternal dismay, she was still an attractive woman."

After being seduced by the sound of pan pipes, Miss Maple is irresistibly drawn to a secluded glade where she engages in sexual activity with a goat-like man-beast that is most likely Pan himself. Despite the fact that she finds herself returning to the forest, night after night, she still hypocritically upholds the rigidly conservative and damaging "moral" viewpoints that had characterized her behavior up to that point. She has, we are told, "developed the facility of detachment to a fine degree." By the end of the story, however, she will pay a high price indeed for her hypocrisy.

The title story in the collection, "The Hunger," has a much more sympathetic protagonist, but again, we have here an unmarried woman whose state is actively equated with loneliness and sexual repression. Julia Landon, 38 years old, lives with her two older sisters (also unmarried) in a small town which is gripped by fear because a murderer is targeting local women. Julia, who is profoundly lonely, and feels that all chance of romantic and sexual fulfillment has passed her by already, becomes increasingly fixated upon the murderer, to the extent that her obsessive fixation increasingly comes to resemble his own violent impulses. She empathizes with what she perceives to be his need for human contact: "You want love so badly you must kill for it." Eventually, in a plot development that anticipates the premise of Muriel Spark's equally chilling 1970 novella *The Driver's Seat*, Julia actively seeks out the killer: "I've been looking for you. Every night, I've thought of you." (Protagonists who actively seek our death also feature in "The Customers," which evokes Ray Bradbury at his finest).

Beaumont's female characters are therefore seen as even more restricted by society and circumstance (as well as by individual circumstances) as the men in his stories. The fact that his unmarried women are all, to a lesser or greater extent, deluded fantasists, suggests that they have been gravely affected by their exclusion from the sphere of the nuclear family, and that Beaumont himself may have internalized his era's belief that such women will never find true fulfillment or happiness. Miss Gentilbelle is, in her own way, merely an even more disturbed version of Miss Maple: a twisted psychotic who is the epitome of the suffocating mother figure contemporary commentators such as Philip Wylie, author of *A Generation of Vipers* (1942), identified as a threat to the future of the very nation itself.

Whilst there are definitely therefore some obvious recurring themes and preoccupations to be found here, however, one of the things that remains impressive about *The Hunger and Other Stories* is the evidence it provides of Beaumont's range. We find here grimly humorous "biter bit" stories such as "Free Dirt" and "The Infernal Bouillabaisse," tales of empowering whimsy such as "The Vanishing American," and impressionistic attempts to evoke African-American and Hispanic culture in "Black Country" and "Tears of the Madonna" respectively, as well as tales of out-right horror such as "Miss Gentilbelle." Beaumont was a talented prose stylist whose stories, at their finest, effectively evoke terror, unease, and pity in equal measure. As such, a critical reappraisal of his literary legacy is long overdue: let us hope that it starts here.

BERNICE M. MURPHY
Dublin

April 19, 2013

THE HUNGER AND OTHER STORIES

FOR HELEN

CONTENTS

MISS GENTILBELLE

ROBERT settled on his favorite branch of the old elm and watched Miss Gentilbelle. The night was very black, but he was not afraid, although he was young enough to be afraid. And he was old enough to hate, but he didn't hate. He merely watched.

Miss Gentilbelle sat straight and stiff in the faded chair by the window. The phonograph had been turned down and she sat, listening. In her hands were a teacup, faintly flowered, and a saucer that did not match. She held them with great care and delicacy and the tea had long ago turned cold.

Robert decided to watch Miss Gentilbelle's hands.

They were thin and delicate, like the cup and saucer. But he saw that they were also wrinkled and not smooth like his own. One of the fingers was encircled by a tarnished yellow band and the skin was very, very white.

Now the phonograph began to repeat toward the end of the record and Miss Gentilbelle let it go for a while before she moved.

When she rose, Robert became frightened and cried loudly. He had forgotten how to climb down from the tree. Miss Gentilbelle heard him crying and after she had replaced the record in its album she went to the window and raised it halfway to the top.

"Roberta," she said, "I'm surprised. Quite surprised." She paused. "Trees are for monkeys and birds, not little girls. Do you remember when I told you that?"

The soft bayou wind took Miss Gentilbelle's words and carried them off. But Robert knew what had been said.

"Yes, Mother. Trees are for monkeys and birds."

"Very well. Come down from there. I wish to speak with you."

"Yes, Mother." Robert remembered. Cautiously at first, and then with greater daring, he grasped small limbs with his hands

5

and descended to the ground. Before the last jump a jagged piece of bark caught on his gown and ripped a long hole in the gauzy cloth.

The jump hurt his feet but he ran up the splintery steps fast because he had recognized the look in Miss Gentilbelle's eyes. When he got to the living room, he tried nervously to hold the torn patch of cloth together.

He knocked.

"Come in, Roberta." The pale woman beckoned, gestured. "Sit over there, please, in the big chair." Her eyes were expressionless, without color, like clots of mucus. She folded her hands. "I see that you have ruined your best gown," she whispered. "A pity: it once belonged to your grandmother. You should have been in bed, asleep, but instead you were climbing trees and that is why you ruined your gown. It's made of silk—did you know that, Roberta? Pure silk. Soft and fragile, like the wings of a dove; not of the coarse burlap they're using nowadays. Such a pity. . . . It can never be replaced." She was quiet for a time; then she leaned forward. "Tell me, Roberta—what did you promise when I gave you the gown?"

Robert hesitated. There were no words to come. He stared at the frayed Oriental rug and listened to his heart.

"Roberta, don't you think you ought to answer me? What did you promise?"

"That—" Robert's voice was mechanical. "That I would take good care of it."

"And have you taken good care of it?"

"No, Mother, I . . . haven't."

"Indeed you have not. You have been a wicked girl."

Robert bit flesh away from the inside of his mouth. "Can't it be mended?" he asked.

Miss Gentilbelle put a finely woven handkerchief to her mouth and gasped. "Mended! Shall I take it to a tailor and have him sew a patch?" Her eyes came to life, flashing. "When a butterfly has lost its wings, what happens?"

"It can't fly."

"True. It cannot fly. It is dead, it is no longer a butterfly.

Roberta—there are few things that can ever be mended. None of the really worthwhile things can be." She sat thoughtfully silent for several minutes, sipping her cold tea.

Robert waited. His bladder began to ache.

"You have been an exceedingly wicked girl, Roberta, and you must be punished. Do you know how I shall punish you?"

Robert looked up and saw his mother's face. "Shall you beat me?"

"Beat you? Really, do I seem so crude? When have I ever beaten you? No. What are a few little bruises? They disappear and are forgotten. You must be taught a lesson. You must be taught never to play tricks again."

The hot night air went through the great house and into his body, but when Miss Gentilbelle took his hand in hers, he felt cold. Her fingers seemed suddenly to be made of iron. They hurt his hand.

Then, in silence, the two walked from the living room, down the vast dark hall, past the many dirty doorways and, finally, into the kitchen.

"Now, Roberta," Miss Gentilbelle said, "run up to your room and bring Margaret to me. Instantly."

He had stopped crying: now he felt ill. Robert knew what his mother was going to do.

He reached up and clutched her arm. "But—"

"I shall count up to thirty-five."

Robert ran out of the room and up the stairs, counting quickly to himself. When he entered his bedroom he went to the small cage and took it from the high shelf. He shook it. The parakeet inside fluttered white and green wings, moved its head in tiny machine movements.

Twenty seconds had passed.

Robert inserted his finger through the slender bars, touched the parakeet's hard bill. "I'm sorry, Margaret," he said. "I'm sorry." He put his face up close to the cage and allowed the bird to nip gently at his nose.

Then he shook the confusion from his head, and ran back downstairs.

Miss Gentilbelle was waiting. In her right hand was a large butcher knife. "Give Margaret to me," she said.

Robert gave the cage to his mother.

"Why do you force me to do these things, child?" asked Miss Gentilbelle.

She took the parakeet from its cage and watched the bird struggle.

Robert's heart beat very fast and he couldn't move; but, he did not hate, yet.

Miss Gentilbelle held the parakeet in her left hand so that one wing was free. The only sound was the frantic fluttering of this wing.

She put the blade of the knife up close to the joint of the wing.

Robert tried not to look. He managed to stare away from Margaret's eyes; his gaze held on his mother's hands.

She held the knife stationary, frozen, touching the feathers.

Why didn't she do it! Get it over with! It was like the time she had killed Edna, holding the knife above the puppy's belly until—

"And now, when you wish you had your little friend, perhaps you will think twice before you climb trees."

There was a quick movement, a glint of silver, an unearthly series of small sounds.

The wing fluttered to the floor.

"Margaret!"

The parakeet screamed for a considerable time before Miss Gentilbelle pressed the life from it. When it was silent, at last, the white fingers that clutched it were stained with a dark, thin fluid.

Miss Gentilbelle put down the butcher knife, and took Robert's hand.

"Here is Margaret," she said. "Take her. Yes. Now: Shall we mend Margaret?"

Robert did not answer.

"Shall we put her together again, glue back her pretty little wing?"

"No, Mother. Nothing can be mended."

"Very good. Perhaps you will learn." Miss Gentilbelle smiled. "Now take the bird and throw it into the stove."

Robert held the dead parakeet gently in his hands, and secretly stroked its back. Then he dropped it into the ashes.

"Take off your gown and put it in, also."

As Robert drew off the thin blue nightgown, he looked directly into his mother's eyes.

"Something you would like to say to me, Roberta?"

"No, Mother."

"Excellent. Put in some papers and light them. And when you've finished that, get a rag from the broom closet and wipe the floor. Then put the rag into the stove."

"Yes, Mother."

"Roberta."

"Yes?"

"Do you understand why Margaret was killed?"

This time he wanted to say no, he did not understand. Not at all. There was such confusion in his head.

"Yes, Mother. I understand."

"And will you climb trees any more when you ought to be in bed?"

"No. I won't climb any more trees."

"I think that is true. Good night, Roberta. You may go to your room, afterwards."

"Good night, Mother."

Miss Gentilbelle walked to the sink and carefully washed her hands. She then returned to the living room and put a record on the phonograph.

When Robert went upstairs, she smiled at him.

He lay still in the bed. The swamp wind was slamming shutters and creaking boards throughout the house, so he could not sleep. From a broken slat in his own shutter, moonlight shredded in upon the room, making of everything dark shadows.

He watched the moonlight and thought about the things he was beginning to know.

They frightened him. The books— The pictures of the people who looked like him and were called boys, and who looked like Miss Gentilbelle and were called girls, or ladies, or women. . . .

He rose from the bed, put his bathrobe about him, and walked to the door. It opened noiselessly, and when it did, he saw that the entire hallway was streaming with dark, cold light. The old Indian's head on the wall looked down at him with a plaster frown, and he could make out most of the stained photographs and wrinkled paintings.

It was so quiet, so quiet that he could hear the frogs and the crickets outside; and the moths, bumping and thrashing against the walls, the windows.

Softly he tiptoed down the long hall to the last doorway and then back again to his room. Perspiration began to form under his arms and between his legs, and he lay down once more.

But sleep would not come. Only the books, the knowledge, the confusion. Dancing. Burning.

Finally, his heart jabbing, loud, Robert rose and silently retraced his footsteps to the door.

He rapped, softly, and waited.

There was no answer.

He rapped again, somewhat harder than before; but only once.

He cupped his hands to his mouth and whispered into the keyhole: *"Drake!"*

Silence. He touched the doorknob. It turned.

He went into the room.

A large man was lying across a bulky, posterless bed. Robert could hear the heavy guttural breathing, and it made him feel good.

"Drake. Please wake up."

Robert continued to whisper. The large man moved, jerked, turned around. "Minnie?"

"No, Drake. It's me."

The man sat upright, shook his head violently, and pulled open a shutter. The room lit up.

"Do you know what will happen if she finds you here?"

Robert sat down on the bed, close to the man. "I couldn't sleep. I wanted to talk to you. She won't hear—"

"You shouldn't be here. You know what she'll say."

"Just a little while. Won't you talk a little while with me, like you used to?"

The man took a bottle from beneath the bed, filled a glass, drank half. "Look here," he said. "Your mother doesn't like us to be talking together. Don't you remember what she did last time? You wouldn't want that to happen again, would you?"

Robert smiled. "It won't. I don't have anything left for her to kill. She could only hit me now and she wouldn't hit you. She never hits you."

The man smiled, strangely.

"Drake."

"What?"

"Why doesn't she want me to talk to you?"

The man coughed. "It's a long story. Say I'm the gardener and she's the mistress of the house and you're her . . . daughter, and it isn't right that we should mix."

"But why?"

"Never mind."

"Tell me."

"Go back to bed, Bobbie. I'll see next week when your mother takes her trip into town."

"No, Drake, please talk a little more with me. Tell me about town; please tell me about town."

"You'll see some day—"

"Why do you always call me 'Bobbie'? Mother calls me Roberta. Is my name Bobbie?"

The man shrugged. "No. Your name is Roberta."

"Then why do you call me Bobbie? Mother says there is no such name."

The man said nothing, and his hand trembled more.

"Drake."

"Yes?"

"Drake, am I *really* a little girl?"

The man got up and walked over to the window. He opened the other shutter and stood for a long while staring into the night. When he turned around, Robert saw that his face was wet.

"Bobbie, what do you know about God?"

"Not very much. It is mentioned in the George Bernard Shaw book I am reading, but I don't understand."

"Well, God is who must help your mother now, Bobbie boy!"

Robert's fists tightened. He knew—he'd known it for a long time. A *boy* . . .

The man had fallen onto the bed. His hand reached for the bottle, but it was empty.

"It's good," the man said. "Ask your questions. But don't ask them of me. Go away now. Go back to your room!"

Robert wondered if his friend were ill, but he felt too strange to be with anyone. He opened the door and hurried back to his room.

And as he lay down, his brain hurt with the new thoughts. He had learned many wonderful things this night. He could almost identify the feeling that gnawed at the pit of his stomach whenever he thought of Miss Gentilbelle. . . .

Robert did not sleep before the first signs of dawn appeared. And then he dreamed of dead puppies and dead birds.

They were whispering something to him.

"Why, Roberta," said Miss Gentilbelle, in a soft, shocked voice. "You haven't worn your scent this morning. Did you forget it?"

"Yes."

"A pity. There's nothing like the essence of blossoms to put a touch of freshness about everything."

"I'm sorry."

"I should be displeased if you were to forget your scent again. It's not ladylike to go about smelling of your flesh."

"Yes, Mother."

Miss Gentilbelle munched her toast slowly and looked into Robert's flushed face.

"Roberta, do you feel quite well?"

"Yes."

Miss Gentilbelle put her hand to Robert's forehead. "You do seem somewhat feverish. I think we will dispense with today's lesson in Jeanne d'Arc. Immediately following your criticism on the Buxtehude you will go to bed."

The breakfast was finished in silence as Miss Gentilbelle read a book. Then they went into the living room.

Robert hated the music. It sounded in the faded room like the crunch of shoes on gravel, and the bass notes were all dissolved into an ugly roar.

They listened for one hour without speaking, and Robert moved only to change the records.

"Now, then, Roberta," Miss Gentilbelle said. "Would you agree with Mr. Locke that Buxtehude in these works surpasses the bulk of Bach's organ music?"

Robert shook his head. He knew he would have to answer. "I think Mr. Locke is right."

And then it struck him that he had actually lied before, many times. But perhaps he never knew before that he disliked music.

"Very good. No need to continue. The facts are self-evident. Go to your room now and undress. Dinner will be prepared at twelve-thirty."

Robert curtsied and began to walk to the stairway.

"Oh, Roberta."

"Yes, Mother?"

"Did you by any chance see Mr. Franklin last night?"

Robert's throat went dry. It was difficult to hold on to his thoughts. "No, Mother, I did not."

"You know you should never see that evil man, don't you? You must always avoid him, never speak a word to him. You remember when I told you that, don't you?"

"Yes, Mother."

"You disobeyed me once. You would never dream of doing that again, would you, Roberta?"

"No, Mother."

"Very good. Retire to your room and be dressed for dinner by twelve."

Robert went up the stairs slowly, for he could not see them. Tears welled in his eyes and burned them, and he thought he would never reach the top.

When he went into his room he saw Margaret for a moment and then she was gone.

He sat on the bed and proceeded to remove his clothes. They were dainty clothes, thin and worn, demanding of great care. He took them off lightly with a light touch and looked at each garment for a long time.

The patent leather shoes, the pink stockings, the pale yellow dress—he laid them neatly on the sofa and looked at them. Then, when all the clothes had been removed, he went to the mirror and looked into it.

Robert didn't know what he saw and he shook his head. Nothing seemed clear; one moment he felt like shouting and another, like going to sleep. Then he became frightened and leapt into the large easy chair, where he drew his legs and arms about him. He sat whimpering softly, with his eyes open, dreaming.

A little bird flew out of a corner and fluttered its wings at him. Margaret's wing, the one Miss Gentilbelle had cut off, fell from the ceiling into his lap and he held it to his face before it disappeared.

Presently the room was full of birds, all fluttering their wings and crying, crying to Robert. He cried, too, but softly.

He pulled his arms and legs closer to him and wrenched at the blond curls that fell across his eyes. The birds flew at him and around him and then their wings started to fall off. And as they did, the brown liquid he remembered soaked into all the feathers. Some of it got on Robert and when it did, he cried aloud and shut his eyes.

Then the room seemed empty. There were no birds. Just a puppy. A little dog with its belly laid open, crawling up to Robert in a wake of spilled entrails, looking into his eyes.

Robert fell to the floor and rolled over several times, his body quivering, flecks of saliva streaming from his lips.

"Edna, Edna, don't go away."

The puppy tried to walk further but could not. Its round low body twitched like Robert's, and it made snuffling noises.

Robert crawled to a corner.

"Edna, please. It wasn't me, it wasn't, really . . ."

And then a cloud of blackness covered Robert's mind, and he dropped his head on his breast.

When awakened he was in bed and Drake was standing over him, shaking his shoulders.

"Bobbie, what is it?"

"I don't know. All of a sudden I saw Margaret and Edna and all the birds. They were mad, Drake. They were mad!"

The man stroked Robert's forehead gently.

"It's all right. You don't have to be afraid now. You just had a bad nightmare, that's all. I found you laying on the floor."

"It seemed very real this time."

"I know. They sometimes do. Why, I could hear you crying all the way down the hall!"

"She didn't hear me, did she?"

"No, she didn't hear you."

Then Robert saw the heavy brown bag. "Drake, why have you got that suitcase?"

The man coughed and tried to kick the bag underneath the bed. "It's nothing. Just some equipment for the yard."

"No, no it isn't, Drake. I can tell. You're going away!"

"It's equipment for the yard, I tell you."

"Please don't go away, Drake. Please don't. Please don't."

The man tightened his fists and coughed again.

"Now you look, Bobbie. I've just got to go away for a little trip, and I'll be back before you know it. And maybe then we can go off somewhere together. I'm going to find out about it, but you mustn't say a word to your mother. Hear?"

Robert looked up, confused. Something fluttered. He could see it, from the corner of his eye.

The man was dirty and he smelled of alcohol, but it made Robert feel good when he touched him.

"Really? You mean *us*?"

"Bobbie. You've got to tell me something first. Do you love your mother?"

He didn't have to think about it. "No, she always kills things, and always hurts things. I don't love her."

The man spoke under his breath. "I've wanted to do this for a long time."

Something crawled in a corner. Robert could almost see it. "Drake," he said, "have you ever killed anything?"

Perspiration stood out on the man's forehead. He answered as if he had not heard.

"Only once, Bobbie. Only once did I kill."

"What was it? An animal?"

"No. It was worse, Bobbie. I killed a human spirit—a soul."

"Mother does it all the time!"

"I know. There's been a lot of death in this house. . . . But here now, lad, are you over your nightmare?"

Robert tried not to look up.

"Are we really going away when you get back? Away from Mother and this place, just you and me, Drake? Promise me?"

"Yes, boy. Yes, we are!"

The man took Robert's hand in his and held it hard.

"Now you see here. If she learns of this there'll be a lot of trouble. Something might go wrong. So, whatever you do, don't you let on to her what's happened. I'll see the authorities and tell them everything and you'll get out of here. And we'll be free, you and me, boy!"

Robert didn't say anything. He was looking at a corner.

"Bobbie, you're not old enough yet to know everything about your mother. She wasn't always like she is now. And I wasn't, either. Something just happened and . . . well, I'll tell you about it later so you'll understand. But right now, I want you to do something. After I leave, you get yourself another little pet, a frog or something. Keep it in this room. She'll know nothing's changed, then. She'll know you haven't been talking to me. Get that frog, Bobbie, and I'll be back so that you can have it always as a friend. Always.

"Goodbye, lad. You'll not be staying with that crazy woman much longer, I promise you."

Robert smiled and watched Drake go toward the door.

"Will you really come back, Drake?"

"Nothing on earth is going to stop me, son. I knew that when I saw you last night; I knew it when you asked me those questions. The first normal things I'd heard for . . . Yes, son, I'll be back for you."

Robert did not understand much. Only about the frog. He would find himself a pet and keep it.

The movement in the corners had stopped, and Robert could think for only a little while before he fell into a sound sleep. So sound a sleep that he did not hear Miss Gentilbelle coming up the stairs and he did not see her face when she stepped into the room.

"Roberta, you're late. You were told to be downstairs promptly at twelve thirty and instead I find you resting like a lady of great leisure. Get up, girl!"

Robert's eyes opened and he wanted to scream.

Then he apologized, remembering to mention nothing of Drake. He put on his dress quickly and went downstairs after Miss Gentilbelle.

He scarcely knew what he was eating; the food was tasteless in his mouth. But he remembered things and answered questions as he always had before.

During dessert Miss Gentilbelle folded her book and laid it aside.

"Mr. Franklin has gone away. Did you know that?"

"No, Mother, I did not. Where has he gone?"

"Not very far—he will be back. He's sure to come back; he always does. Roberta, did Mr. Franklin say anything to you before he left?"

"No, Mother, he did not. I didn't know Mr. Franklin had gone away."

Robert looked at Miss Gentilbelle's hands, watched the way the thin fingers curled about themselves, how they arched delicately in the air.

He looked at the yellow band and again at the fingers. Such white fingers, such dry, white fingers. . . .

"Mother."

"Yes?"

"May I go into the yard for a little while?"

"Yes. You have been naughty and kept me waiting dinner but I shall not punish you. See you remember the kindness and be in the living room in one half hour. You have your criticism to write."

"Yes, Mother."

Robert walked down the steps and into the yard. A soft breeze went through his hair and lifted the golden curls and billowed out his dress. The sun shone hotly but he did not notice. He walked to the first clump of trees and sat carefully on the grass. He waited.

And then, after a time, a plump frog hopped into the clearing and Robert quickly cupped his hands over it. The frog leapt about violently, bumping its body against Robert's palms, and then it was still.

Robert loosened the thin cloth belt around his waist and put the frog under his dress, so that it did not protrude noticeably.

Then he stroked its back from outside the dress. The frog did not squirm or resist.

Robert thought a while.

"I shall call you Drake," he said.

When Robert re-entered the kitchen he saw that Miss Gentilbelle was still reading. He excused himself and went up to his bedroom, softly, so that he would not be heard, and hid the frog in his dresser.

He began to feel odd then. Saliva was forming inside his mouth, boiling hot.

The corners of the room looked alive.

He went downstairs.

". . . and Jeanne d'Arc was burned at the stake, her body consumed by flames. And there was only the sound of the flames, and of crackling straw and wood: she did not cry out once." Miss Gentilbelle sighed. "There was punishment for you, Roberta. Do you profit from her story?"

Robert said yes, he had profited.

"So it is with life. The Maid of Orleans was innocent of any crime; she was filled with the greatest virtue and goodness, yet they murdered her. Her own people turned upon her and burnt the flesh away from her bones! Roberta—this is my question. What would *you* have done if you'd been Jeanne d'Arc and could have lived beyond the stake?"

"I—don't know."

"That," said Miss Gentilbelle, "is your misfortune. I must speak with you now. I've purposely put off this discussion so that you might think. But you've thought and remain bathed in your own iniquity. Child, did you honestly suspect that you could go babbling about the house with that drunken fool without my knowledge?"

Robert's heart froze; the hurting needles came.

"I listened to you, and heard a great deal of what was said. First, let us have an answer to a question. Do you think that you are a boy?"

Robert did not answer.

"You do." Miss Gentilbelle moved close. "Well, as it happens, you are not. Not in any sense of the word. For men are animals— do you understand? Tell me, are you an animal or a human being, Roberta?"

"A human being."

"Exactly! Then obviously you cannot be a boy, isn't that so? You are a girl, a young lady: never, never forget that. Do you hear?"

"Yes, Mother."

"That, however, is not the purpose of this discussion." Miss Gentilbelle calmed swiftly. "I am not disturbed that your mind plays tricks on you. No. What does disturb me is that you should lie and cheat so blatantly to your mother. You see, I heard your talking."

Robert's head throbbed uncontrollably. His temples seemed about to burst with pain.

"So—he has gone to get authorities to take you away from me! Because your mother is so cruel to you, so viciously cruel to the innocent young child! And you will both ride off on a white horse to wonderful lands where no one is mean. . . ." Her cheeks trembled. Her eyes seemed glazed. "Roberta, can you be so naïve? Mr. Franklin is *accustomed* to such promises: I know." She put a hand to her brow, moved thin fingers across the flesh. "At this moment," she said, distantly, "he is in a bar, drinking himself into a stupor. Or perhaps one of the Negro brothels—I understand he's a well-known figure there."

Miss Gentilbelle did not smile. Robert was confused: this was unlike her. He could catch just a little something in her eyes.

"And so you listened to him and loved him and you wait for him. I understand, Roberta; I understand very well indeed. You love the gardener and you will go away with him!" Something happened; her tone changed, abruptly. It was no longer soft and distant. "You must be punished. It ought to be enough when you finally realize that your Drake will never come back to carry you off. But—it is not enough. There must be more."

Robert heard very little now.

"Stop gazing off as if you didn't hear me. Now—bring your little friend here."

Robert felt the seed growing within him. He could feel it hard and growing inside his heart. And he couldn't think now.

Miss Gentilbelle took Robert's wrist in her hand and clutched it until her nails bit deep into the flesh. "I saw you put that animal in your dress and take it upstairs. Fetch it to me this instant."

Robert looked into his mother's eyes. Miss Gentilbelle stood above him, her hands clasped now to the frayed white collars of her dress. She was trembling and her words did not quite knit together.

"Get it, bring it to me, to me. Do you hear?"

Robert nodded dumbly, and went upstairs to his room. It was alive. Birds filled it, and puppies. Little puppies, crying, whimpering with pain.

He walked straight to the dresser and withdrew the frog, holding it securely in his hand.

Green and white wings brushed his face as he went back toward the door.

He walked downstairs and into the living room. Miss Gentilbelle was standing in the doorway; her eyes danced over the wriggling animal.

Robert said nothing as they walked into the kitchen.

"I am sure, Roberta, that when you see this—and when you see that no one ever comes to take you away—that the best thing is merely to be a good girl. It is enough. To be a good girl and do as Mother says."

She took the frog and held it tightly. She did not seem to notice that Robert's mouth was moist, that his eyes stared directly through her.

She did not seem to hear the birds and the puppies whispering to Robert, or see them clustering about him.

She held the frog in one hand, and with the other pulled a large knife from the knife-holder. It was rusted and without luster, but its edge was keen enough, and its point sharp.

"You must think about this, child. About how you forced your mother into punishing you." She smiled. "Tell me this: have you named your little friend?"

"Yes. His name is Drake."

"Drake! How very appropriate!"

Miss Gentilbelle did not look at her son. She put the frog on the table and turned it over on its back. The creature thrashed violently.

Then she put the point of the knife on the frog's belly, paused, waited, and pushed inwards. The frog twitched as she held it and drew the blade slowly across, slowly, deep inside the animal.

In a while, when it had quieted, she dropped the frog into a box of kindling.

She did not see Robert pick up the knife and hold it in his hand.

Robert had stopped thinking. Snowy flecks of saliva dotted his face, and his eyes had no life to them. He listened to his friends. The puppies, crawling about his feet, yipping painfully. The birds, dropping their bloody wings, flying crazily about his head, screaming, calling. And now the frogs, hopping, croaking. . . .

He did not think. He listened.

"Yes . . . yes."

Miss Gentilbelle turned quickly, and her laughter died as she did so. She threw her hands out and cried—but the knife was already sliding through her pale dress, and through her pale flesh.

The birds screeched and the puppies howled and the frogs croaked. Yes, yes, yes, yes!

And the knife came out and went in again, it came out and went in again.

Then Robert slipped on the wet floor and fell. He rolled over and over, crying softly, and laughing, and making other sounds.

Miss Gentilbelle said nothing. Her thin white fingers were

curled about the handle of the butcher knife, but she no longer tried to pull it from her stomach.

Presently her wracked breathing stopped.

Robert rolled into a corner, and drew his legs and arms about him, tight.

He held the dead frog to his face and whispered to it. . . .

The large red-faced man walked heavily through the cypressed land. He skillfully avoided bushes and pits and came, finally, to the clearing that was the entrance to the great house.

He walked to the wrought-iron gate that joined to the high brick wall that was topped with broken glass and curved spikes.

He opened the gate, crossed the yard, and went up the decaying, splintered steps.

He applied a key to the old oak door.

"Minnie!" he called. "Got a little news for you! Hey, Minnie!"

The silent stairs answered him.

He went into the living room, upstairs to Robert's room.

"Minnie!"

He walked back to the hallway. An uncertain grin covered his face. "They're not going to let you keep him! How's that? How do you like it?"

The warm bayou wind sighed through the shutters.

The man made fists with his fingers, paused, walked down the hall, and opened the kitchen door.

The sickly odor went to his nostrils first. The words "Jesus God" formed on his lips, but he made no sound.

He stood very still, for a long time.

The blood on Miss Gentilbelle's face had dried, but on her hands and where it had gathered on the floor, it was still moist.

Her fingers were stiff around the knife.

The man's eyes traveled to the far corner. Robert was huddled there, chanting softly—flat, dead, singsong words.

". . . wicked . . . must be punished . . . wicked girl . . ."

Robert threw his head back and smiled up at the ceiling.

The man walked to the corner and lifted Robert to his chest and held him tightly, crushingly.

"Bobbie," he said. "Bobbie. Bobbie. Bobbie."

The warm night wind turned cold.

It sang through the halls and through the rooms of the great house in the forest.

And then it left, frightened and alone.

THE VANISHING AMERICAN

HE got the notion shortly after five o'clock; at least, a part of him did, a small part hidden down beneath all the conscious cells—*he* didn't get the notion until some time later. At exactly five P.M., the bell rang. At two minutes after, the chairs began to empty. There was the vast slamming of drawers, the straightening of rulers, the sound of bones snapping and mouths yawning and feet shuffling tiredly.

Mr. Minchell relaxed. He rubbed his hands together and relaxed and thought how nice it would be to get up and go home, like the others. But of course there was the tape, only three-quarters finished. He would have to stay.

He stretched and said good night to the people who filed past him. As usual, no one answered. When they had gone, he set his fingers pecking again over the keyboard. The *click-clicking* grew loud in the suddenly still office, but Mr. Minchell did not notice. He was lost in the work. Soon, he knew, it would be time for the totaling, and his pulse quickened at the thought of this.

He lit a cigarette. Heart tapping, he drew in smoke and released it.

He extended his right hand and rested his index and middle fingers on the metal bar marked TOTAL. A mile-long ribbon of paper lay gathered on the desk, strangely festive. He glanced at it, then at the manifest sheet. The figure 18037448 was circled in red. He pulled breath into his lungs, locked it there; then he closed his eyes and pressed the TOTAL bar.

There was a smooth low metallic grinding, followed by absolute silence.

Mr. Minchell opened one eye, dragged it from the ceiling on down to the adding machine.

He groaned, slightly.

The total read: 18037447.

"God." He stared at the figure and thought of the fifty-three pages of manifest, the three thousand separate rows of figures that would have to be checked again. "God."

The day was lost, now. Irretrievably. It was too late to do anything. Madge would have supper waiting, and F. J. didn't approve of overtime; also . . .

He looked at the total again. At the last two digits.

He sighed. Forty-seven. And thought, startled: Today, for the Lord's sake, is my birthday! Today I am forty—what?—forty-seven. And that explains the mistake, I suppose. Subconscious kind of thing. . . .

Slowly he got up and looked around the deserted office.

Then he went to the dressing room and got his hat and his coat and put them on, carefully.

"Pushing fifty now . . ."

The outside hall was dark. Mr. Minchell walked softly to the elevator and punched the *Down* button. "Forty-seven," he said, aloud; then, almost immediately, the light turned red and the thick door slid back noisily. The elevator operator, a bird-thin, tan-fleshed girl, swiveled her head, looking up and down the hall. "Going down," she said.

"Yes," Mr. Minchell said, stepping forward.

"Going down." The girl clicked her tongue and muttered, "Damn kids." She gave the lattice gate a tired push and moved the smooth wooden-handled lever in its slot.

Odd, Mr. Minchell decided, was the word for this particular girl. He wished now that he had taken the stairs. Being alone with only one other person in an elevator had always made him nervous: now it made him very nervous. He felt the tension growing. When it became unbearable, he cleared his throat and said, "Long day."

The girl said nothing. She had a surly look, and she seemed to be humming something deep in her throat.

Mr. Minchell closed his eyes. In less than a minute—during which time he dreamed of the cable snarling, of the car being caught between floors, of himself trying to make small talk with the odd girl for six straight hours—he opened his eyes again and walked into the lobby, briskly.

The gate slammed.

He turned and started for the doorway. Then he paused, feeling a sharp increase in his heartbeat. A large, red-faced, magnificently groomed man of middle years stood directly beyond the glass, talking with another man.

Mr. Minchell pushed through the door, with effort. He's seen me now, he thought. If he asks any questions, though, or anything, I'll just say I didn't put it on the time card; that ought to make it all right. . . .

He nodded and smiled at the large man. "Good night, Mr. Diemel."

The man looked up briefly, blinked, and returned to his conversation.

Mr. Minchell felt a burning come into his face. He hurried on down the street. Now the notion—though it was not even that yet, strictly: it was more a vague feeling—swam up from the bottom of his brain. He remembered that he had not spoken directly to F. J. Diemel for over ten years, beyond a "Good morning". . . .

Ice-cold shadows fell off the tall buildings, staining the streets, now. Crowds of shoppers moved along the pavement like juggernauts, exhaustedly, but with great determination. Mr. Minchell looked at them. They all had furtive appearances, it seemed to him suddenly, even the children, as if each was fleeing from some hideous crime. They hurried along, staring.

But not, Mr. Minchell noticed, at him. Through him, yes. Past him. As the elevator operator had done, and now F. J. And had anyone said good night?

He pulled up his coat collar and walked toward the drugstore, thinking. He was forty-seven years old. At the current life-expectancy rate, he might have another seventeen or eighteen years left. And then death.

If you're not dead already.

He paused and for some reason remembered a story he'd once read in a magazine. Something about a man who dies and whose ghost takes up his duties, or something; anyway, the man didn't know he was dead—that was it. And at the end of the story, he runs into his own corpse.

Which is pretty absurd: he glanced down at his body. Ghosts don't wear $36 suits, nor do they have trouble pushing doors open, nor do their corns ache like blazes, and what the devil is wrong with me today?

He shook his head.

It was the tape, of course, and the fact that it was his birthday. That was why his mind was behaving so foolishly.

He went into the drugstore. It was an immense place, packed with people. He walked to the cigar counter, trying not to feel intimidated, and reached into his pocket. A small man elbowed in front of him and called loudly: "Gimme coupla nickels, will you, Jack?" The clerk scowled and scooped the change out of his cash register. The small man scurried off. Others took his place. Mr. Minchell thrust his arm forward. "A pack of Luckies, please," he said. The clerk whipped his fingers around a pile of cellophaned packages and, looking elsewhere, droned: "Twenty-six." Mr. Minchell put his twenty-six-cents-exactly on the glass shelf. The clerk shoved the cigarettes toward the edge and picked up the money, deftly. Not once did he lift his eyes.

Mr. Minchell pocketed the Luckies and went back out of the store. He was perspiring now, slightly, despite the chill wind. The word "ridiculous" lodged in his mind and stayed there. Ridiculous, yes, for heaven's sake. Still, he thought—now just answer the question—isn't it true? Can you honestly say that that clerk saw you?

Or that anybody saw you today?

Swallowing dryly, he walked another two blocks, always in the direction of the subway, and went into a bar called the Chez When. One drink would not hurt, one small, stiff, steadying shot.

The bar was a gloomy place, and not very warm, but there was a good crowd. Mr. Minchell sat down on a stool and folded his hands. The bartender was talking animatedly with an old woman, laughing with boisterous good humor from time to time. Mr. Minchell waited. Minutes passed. The bartender looked up several times, but never made a move to indicate that he had seen a customer.

Mr. Minchell looked at his old gray overcoat, the humbly floraled tie, the cheap sharkskin suit-cloth, and became aware of the extent to which he detested this ensemble. He sat there and detested his clothes for a long time. Then he glanced around. The bartender was wiping a glass, slowly.

All right, the hell with you. I'll go somewhere else.

He slid off the stool. Just as he was about to turn he saw the mirrored wall, pink-tinted and curved. He stopped, peering. Then he almost ran out of the bar.

Cold wind went into his head.

Ridiculous. The mirror was curved, you jackass. How do you expect to see yourself in curved mirrors?

He walked past high buildings, and now past the library and the stone lion he had once, long ago, named King Richard; and he did not look at the lion, because he'd always wanted to ride the lion, ever since he was a child, and he'd promised himself he would do that, but he never did.

He hurried on to the subway, took the stairs by twos, and clattered across the platform in time to board the express.

It roared and thundered. Mr. Minchell held onto the strap and kept himself from staring. No one watched him. No one even glanced at him when he pushed his way to the door and went out onto the empty platform.

He waited. Then the train was gone, and he was alone.

He walked up the stairs. It was fully night now, a soft, unshadowed darkness. He thought about the day and the strange things that were gouging into his mind and thought about all this as he turned down a familiar street which led to his familiar apartment.

The door opened.

His wife was in the kitchen, he could see. Her apron flashed across the arch, and back, and across. He called: "Madge, I'm home."

Madge did not answer. Her movements were regular. Jimmy was sitting at the table, drooling over a glass of pop, whispering to himself.

"I said—" Mr. Minchell began.

"Jimmy, get up and go to the bathroom, you hear? I've got your water drawn."

Jimmy promptly broke into tears. He jumped off the chair and ran past Mr. Minchell into the bedroom. The door slammed viciously.

"Madge."

Madge Minchell came into the room, tired and lined and heavy. Her eyes did not waver. She went into the bedroom, and there was a silence; then a sharp slapping noise, and a yelling.

Mr. Minchell walked to the bathroom, fighting down the small terror. He closed the door and locked it and wiped his forehead with a handkerchief. Ridiculous, he thought, and ridiculous and ridiculous. I am making something utterly foolish out of nothing. All I have to do is look in the mirror, and—

He held the handkerchief to his lips. It was difficult to breathe.

Then he knew that he was afraid, more so than ever before in a lifetime of being afraid.

Look at it this way, Minchell: why shouldn't *you vanish?*

"Young man, just you wait until your father gets here!"

He pushed the handkerchief against his mouth and leaned on the door and gasped.

"What do you mean, vanish?"

Go on, take a look. You'll see what I mean.

He tried to swallow, couldn't. Tried to wet his lips, found that they stayed dry.

"Lord—"

He slitted his eyes and walked to the shaving mirror and looked in.

His mouth fell open.

The mirror reflected nothing. It held nothing. It was dull and gray and empty.

Mr. Minchell stared at the glass, put out his hand, drew it back hastily.

He squinted. Inches away. There was a form now: vague, indistinct, featureless: but a form.

"Lord," he said. He understood why the elevator girl hadn't seen him, and why F. J. hadn't answered him, and why the clerk at the drugstore and the bartender and Madge . . .

"I'm not dead."

Of course you're not dead—not that way.

"—tan your hide, Jimmy Minchell, when he gets home."

Mr. Minchell suddenly wheeled and clicked the lock. He rushed out of the steam-filled bathroom, across the room, down the stairs, into the street, into the cool night.

A block from home he slowed to a walk.

Invisible! He said the word over and over, in a half-voice. He said it and tried to control the panic that pulled at his legs, and at his brain, and filled him.

Why?

A fat woman and a little girl passed by. Neither of them looked up. He started to call out and checked himself. No. That wouldn't do any good. There was no question about it now. He was invisible.

He walked on. As he did, forgotten things returned; they came and they left, too fast. He couldn't hold onto them. He could only watch, and remember. Himself as a youngster, reading: the Oz books, and Tarzan, and Mr. Wells. Himself, going to the University, wanting to teach, and meeting Madge; then not planning any more, and Madge changing, and all the dreams put away. For later. For the right time. And then Jimmy—little strange Jimmy, who ate filth and picked his nose and watched television, who never read books, never; Jimmy, his son, whom he would never understand. . . .

He walked by the edge of the park now. Then on past the park, through a maze of familiar and unfamiliar neighborhoods. Walking, remembering, looking at the people and feeling pain because he knew that they could not see him, not now or ever again, because he had vanished. He walked and remembered and felt pain.

All the stagnant dreams came back. Fully. The trip to Italy he'd planned. The open sports car, bad weather be damned. The first-hand knowledge that would tell him whether he did or did not approve of bullfighting. The book . . .

Then something occurred to him. It occurred to Mr. Minchell that he had not just suddenly vanished, like that, after all. No; he had been vanishing gradually for a long while. Every time he said good morning to that bastard Diemel he got a little harder to see.

Every time he put on this horrible suit he faded. The process of disappearing was set into action every time he brought his pay check home and turned it over to Madge, every time he kissed her, or listened to her vicious unending complaints, or decided against buying that novel, or punched the adding machine he hated so, or . . .

Certainly.

He had vanished for Diemel and the others in the office years ago. And for strangers right afterwards. Now even Madge and Jimmy couldn't see him. And he could barely see himself, even in a mirror.

It made terrible sense to him. *Why* shouldn't *you* *disappear?* Well, why, indeed? There wasn't any very good reason, actually. None. And this, in a nightmarish sort of a way, made it as brutally logical as a perfect tape.

Then he thought about going back to work tomorrow and the next day and the day after that. He'd have to, of course. He couldn't let Madge and Jimmy starve; and, besides, what else would he do? It wasn't as if anything important had changed. He'd go on punching the clock and saying good morning to people who didn't see him, and he'd run the tapes and come home beat, nothing altered, and some day he'd die and that would be that.

All at once he felt tired.

He sat down on a cement step and sighed. Distantly he realized that he had come to the library. He sat there, watching the people, feeling the tiredness seep through him, thickly.

Then he looked up.

Above him, black and regal against the sky, stood the huge stone lion. Its mouth was open, and the great head was raised proudly.

Mr. Minchell smiled. King Richard. Memories scattered in his mind: old King Richard, well, my God, here we are.

He got to his feet. Fifty thousand times, at least, he had passed this spot, and every time he had experienced that instant of wild craving. Less so of late, but still, had it ever completely gone? He was amazed to find that now the childish desire was welling up again, stronger than ever before. Urgently.

He rubbed his cheek and stood there for several minutes. It's the most ridiculous thing in the world, he thought, and I must be going out of my mind, and that must explain everything. But, he inquired of himself, even so, why not?

After all, I'm invisible. No one can see me. Of course, it didn't have to be this way, not really. I don't know, he went on, I mean, I believed that I was doing the right thing. Would it have been right to go back to the University and the hell with Madge? I couldn't change that, could I? Could I have done anything about that, even if I'd known?

He nodded sadly.

All right, but don't make it any worse. Don't for God's sake *dwell* on it!

To his surprise, Mr. Minchell found that he was climbing up the concrete base of the statue. It ripped the breath from his lungs—and he saw that he could much more easily have gone up a few extra steps and simply stepped on—but there didn't seem anything else to do but just this, what he was doing. Once upright, he passed his hand over the statue's flank. The surface was incredibly sleek and cold, hard as a lion's muscles ought to be, and tawny.

He took a step backwards. Lord! Had there ever been such power? Such marvelous downright power and—majesty, as was here? From stone—no, indeed. It fooled a good many people, but it did not fool Mr. Minchell. He knew. This lion was no mere library decoration. It was an animal, of deadly cunning and fantastic strength and unbelievable ferocity. And it didn't move for the simple reason that it did not care to move. It was waiting. Some day it would see what it was waiting for, its enemy, coming down the street. Then look out, people!

He remembered the whole yarn now. Of everyone on Earth, only he, Henry Minchell, knew the secret of the lion. And only he was allowed to sit astride this mighty back.

He stepped onto the tail, experimentally. He hesitated, gulped, and swung forward, swiftly, on up to the curved rump.

Trembling, he slid forward, until finally he was over the shoulders of the lion, just behind the raised head.

His breath came very fast.

He closed his eyes.

It was not long before he was breathing regularly again. Only now it was the hot, fetid air of the jungle that went into his nostrils. He felt the great muscles ripple beneath him and he listened to the fast crackle of crushed foliage, and he whispered:

"Easy, fellow."

The flying spears did not frighten him; he sat straight, smiling, with his fingers buried in the rich tawny mane of King Richard, while the wind tore at his hair. . . .

Then, abruptly, he opened his eyes.

The city stretched before him, and the people, and the lights. He tried quite hard not to cry, because he knew that forty-seven-year-old men never cried, not even when they had vanished, but he couldn't help it. So he sat on the stone lion and lowered his head and cried.

He didn't hear the laughter at first.

When he did hear it, he thought that he was dreaming. But it was true: somebody was laughing.

He grasped one of the statue's ears for balance and leaned forward. He blinked. Below, some fifteen feet, there were people. Young people. Some of them with books. They were looking up and smiling and laughing.

Mr. Minchell wiped his eyes.

A slight horror came over him, and fell away. He leaned farther out.

One of the boys waved and shouted: "Ride him, Pop!"

Mr. Minchell almost toppled. Then, without understanding, without even trying to understand—merely knowing—he grinned widely, showing his teeth, which were his own and very white.

"You—see me?" he called.

The young people roared.

"You do!" Mr. Minchell's face seemed to melt upwards. He let out a yell and gave King Richard's shaggy stone mane an enormous hug.

Below, other people stopped in their walking and a small crowd began to form. Dozens of eyes peered sharply, quizzically.

A woman in gray furs giggled.

A thin man in a blue suit grunted something about these damned exhibitionists.

"You pipe down," another man said. "Guy wants to ride the goddamn lion it's his own business."

There were murmurings. The man who had said pipe down was small and he wore black-rimmed glasses. "I used to do it all the time." He turned to Mr. Minchell and cried: "How is it?"

Mr. Minchell grinned. Somehow, he realized, in some mysterious way, he had been given a second chance. And this time he knew what he would do with it. "Fine!" he shouted, and stood upon King Richard's back and sent his derby spinning out over the heads of the people. "Come on up!"

"Can't do it," the man said. "Got a date." There was a look of profound admiration in his eyes as he strode off. Away from the crowd he stopped and cupped his hands and cried: "I'll be seeing you!"

"That's right," Mr. Minchell said, feeling the cold new wind on his face. "You'll be seeing me."

Later, when he was good and ready, he got down off the lion.

A POINT OF HONOR

TODAY Mrs. Martinez did not practice on the organ, so St. Christopher's was full of the quiet that made Julio feel strange and afraid. He hated this feeling, and, when he touched the sponge in the fountain of Holy Water—brittle and gray-caked, like an old woman's wrist—he thought of sitting alone in the big church and decided that tomorrow would be time enough to pray. Making the Sign of the Cross, he put a dime and two pennies into the poor box and went back down the stone stairs.

The rain was not much. It drifted in fine mist from the high iron-colored clouds, freckling the dry streets briefly, then disappearing.

Julio wished that it would rain or that it would not rain.

He hurried over to the young man who was still leaning against the fender of a car, still cleaning his fingernails with a pocket knife. The young man looked up, surprised.

"So let's go," Julio said, and they started to walk.

"That was a quickie," the young man said.

Julio didn't answer. He should have gone in and prayed and then he wouldn't be so scared now. He thought of the next few hours, of Paco and what would be said if it were known how scared he really was.

"I could say your mom got sick, or something. That's what Shark pulled and he got out of it, remember."

"So?"

"So nothing, for Chrissakes. You want me to mind my own business—all right."

Danny Arriaga was Julio's best friend. You can't hide things from your best friend. Besides, Danny was older, old enough to start a mustache, and he'd been around: he had even been in trouble with a woman once and there was a child, which had shocked Julio when he first heard about it, though later he was filled with great envy. Danny was smart and he wasn't soft. He'd take over, some day. So Julio would have to pretend.

"Look, I'm sorry—okay by you?"

"Jimdandy."

"I'm nervous is all. Can't a guy get nervous without he's chicken?"

They walked silently for a while. The heat of the sun and the half-rain had left the evening airless and sticky, and both boys were perspiring. They wore faded blue jeans which hung tight to their legs, and leather flying jackets with THE ACES crudely lettered in whitewash on the backs. Their hair was deep black, straight and profuse, climbing down their necks to a final point on each; their shoes were brightly shined, but their T-shirts were grimy and speckled with holes. Julio had poked the holes in his shirt with his finger, one night.

They walked across the sidewalk to a lawn, down the lawn's decline to the artificial lake and along the lake's edge. There were no boats out yet.

"Danny," Julio said, "why you suppose Paco picked me?"

Danny Arriaga shrugged. "Your turn."

"Yeah, but what's it going to be?"

"For you one thing, for another guy something else. Who knows? It's all what Paco dreams up."

Julio stopped when he saw that they were approaching the boathouse. "I don't want to do it, I'm chicken—right?"

Danny shrugged again and took out a cigarette. "I told you what I would've told Paco, but you didn't want to. Now it's too late."

"Gimme a bomb," Julio said.

For the first time, suddenly, as he wondered what he had to do tonight, he remembered a crazy old man he had laughed at once in his father's pharmacy on San Julian Street and how hurt his father had been because the old man was a shellshock case from the first world war and couldn't help his infirmity. He felt like the old man now.

"Better not crap around like this," Danny said, "or Paco'll start wondering."

"Let him wonder! All right, all right."

They continued along the edge of the lake. It was almost dark now, and presently they came to the rear door of the park's boathouse. Danny looked at Julio once, stamped out his cigarette and rapped on the door.

"Check the playboys," somebody said, opening the door.

"Cram it," Danny said. "We got held up."

"That's a switch."

Julio began to feel sick in his stomach.

They were all there. And Julio knew why: to see if he would chicken out.

Lined up against the far wall, Gerry Sanchez, Jesús Rivera, Manuel Morales and his two little brothers who always tagged along wherever he went; seated in two of the battery boats, Hernando and Juan Verdugo and Albert Dominguin. All silent and in their leather-jacket-and-jeans uniforms. In the center of the big room was Paco.

Julio gestured a greeting with his hand, and immediately began to fear the eyes that were turned on him.

Paco Maria Christobal y Mendez was a powerfully muscled, dark and dark-haired youth of seventeen. He sat tipped back in a wicker chair, with his arms stretched behind his head, staring at Julio, squinting through the cigarette smoke.

"What, you stop in a museum on the way?" Paco said. Everybody laughed. Julio laughed.

"What are you talking? I ain't so late as all that."

"Forty-five minutes is too late." Paco reached to the table and moved a bottle forward.

"Speech me," Julio said. "Speech me."

"Hey, listen, you guys! Listen. Julio's cracking wise."

"Who's cracking wise? Look, so I'm here, so what should I do?"

Danny was looking at his shoes.

Paco rubbed his face. It glistened with hot sweat and was inflamed where the light beard had caused irritations. "Got a hot job for Julio tonight," he said. "Know what it is?"

"How should I know?" Julio tried hard to keep his voice steady.

"Great kidders, you English," Paco said. "Hey, you guys, he don't know." He looked over at Danny Arriaga. "You didn't tell him?"

"For Chrissakes," Danny said.

"All right, all right, so. You still want in The Aces?"

Julio nodded.

"By which means you got to do whatever I say you got to do, no matter what, right? Okay." Paco drank from the bottle and passed it to Manuel Morales, who drank and gave the bottle to the younger of his brothers, who only wet his lips and gave it back.

Julio knew he'd have to wait, because he remembered Albert's initiation, and how Paco had stalled and watched to see how scared he got. They'd sent Albert to swipe a car that was owned by the manager of Pacific Fruit who always left the key in. That wasn't so bad, even if Albert did wreck the car the same night, driving it back to the club. Swiping a car would be all right.

But from the way Danny looked, it wasn't going to be anything like that. Paco had it in for him ever since he found out about his going to church. Though there must be more to it, because Julio knew that Hernando and Juan went to church, too.

Something deep and strange, hard to figure.

But strong.

"Pretty soon it's time," Paco said, leaning back in the chair. The others were smiling.

The boats rocked uneasily in the small currents, a short drifting.

Julio thought about Paco, about how he'd come to The Aces. It was Danny who joined first, long before, even before Julio was wearing jeans. Paco was later, a new guy on the street. Mr. Mendez was dead, and his mother worked in the Chinese grocery on Aliso Street with the dead cats in the window. No organization to the club, then. Paco moved in and organized. He beat up Vincente Santa Cruz, who was the strongest guy in the Heights, and he introduced the guys to marijuana and showed them where to get it. He'd been booked three times at the jail and was seen with girls tagging after him, even though he wasn't good-looking, only strong and powerful. Danny admired Paco. Julio didn't, but he respected him.

"Charge up, kid." Paco opened a pill box which contained four crude cigarettes.

"Afterwards," Julio said.

"So okay. Afterwards." Paco grinned and winked at the others.

There was silence again: only the water sloshing against the boats and the painful creak of the wicker chair straining back and forth.

The room was very small. THE ACES was whitewashed on the walls, and initials were carved in various places. Except Julio's. His were not on any of the walls. That distinction would come only when he'd finished his job.

No one seemed prepared to break the quiet.

Julio thought, Danny knows. He knew all along, but he wouldn't tell me. Danny was a full-fledged member now. He'd had to break windows out of Major Jewelry and swipe enough watches for the gang. A tough assignment, because of the cops who prowled and wandered around all the time. It took nerve. Julio had broken into a store himself, though—a tire shop—and so he knew he could do it again, although he remembered how afraid he had been.

Why wouldn't they tell him, for Chrissakes? Why stall? If they'd only tell him now, he'd go right out, he was sure. But, any later . . .

"Scared?" Paco asked, lighting another cigarette and taking off his jacket.

"Listen close—you'll hear me shaking," Julio said.

Danny smiled.

Paco frowned and brought his chair forward with a loud noise. "What are you so cocky—I'll give you in the mouth in a minute. I asked a question."

"No. I ain't scared."

"That's a crock of shit. Who you trying to kid, anyway? Me?"

Suddenly Julio hated this leering, posturing Paco as he had never hated a person before. He looked at his friend Danny, but Danny was looking elsewhere.

"Mackerel snapper, isn't it, Julio?" Paco scratched his leg loudly. "What did you, go to confession today or was the priest busy in the back room?" He smiled.

Julio clenched his fists. "Gimme to do, already," he said; and, all at once, he thought of his father, Papa Velasquez. Papa would be working late right now, in the pharmacy, mixing sodas and prescriptions. Business was very good, with the new housing project and all the new trade.

Julio was going to be a pharmacist—everybody knew that, though no one believed it. No one but Father Laurent: he talked to Julio many times, softly, understandingly. And there were many times when Julio wanted to tell the priest what he had done—about the motorcycle or the time he helped the guys push tea—but he could never seem to get the words out.

He waited, hands tight together, listening to the breathing, and thinking: I could go right to the drugstore now, if I wanted. It was only a mile away. . . .

He cleared his throat. Albert Dominguin was staring at him.

And now Danny Arriaga was getting sore, too: Julio could tell.

"You want to know, huh? Guys—think I should tell him?"

"Tell him already," Danny snapped, rising to his feet. He looked a lot bigger than Paco, suddenly. "Now."

"Who asked for your mouth?" Paco said, glaring. He looked quickly away. "All right, Julio. But first you got to see this."

Paco reached in his pocket and took out a large bone-handled knife. Julio didn't move.

"Ever use one, kid?"

"Yeah."

"Hey, no shit? What do you think, guys—Julio's an expert!" Paco pressed a button on the knife with his thumb. A long silver blade flashed out, glittering in the greenish light of the boathouse.

"So?"

"So you're going to use it tonight, Julio," Paco said, grinning broadly and rocking in the chair. The others crouched and held their cigarettes in their mouths.

Danny seemed about to speak up, but he held himself in check.

"On what?" Julio said.

"No, kid—not on *what*. On *who*." Paco flipped the knife toward Julio's foot, but it landed handle-down and slid to a corner. Julio picked it up, pressed the button, folded back the blade and put the knife in his pocket.

"All right, who. On who?"

He remembered what the Kats had done to the old woman over on Pregunta. For eighty-three cents.

"A dirty son of a bitch that's got it coming," Paco said. He waited. "Hey, kid, what's wrong? You look sick."

"What are you talking, for Chrissakes? What do you want I should do?"

"Carry out a very important mission for our group, that's what. You're a very important man, Julio Velasquez. Know that?"

Near Cuernavaca, by the caverns of Cacahuamilpa, Grandfather had seen a man lying still in the bushes. The man was dead. But not only that—he had been dead for a long time. Grandfather used to sit after the coffee and tell about it; and it was always terrifying because Grandfather had a quiet way of talking, without emphasis, without excitement.

—"¿Quien fué el hombre, Papá?"

—"¿Quien ¡Un hombre muy importante en el pueblo!"

Always; then the slow description, unrolling like one of Mama's stringballs. The man had been a rich one of the village, influential and well liked, owner of a beautiful hacienda, over two thousand acres of land. Then one night he didn't come back when he should have, and the next night it was the same, and the next night, and after the searches, he was forgotten. It was Grandfather who found him. But the flies and the vultures had found him first.

—"¿Comó murió el hombre?" He had been murdered. The knife was still between his ribs and the flesh had softened and decayed around the knife.

Death. . . .

Julio always thought of death as the rich man from Cuernavaca.

"What'd he do?" Julio asked. "This guy."

"He got to do something?" Paco said, laughing. Then: "Plenty. You know when we all went to the Orpheum the other night and you had to stay home on account of your old man or something?"

"Yeah. Sure."

"Okay. They got Billy Daniels and a picture that's supposed to be good, y'know? Okay, we start to pay when the chick at the window picks up the phone and says, 'Wait a minute.' Pretty soon the brass comes out and starts to look us over, real cool, see, like he had a bug up or something. I talk to him and it's all right—we go in. Five goddam dollars. So—the show stinks, the movie: it's cornball, and we go to get our loot back. Guy at the window now, no broad. He says 'Nooo.' I ask to see the manager, but he's gone. They won't give us back our loot. What do we do? What would *you* do, Julio?"

"Raise a stink."

"You bet your sweet ass. That's what we do, what happens? Big Jew punk comes barrelin' down the aisle, says he's the assistant manager. We got to blow, see. But no loot, no, man. Then he took Albert by the hair and kicked him. Right, Albert?"

Albert nodded.

"So naturally this isn't for The Aces. I didn't say nothing after that, except I let the schmuck know he'd get his, later on. So we just casually walked out. And here's the thing—" Paco's eyes narrowed dramatically. "That louse is still walking around, Julio, like he never done a thing to anybody, like he never insulted all of us. Know what he said? Know what he called us, Julio?"

"What'd he call you?"

"Pachooks. Wetbacks. Dirty Mex bastards. Crapped his mouth off like that in front of everybody in the show."

"So you want him cut up?"

Paco rocked and smiled. "No, not just cut up. I want that liddle-Yiddle dead, where he can't crap off any more. That's your assignment, Julio. Bring back his ears."

Julio glanced at Danny, who was not smiling. The others were very quiet. They all looked at him.

"When's he get off?" Julio asked, finally.

"Ten-thirty. He walks down Los Angeles Street, then he hits Third, down Third till he's around the junction. It's a break, Julio. We followed him for three nights, and there's never anybody around the junction. Get him when he's passing the boon docks over to Alameda. Nobody'll ever see you."

"How will I know him?"

"Fat slob. Big nose, big ears, curly brown hair. Carries something, maybe his lunch-pail—you might bring that back with you. Albert'll go along and point him out, in case he wants to try to give you trouble. He's big, but you can take him."

Julio felt the knife in his pocket. He nodded.

"All right, so this is it. You and Albert take off in half an hour, wait and hang around the loading docks, but make sure nobody sees you. Then check the time and grab a spot behind the track next to Merchant Truck—you know where it is. He'll pass there around eleven. All right?"

Julio reached for the pill box and controlled his fingers as they removed the last cigarette. Paco grinned.

"So in the meantime, let's have our meeting. Whoever got what, lay it out on the floor."

The boys began reaching into bags and parcels, and into their pockets, and taking out watches and rings and handfuls of money. These items they spread on the floor.

The rich man, Julio thought, lying still in the bushes, with his fat dead face, waiting for the flies, waiting, while a little Mexican boy with red wet hands runs away, fast, fast. . . .

The grating sound of heavy machinery being pushed across cement came muffled through the wooden doors of the freight dock. There were a few indistinct voices, and the distant hum of other machines that never stopped working.

The night was still airless. Julio and Albert Dominguin walked along the vacant land by the boxcar, clinging to the shadows and speaking little.

Finally Julio said, "This guy really do all that that Paco said?"

"He got smart," Albert said.

"Kick you?"

"You could call it that. Just as good."

"So what kind of a stink you guys raise to cause all that?"

"Nothing."

"Nothing my ass."

"Aah, you know Paco. He got p-o'ed at the picture and started to horse around. Dropped a beer bottle off of the balcony or something, I don't know."

"Then this guy booted you guys out?"

"Yeah."

"Did Paco give him a fight?"

"No," Albert said, thoughtfully. They climbed up the side of a car and jumped from the top to the ground. "He's too smart for that. They would of called the cops and all that kind of crap. This way's better."

"Yeah."

"Nervous?"

"Yeah, real nervous. I'm dying to death, I'm so frigging nervous. Listen—when I get through tonight, Paco and all the rest of you guys better lay off me."

"Don't worry."

"So what is it?"

"Twenty-of. This is the place—he went by right over there."

Julio wondered if Albert could hear his heart. And if Albert could read his thoughts. . . .

He felt the greasy knife handle slip in his hands, so he took it out and wiped it on his trousers and tested it. He pushed the point of the blade into the soft wood of a car, pretending it was the Jewish boy's neck.

He pulled the knife out and didn't do that any more.

They sat on the cindery ground beside a huge iron wheel.

"Really a rat, huh?" Julio said.

"The most," Albert said.

"How old?"

"Who knows—twenty-five, thirty. You can't tell with them."

"You don't suppose he—I mean this guy—you don't think he's got a family or anything like that, do you?"

"What the hell kind of a thing is that to say? Christ, no! Who'd marry a greaseball slob like that?" Albert laughed softly, and took from his leather jacket pocket a red-handled knife that had to be operated manually. He opened it and began to clean his fingernails. Every two or three seconds he glanced up toward the dark unpaved street.

"So nobody's going to miss him, right?" Julio said.

"No. We're going to all break down and cry. What's the matter, you chickening out? If you are, I ain't going to sit here on my can all—"

Julio clutched Albert's shirt-front and gathered it in his fist. "Shut up. You hear? Shut your goddam face about that stuff or I'll break it for you."

"Shhh, quiet down . . . we'll talk later. Let go. If you want to screw everything, just keep shooting your mouth."

Julio felt the perspiration course down his legs.

He tried to stop the shudder.

"Okay," he said.

On tracks a mile distant a string of freight cars lumbered clumsily out of a siding, punching with heavy sounds at the night. There were tiny human noises, too, like small birds high out of sight. Otherwise, there was only his own breathing.

"I want to hear 'mackerel snapper' when this is over," Julio said.

"You ain't done nothing yet," Albert said, looking away quickly.

"Screw you," Julio said. But his voice started to crack, so he forced a yawn and stretched out his legs. "So when the hell we going to get a goddam sickle?" he said.

Albert didn't answer.

"Kind of a gang is this, anyway, we don't have any goddam sickles?"

"Five-of. He ought to be along pretty quick now."

Julio grinned, closed his knife, reopened it with a swift soft click, closed it again. His hands were moist and the knife handle was coated with a grimy sweat which made it slippery. He wiped it carefully along the sides of his jeans.

"The Kats have got sickles. Five, for Chrissakes."

"Kats, schmats," Albert said. "Knock it off, will you?"

"What's the matter, Albert? Don't tell me you're scared!"

Albert drew back his fist and hit Julio's shoulder, then quickly put a finger to his lips. "*Shhh!*"

They listened.

It was nothing.

"Hey, little boy, hey, *Albert*, know what?" Julio combed his hair. "Know what I know? Paco, he don't think I'll do it. He wants you and I to come back so he can give with the big-man routine. He don't think I'll do it."

Albert looked interested.

"He's real sharp. Having a great big ball right now. Where's it going to put him when we get back with that Jewboy's ears?" Julio laughed.

In the stillness, footsteps rang sharply on the ground, but ponderously as gravel was crunched and stones were sent snapping.

The footsteps grew louder.

Albert listened, then he rose slowly and brushed the dirt from his jeans. He opened his knife, looked at Julio and Julio got up. They hunched close by the shadow of the boxcar.

The steps were irregular, and for a moment Julio thought it sounded like a woman. For another moment he heard Grandfather's words and saw the carrion in the bushes.

The images scattered and disappeared.

"Dumb jerk don't know what he's walking into, right?" Julio whispered. The words frightened him. Albert wasn't moving. "Wetbacks. Greasers. Mex—right? Okay. Okay, Albert? Okay." The blade sprang out of the handle.

"Shut up," Albert whispered. "There he is. See him?"

There were no streetlamps, so the figure was indistinct. In the darkness it could be determined that the figure was that of a man: heavy set, not old, walking slowly, almost as if he were afraid of something.

"That's him," Albert said, letting out a stream of breath.

Julio's throat was dry. It pained him when he tried to swallow. "Okay," he said.

Albert said, "Okay, look. Go up and pretend you want a handout, y'know? Make it good. Then let him have it, right away."

"I thought I saw something," Julio said.

"What's that supposed to mean?"

"I thought I saw something, I thought I saw something. You mind?"

"Where?"

"I couldn't make out."

"Who you bulling? You want to go back?"

"All right, so I was wrong."

The figure had passed the boxcar and disappeared into shadows, but the footsteps were still clear.

"You ready?" Albert said.

Julio paused, then he nodded.

"The hell," Albert said. "You're scared green. You'll probably louse it all up. Let's go back."

Julio thought of going back. Of what would be said, of all the eyes turned on him like ominous spotlights. The laughter he heard was what he hated most.

Albert looked anxious; the footsteps were dying away.

"Screw you," Julio said. "You coming with, or not?" He put the knife up his sleeve and held it there with his palm cupped underneath.

Albert rubbed his hands along his shirt. "All right, I'll follow you—about a minute. Sixty seconds."

Julio listened. Suddenly he didn't tremble any more, though his throat was still dry. There were no more pictures in his mind.

He waited, counting.

Then he smiled at Albert and started to walk.

It will take only a few minutes, he thought. No one will see. No one will give Julio Velasquez the old crap about chicken after this. No one . . .

Up ahead, he could see the man. No one else: just the man who was a louse and who didn't deserve to live.

And the long shadows.

He looked over his shoulder once, but the darkness seemed alive, so he jerked his head around and walked faster, with less care.

At last he caught up with the man.

"Hey, mister," Julio said.

FAIR LADY

"Go to Mexico, Elouise," they had told her. "You'll find him there." So she had gone to Mexico and searched the little dry villages and the big dry cities, searched carefully; but she did not find him. So she left Mexico and came home.

Then they said, "Paris! That's the place he'll be. Only, hurry, Elouise! It's getting late." But Paris was across an ocean: it didn't exist, except in young girls' hearts and old women's minds, and if she were to see him there, a *boulevardier*, a gay charmer with a wine bottle—no, they were wrong. He wasn't in Paris.

In fact—it came to her one day in class, when the sun was not bright and autumn was a dead cold thing outside—Duane wasn't anywhere. She knew this to be true because a young man with golden hair and smooth cheeks was standing up reading Agamemnon, and she listened *and did not dream.*

She did not even think of Duane—or, as it may have been, Michael or William or Gregory.

She went home after grading the papers and thought and tried to recall his features. Then she looked about her room, almost, it seemed, for the first time: at the faded orange wallpaper, the darkwood chiffonier, the thin rows of books turned gray and worn by gentle handling over the years. The years . . .

She discovered her wrists and the trailing spongy blue veins, the tiny wrinkled skin that was no longer taut about the hands; and her face, she studied it, too, in the mirror, and saw the face the mirror gave back to her. Not ugly, not hard, but . . . unbeautiful, and old. And what is a thing, after all, when it is no longer young, if it is not old?

She searched, pulled out memories from the cedar chest, and listened in the quiet room to her heart. But he was not there, the tall stranger who waited to love her, only her, Miss Elouise Baker, and she knew now that he never would be. Because he never was.

It was on that night that Miss Elouise wept softly for death to come and take her away.

And it was on the next morning that she met, and fell in love with, Mr. Oliver O'Shaugnessy.

It happened this way. Miss Elouise was seated at the bus stop waiting for the 7:25, seated there as on years of other mornings; only now she thought of death whereas before she'd thought of life, full and abundant. She was an elderly schoolteacher now, dried-up and desiccated, like Mrs. Ritter or Miss Ackwright; cold in the morning air, unwarmed by dreams, cold and heavy-lidded from a night of staring, frightened, into darkness. She sat alone, waiting for the 7:25.

It came out of the mist with ponderous grace, its old motor loud with the cold. It rumbled down the street, then swerved and groaned to a stop before the triangular yellow sign. The doors hissed open and it paused, breathing heavily.

But Miss Elouise stared right into the red paint, sat and stared in the noise and the smoke and didn't move at all or even blink.

The voice came to her soft and unalarmed, almost soothing:

"You wouldn't be sitting there thinking up ways to keep the kiddies after school, would you?"

She looked up and saw the driver.

"I'm sorry. I . . . must have dozed off."

She got inside and began to walk to her seat, the one she'd occupied every morning for a million years.

Then it happened. A rushing into existence, a running, a being. Later she tried to remember her impressions of the surrounding few seconds. She recalled that the bus was empty of passengers. That the advertising signs up above had been changed. That the floor had not been properly swept out. Willed or unwilled, it happened then, at the moment she reached her seat and the doors hissed closed. With these words it happened:

Fair Lady.

"What did you say?"

"Unless you're under twelve years of age, which you'd have a hard time persuading me of, miss, I'll have to ask the company's rightful fare." Then gently, softly, like the laughter of elves: "It's a wicked, money-minded world, and me probably the worst of all, but that's what makes it spin."

Miss Elouise looked at the large red-faced man in the early-morning fresh uniform creased from the iron and crisp. The cap, tilted back over the gray locks of hair; the chunks of flesh straining the clothes tight and rolling out over the belt; at the big, broad, burly man behind the wheel who smiled at her with his eyes. She looked at Oliver O'Shaugnessy, whom she'd seen before and before and never seen before this moment.

Then she dropped a dime into the old-fashioned black coin box and sat down.

But not in her usual seat. She sat down in the seat first back from the man who'd said Fair Lady when it took just those words out of a fat dictionary of words to bring her to life.

That's how it happened. As mysteriously, as unreasonably as any great love has ever happened. And Miss Elouise, from that time on, didn't question or doubt or, for that matter, even think about it much. She just accepted.

And it made the old dream an embarrassed little thing. A pale, dated matinee illusion—she couldn't even bear to think of it, now, with its randy smell of sheiks on horseback and dark strangers from a cardboard nowhere. Duane . . . what an effete ass *he* turned out to be, and to think: she might actually have met him and been crushed and forsaken and forever lost. . . .

Now, she could once again take up her interest in books and art and music, and, in a little while, it all came—she was loving her job—loving it. And before, she'd hated it with her soul. Since falling in love with Oliver O'Shaugnessy, these things were hers. She grew young and healthy and wore a secret smile wherever she went.

Every morning, then, Miss Elouise would hurry to the bus stop and wait while her heart rattled fast. And, sure enough, the bus would come and it would be empty—most of the time, anyway: when it was not empty, she felt that intruders or in-laws had moved in for a visit. But, mostly it was empty.

For thirty minutes every morning, she would live years of life. And slowly, deliciously, she came to know Oliver as well as to love him. He grew dearer to her as she found, each day, new sides to him, new facets of his great personality. For example, his moods became more readily apparent, though hidden behind the smile he always wore for her: she came to know his moods. On some days he felt perfectly wretched; on others, tired and vaguely disturbed; still other days found him bursting with spring cheer, happy as a fed child. Once, even, Oliver was deeply introspective and his smile was weary and forced as he revolved the large wedding ring on his third finger left hand. Through all, he changed and broadened and grew tall, and she loved him with all her heart.

Of course she never spoke of these things. Ever. In fact, they conversed practically not at all. He had no way of guessing the truth, though at times Miss Elouise thought perhaps he did.

Together, it was perfect. And what more can be said?

For three years Miss Elouise rode with Oliver O'Shaugnessy, her lover, every morning, every morning without fail. Except for that awful day each week when he did not work—and these were dark, empty days, full of longing. But they passed. And it gave such wings to her spirit that she felt truly no one in the world could be quite so happy. Fulfillment there was, and quiet contentment. No wife in bed with her husband had ever known one tenth this intimacy; no youngsters in the country under August stars had ever come near to the romance that was hers; nor had ever a woman known such felicity, unspoken, undemanded, but so richly there.

For three magic years. And who could speak with her about love and be on fair ground?

Then, there came a morning. A morning cold as the one of years before, when she had thought of death, and Miss Elouise felt a chill enter her heart and lodge there. She glanced at her watch and looked at the street, misted and empty and wet gray. It was not late, it was not Oliver's day off, nothing had happened—therefore, why should she be afraid? Nevertheless, she was afraid.

The bus came. It swung around the corner far ahead and rolled toward her and came to its stop and, without thinking or looking, she got on.

And saw.

Oliver O'Shaugnessy was not there.

A strange young man with blond hair and thick glasses sat at the wheel. Miss Elouise felt everything loosen and break apart and start to drift off. She was terrified, suddenly, frozen like a china figurine, and she did not even try to move or understand.

It was not merely that something had been taken—as her father had been taken, her father whom she loved so very much. Not merely that. It was knowing, all at once, that she *herself* was being taken, pushed out of a world she'd believed in and told to stay away.

Once she'd known a woman who was insane. They would say to this woman, "You were walking through the house last night, and laughing," and the woman, who never laughed, she wouldn't remember and her eyes would widen in fear and she would say, later, in a lost voice: "I wonder what I could have been laughing at. . . ."

There was a throaty noise, a loud cough.

"Who are you?" Miss Elouise said.

"Beg pardon?" the young man said.

"Where is Oliver?"

"O'Shaugnessy? Got transferred. Takes the Randolphe route now."

Transferred. . . .

Miss Elouise felt that a cageful of little black ugly birds had suddenly been released and that they beat their wings against her heart. She remembered the loneliness and how the loneliness had died and been replaced with something good and clean and fine and built of every lovely dream in all the world.

She got off the bus at the next stop and went home and thought all that day and into the night. Very late into the night . . .

Then, the birds went away.

She smiled, as she had been smiling for these three years, and, when the morning came again, she made a telephone call. Retirement—for Miss Elouise? Why certainly she was due it, but—

She worked busily as a housewife, packing, moving, setting straight the vacant room, telling her goodbyes.

It took time. But not much, really, and she worked so fast and so hard she had little time to think. The days flew.

And then it was done.

And, smiling, she sat one morning in new air, on a new corner two blocks from her new home, and she waited for the bus.

And presently, as lovers will, her lover came to her.

FREE DIRT

No fowl had ever looked so posthumous. Its bones lay stacked to one side of the plate like kindling: white, dry and naked in the soft light of the restaurant. Bones only, with every shard and filament of meat stripped methodically off. Otherwise, the plate was a vast glistening plain.

The other, smaller dishes and bowls were equally virginal. They shone fiercely against one another. And all a pale cream color fixed upon the snowy white of a tablecloth unstained by gravies and unspotted by coffee and free from the stigmata of breadcrumbs, cigarette ash and fingernail lint.

Only the dead fowl's bones and the stippled traceries of hardened red gelatine clinging timidly to the bottom of a dessert cup gave evidence that these ruins had once been a dinner.

Mr. Aorta, not a small man, permitted a mild belch, folded the newspaper he had found on the chair, inspected his vest for food leavings and then made his way briskly to the cashier.

The old woman glanced at his check.

"Yes, sir," she said.

"All righty," Mr. Aorta said and removed from his hip pocket a large black wallet. He opened it casually, whistling The Seven Joys of Mary through the space provided by his two front teeth.

The melody stopped, abruptly. Mr. Aorta looked concerned. He peered into his wallet, then began removing things; presently its entire contents were spread out.

He frowned.

"What seems to be the difficulty, sir?"

"Oh, no difficulty," the fat man said, "exactly." Though the wallet was manifestly empty, he flapped its sides apart, held it upside down and continued to shake it, suggesting the picture of a hydrophobic bat suddenly seized in mid-air.

54

Mr. Aorta smiled a weak harassed smile and proceeded to empty all of his fourteen separate pockets. In a time the counter was piled high with miscellany.

"Well!" he said impatiently. "What nonsense! What bother! Do you know what's happened? My wife's gone off and forgotten to leave me any change! Heigh-ho, well—my name is James Brockelhurst: I'm with the Pliofilm Corporation. I generally don't eat out, and—here, no, I insist. This is embarrassing for you as well as for myself. I *insist* upon leaving my card. If you will retain it, I shall return tomorrow evening at this time and reimburse you."

Mr. Aorta shoved the pasteboard into the cashier's hands, shook his head, shoveled the residue back into his pockets and, plucking a toothpick from a box, left the restaurant.

He was quite pleased with himself—an invariable reaction to the acquisition of something for nothing in return. It had all gone smoothly, and what a delightful meal!

He strolled in the direction of the streetcar stop, casting occasional licentious glances at undressed mannequins in department store windows.

The prolonged fumbling for his car token worked as efficiently as ever. (Get in the middle of the crowd, look bewildered, inconspicuous, search your pockets earnestly, the while edging from the vision of the conductor—then, take a far seat and read a newspaper.) In four years' traveling time, Mr. Aorta computed he had saved a total of $211.20.

The electric's ancient list did not jar his warm feeling of serenity. He studied the amusements briefly, then went to work on the current puzzle, whose prize ran into the thousands. Thousands of dollars, actually for nothing. Something for nothing. Mr. Aorta loved puzzles.

But the fine print made reading impossible.

Mr. Aorta glanced at the elderly woman standing near his seat; then, because the woman's eyes were full of tired pleading and insinuation, he refocused out the wire crosshatch windows.

What he saw caused his heart to throb. The section of town was one he passed every day, so it was a wonder he'd not noticed it before—though generally there was little provocation to sightsee on what was irreverently called "Death Row"—a dreary round of mortuaries, columbariums, crematories and the like, all crowded into a five-block area.

He yanked the stop-signal, hurried to the rear of the streetcar and depressed the exit plate. In a few moments he had walked to what he'd seen.

It was a sign, artlessly lettered though spelled correctly enough. It was not new, for the white paint had swollen and cracked and the rusted nails had dripped trails of dirty orange over the face of it.

The sign read:

FREE DIRT
APPLY WITHIN
Lilyvale
Cemetery

and was posted upon the moldering green of a woodboard wall.

Now Mr. Aorta felt a familiar sensation come over him. It happened whenever he encountered the word FREE—a magic word that did strange and wonderful things to his metabolism.

Free. What was the meaning, the *essence* of free? Why, something for nothing. And to get something for nothing was Mr. Aorta's chiefest pleasure in this mortal life.

The fact that it was dirt which was being offered Free did not oppress him. He seldom gave more than a fleeting thought to these things; for, he reasoned, nothing is without its use.

The other, subtler circumstances surrounding the sign scarcely occurred to him: why the dirt was being offered, where free dirt from a cemetery would logically come from; et cetera. In this connection he considered only the probable richness of the soil, for reasons he did not care to speculate upon.

Mr. Aorta's solitary hesitation encircled such problems as: Was this offer an honest one, without strings where he would have to buy something? Was there a limit on how much he could take home? If not, what would be the best method of transporting it?

Petty problems: all solvable.

Mr. Aorta did something inwardly that resembled a smile, looked about and finally located the entrance to the Lilyvale Cemetery.

These desolate grounds, which had once accommodated a twine factory, an upholstering firm and an outlet for ladies' shoes, now lay swathed in a miasmic vapor—accreditable, in the absence of nearby bogs, to a profusion of windward smokestacks. The blistered hummocks, peaked with crosses, slabs and stones, loomed gray and sad in the gloaming: withal, a place purely delightful to describe, and a pity it cannot be—for how it looked there that evening has little to do with the fat man and what was to become of him.

Important only that it was a place full of dead people on their backs under ground, moldering and moldered.

Mr. Aorta hurried because he despised to waste, along with everything else, time. It was not long before he had encountered the proper party and had this sort of conversation:

"I understand you're offering free dirt."

"That's right."

"How much may one have?"

"Much as one wants."

"On what days?"

"Any days; most likely there'll always be some fresh."

Mr. Aorta sighed in the manner of one who has just acquired a lifetime inheritance or a measured checking account. He then made an appointment for the following Saturday and went home to ruminate agreeable ruminations.

At a quarter past nine that night he hit upon an excellent use to which the dirt might be put.

His back yard, an ochre waste, lay chunked and dry, a barren stretch repulsive to all but the grossest weeds. A tree had once flourished there, in better days, a haven for suburbanite birds, but then the birds disappeared for no good reason except that this was when Mr. Aorta moved into the house, and the tree became an ugly naked thing.

No children played in this yard.

Mr. Aorta was intrigued. Who could say? Perhaps something might be made to grow! He had long ago written an enterprising firm for free samples of seeds, and received enough to feed an army. But the first experiments had shriveled into hard useless pips and, seized by lassitude, Mr. Aorta had shelved the project. Now . . .

A neighbor named Joseph William Santucci permitted himself to be intimidated. He lent his old Reo truck, and after a few hours the first load of dirt had arrived and been shoveled into a tidy mound. It looked beautiful to Mr. Aorta, whose passion overcompensated for his weariness with the task. The second load followed, and the third, and the fourth, and it was dark as a coalbin out when the very last was dumped.

Mr. Aorta returned the truck and fell into an exhausted, though not unpleasant, sleep.

The next day was heralded by the distant clangor of church bells and the *chink-chink* of Mr. Aorta's spade, leveling the displaced graveyard soil, distributing it and grinding it in with the crusty earth. It had a continental look, this new dirt: swarthy, it seemed, black and saturnine: not at all dry, though the sun was already quite hot.

Soon the greater portion of the yard was covered, and Mr. Aorta returned to his sitting room.

He turned on the radio in time to identify a popular song, marked his discovery on a post card and mailed this away, confident that he would receive either a toaster or a set of nylon hose for his trouble.

Then he wrapped four bundles containing, respectively: a can of vitamin capsules, half of them gone; a half-tin of coffee; a half-full bottle of spot remover; and a box of soap flakes with most of the soap flakes missing. These he mailed, each with a note curtly expressing his total dissatisfaction, to the companies that had offered them to him on a money-back guarantee.

Now it was dinnertime, and Mr. Aorta beamed in anticipation. He sat down to a meal of sundry delicacies such as anchovies, sardines, mushrooms, caviar, olives and pearl onions. It was not, however, that he enjoyed this type of food for any aesthetic reasons: only that it had all come in packages small enough to be slipped into one's pocket without attracting the attention of busy grocers.

Mr. Aorta cleaned his plates so thoroughly no cat would care to lick them; the empty tins also looked new and bright: even their lids gleamed iridescently.

Mr. Aorta glanced at his checkbook balance, grinned indecently, and went to look out the back window.

The moon was cold upon the yard. Its rays passed over the high fence Mr. Aorta had constructed from free rocks, and splashed moodily onto the now black earth.

Mr. Aorta thought a bit, put away his checkbook and got out the boxes containing the garden seeds.

They were good as new.

Joseph William Santucci's truck was in use every Saturday thereafter for five weeks. This good man watched curiously as his neighbor returned each time with more dirt and yet more, and he made several remarks to his wife about the oddness of it all, but she could not bear even to talk about Mr. Aorta.

"He's robbed us blind," she said. "Look! He wears your old clothes, he uses my sugar, and spices and borrows everything else he can think of! Borrows, did I say? I mean *steals*. For years! I have not seen the man pay for a thing yet! Where does he work he makes so little money?"

Neither Mr. nor Mrs. Santucci knew that Mr. Aorta's daily labors involved sitting on the sidewalk downtown, with dark glasses on and a battered tin cup in front of him. They'd both passed him several times, though, and given him pennies, both unable to penetrate the clever disguise. It was all kept, the disguise, in a free locker at the railroad terminal.

"Here he comes again, that loony!" Mrs. Santucci wailed.

Soon it was time to plant the seeds, and Mr. Aorta went about this with ponderous precision, after having consulted numerous books at the library. Neat rows of summer squash were sown in the richly dark soil; and peas, corn, beans, onions, beets, rhubarb, asparagus, water cress and much more, actually. When the rows were filled and Mr. Aorta was stuck with extra packs, he smiled and dispersed strawberry seeds and watermelon seeds and seeds without clear description. Shortly the paper packages were all empty.

A few days passed and it was getting time to go to the cemetery again for a fresh load, when Mr. Aorta noticed an odd thing.

The dark ground had begun to yield to tiny eruptions. Closer inspection revealed that things had begun to grow. In the soil.

Now Mr. Aorta knew very little about gardening, when you got right down to it. He thought it strange, of course, but he was not alarmed. He saw things growing, that was the important point. Things that would become food.

Praising his fortune, he hurried to Lilyvale and there received a singular disappointment: Not many people had died lately. There was scant little dirt to be had: hardly one truckful.

Ah well, he thought, things are bound to pick up over the holidays; and he took home what there was.

Its addition marked the improvement of the garden's growth. Shoots and buds came higher, and the expanse was far less bleak.

He could not contain himself until the next Saturday, for obviously this dirt was acting as some sort of fertilizer on his plants—the free food called out for more.

But the next Saturday came a cropper. Not even a shovel's load. And the garden was beginning to desiccate. . . .

Mr. Aorta's startling decision came as a result of trying all kinds of new dirt and fertilizers of every imaginable description (all charged under the name of Uriah Gringsby). Nothing worked. His garden, which had promised a full bounty of edibles, had sunk to new lows: it was almost back to its original state. And this Mr. Aorta could not abide, for he had put in considerable labor on the project and this labor must not be wasted. It had deeply affected his other enterprises.

So—with the caution born of desperateness, he entered the gray quiet place with the tombstones one night, located freshly dug but unoccupied graves and added to their six-foot depth yet another foot. It was not noticeable to anyone who was not looking for such a discrepancy.

No need to mention the many trips involved: it is enough to say that in time Mr. Santucci's truck, parked a block away, was a quarter filled.

The following morning saw a rebirth in the garden.

And so it went. When dirt was to be had, Mr. Aorta was obliged; when it was not—well, it wasn't missed. And the garden kept growing and growing, until—

As if overnight, everything opened up! Where so short a time past had been a parched little prairie, was now a multifloral, multi-vegetable paradise. Corn bulged yellow from its spiny green husks; peas were brilliant green in their half-split pods, and all the other wonderful foodstuffs glowed full rich with life and showcase vigor. Rows and rows of them, and cross rows!

Mr. Aorta was almost felled by enthusiasm.

A liver for the moment and an idiot in the art of canning, he knew what he had to do.

It took a while to systematically gather up the morsels, but with patience, he at last had the garden stripped clean of all but weeds and leaves and other unedibles.

He cleaned. He peeled. He stringed. He cooked. He boiled. He took all the good free food and piled it geometrically on tables and chairs and continued with this until it was all ready to be eaten.

Then he began. Starting with the asparagus—he decided to do it in alphabetical order—he ate and ate clear through beets and celery and parsley and rhubarb, paused there for a drink of water, and went on eating, being careful not to waste a jot, until he came to water cress. By this time his stomach was twisting painfully, but it was a sweet pain, so he took a deep breath and, by chewing slowly, did away with the final vestigial bit of food.

The plates sparkled white, like a series of bloated snowflakes. It was all gone.

Mr. Aorta felt an almost sexual satisfaction—by which is meant, he had had enough . . . for now. He couldn't even belch.

Happy thoughts assailed his mind, as follows: His two greatest passions had been fulfilled; life's meaning acted out symbolically, like a condensed *Everyman*. These two things only are what this man thought of.

He chanced to look out the window.

What he saw was a bright speck in the middle of blackness. Small, somewhere at the end of the garden—faint yet distinct.

With the effort of a brontosaurus emerging from a tar pit Mr. Aorta rose from his chair, walked to the door and went out into his emasculated garden. He lumbered past dangling grotesqueries formed by shucks and husks and vines.

The speck seemed to have disappeared, and he looked carefully in all directions, slitting his eyes, trying to get accustomed to the moonlight.

Then he saw it. A white fronded thing, a plant, perhaps only a flower; but there, certainly, and all that was left.

Mr. Aorta was surprised to see that it was located at the bottom of a shallow declivity in the ground, very near the dead tree. He couldn't remember how a hole could have got dug in his garden, but there were always neighborhood kids and their pranks. A lucky thing he'd grabbed the food when he did!

Mr. Aorta leaned over the edge of the small pit and reached down his hand toward the shining plant. It resisted his touch, somehow. He leaned farther over and still a little farther, and still he couldn't lay fingers on the thing.

Mr. Aorta was not an agile man. However, with the intensity of a painter trying to cover one last tiny spot awkwardly placed, he leaned just a mite farther and plosh! he'd toppled over the edge and landed with a peculiarly wet thud. A ridiculous damned bother, too: now he'd have to make a fool of himself, clambering out again. But, the plant: He searched the floor of the pit, and searched it, and no plant could be found. Then he looked up and was appalled by two things: Number One, the pit had been deeper than he'd thought; Number Two, the plant was wavering in the wind above him, on the rim he had so recently occupied.

The pains in Mr. Aorta's stomach got progressively worse.

Movement increased the pains. He began to feel an overwhelming pressure in his ribs and chest.

It was at this moment of his discovery that the top of the hole was up beyond his reach that he saw the white plant in full moon-glow. It looked rather like a hand, a big human hand, waxy and stiff and attached to the earth. The wind hit it and it moved slightly, causing a rain of dirt pellets to fall upon Mr. Aorta's face.

He thought a moment, judged the whole situation, and began to climb. But the pains were too much and he fell, writhing.

The wind came again and more dirt was scattered down into the hole: soon the strange plant was being pushed to and fro against the soil, and the dirt fell more and more heavily. More and more, more heavily and more heavily.

Mr. Aorta, who had never up to this point found occasion to scream, screamed. It was quite successful, despite the fact that no one heard it.

The dirt came down, and presently Mr. Aorta was to his knees in damp soil. He tried rising, and could not.

And the dirt came down from that big white plant flip-flopping in the moonlight and the wind.

After a while Mr. Aorta's screams took on a muffled quality.

For a very good reason.

Then, some time later, the garden was just as still and quiet as it could be.

Mr. and Mrs. Joseph William Santucci found Mr. Aorta. He was lying on the floor in front of several tables. On the tables were many plates. The plates on the tables were clean and shining.

Mr. Aorta's stomach was distended past burst belt buckle, popped buttons and forced zipper. It was not unlike the image of a great white whale rising curiously from placid, forlorn waters.

"Ate hisself to death," Mrs. Santucci said in the fashion of the concluding line of a complex joke.

Mr. Santucci reached down and plucked a tiny ball of soil from the fat man's dead lips. He studied it. And an idea came to him. . . .

He tried to get rid of the idea, but when the doctors found Mr.

Aorta's stomach to contain many pounds of dirt—and nothing else, to speak of—Mr. Santucci slept badly, for almost a week.

They carried Mr. Aorta's body through the weeded but otherwise empty and desolate back yard, past the mournful dead tree and the rock fence.

They gave him a decent funeral, out of the goodness of their hearts, since no provision had been made.

And then they laid him to rest in a place with a moldering green woodboard wall: the wall had a little sign nailed to it.

And the wind blew absolutely Free.

OPEN HOUSE

THERE was a knock. Only one, but the glass-squared door shook in its poor-fitting jamb and sent sharp sounds trembling throughout the apartment.

Mr. Pierce froze. His head jerked up like the head of a feeding animal suddenly startled; then he recognized the sound and fear began to rearrange him, draining the blood from his head, stoppering his throat, popping his heart up into his craw. He listened and watched his nerves and his courage and his future all eddy away, like rotted lace in a quick wind.

The knock rang again, louder this time.

"Wait!" The word choked loose so softly he could scarcely hear it; it was a prayer. "Wait—just a second. I'll be there in just a second!" Then there was another sound: the tinny clatter of the carving knife that had slipped slowly from his hands and fallen to the pink tile floor.

Mr. Pierce rose and looked at the bathtub. At the water that was not water any longer but, instead, bright red ink, burning red against the glistening white porcelain sides. At the pale things floating in the bright red water, the pale soft things, floating, drifting, turning, like pieces of lamb in a simmering stew.

"Hey, Eddie!" The voice came muffled from behind the knockings. "Anybody home?"

The little man let some air come out of his lungs. He tried to swallow and then started from the bathroom. "Just a minute, will you!" He was almost to the door when he stopped, returned and washed his hands and removed the oilcloth apron that had once been yellow and was now other colors. He dropped the apron to the floor, pulled the shower curtain across the tub—or very nearly across; it had never fit quite snug—inspected himself for stains and went out, closing the door.

Be logical, he told himself. Be calm. And quiet. And cool.

Everything is all right. Nothing has happened. Nothing whatever. Emma is . . . visiting friends. Yes.

He opened the door.

"*Wie Geht's!*"

Two grinning men of nearly middle years stood at the threshold. Mr. Pierce eyed them, closely.

It was Lew Hoover, in soup-and-fish and a new mustache, and someone else whom Mr. Pierce had never seen before.

"*Was ist los mit der gesundheit?*"

"My God, Lew!" How long had it been? A year?

"Eddie, you old son-of-a-gun!" Hoover turned to his companion and delivered a sharp elbow. "This is him, pal. Greatest guy there is. Eddie Pierce. God damn. Eddie, want you to meet—man, what's your name?"

"Vernon," the other said. "Vernon F. Fein. I've told you that seventy-three times."

"All right; don't get smart." Hoover leaned forward and whispered hoarsely: "Just met him tonight. At the bar. Square."

Mr. Pierce said nothing. His throat was calcified. He felt a pressure on his hand.

"Didn't get you up or anything, did we?" Hoover asked.

"Oh, no. No. I was just sort of cleaning up a little."

"We come in for a few minutes?"

"Well . . ." Mr. Pierce dropped his eyes. He thought of the times he had prayed to see the face of Lew Hoover, or Len Brooks, or Jimmy Vandergrift, or any of the old gang. How many times. He thought of all the lonely nights alone, with Emma, here . . . "Well, isn't it kind of late, fellows?"

"Shank of the evening! Fein, I want you to look at a guy that didn't used to even know what late was. Three o'clock, four o'clock, five—God, Eddie, remember?"

Mr. Pierce smiled and nodded.

"Then come on—for old time's sake, what do you say? One drink. Then we'll blow. All right?"

"It's awfully late, Lew."

Hoover giggled and belched. His breath smelled strongly of gin. Vernon F. Fein looked pleasantly noncommittal.

"Eddie, I promised my pal here, George, that we'd all have one short one together. I promised him. Don't make me out a liar, huh? Or"—Hoover's voice lowered—"would it disturb the little woman?"

"No, as a matter of fact that isn't it at all. Emma's away, visiting. She's not here."

"*Not here!*" Hoover pushed past and weaved across the room to the couch. He made a face and said: "*Was ist los mit der gesundheit?*"

Mr. Pierce fought down the hysteria. He beckoned the stranger in and closed the door. "Well," he said; "just a short one, Lew. Got to rise and shine in the morning."

"That's what I was talking about, one short one, isn't it?"

Mr. Pierce went into the kitchen and quickly made three Scotch-and-waters. When he returned, his visitors were laughing.

"Eddie," Hoover chuckled. "Lordy—I can't believe it's been so long." He stopped chuckling. "Man, what *happened?*"

"I don't know what you mean, Lew."

"Don't know what I mean! George, what your bloodshot orbs envisage tonight is a miracle in the flesh. You wouldn't believe it, George."

Vernon F. Fein took a large swallow and shifted uncomfortably.

"You see that dried-up mess of bones there?" Hoover renewed his giggling. "That, Fred, was once the sweetest bastard that ever walked on two legs. Fun? Oh my God. Just two years ago. Two stinking years. Every night, a ball. Right, Eddie? Am I right or wrong, every night a ball?"

Mr. Pierce threw down some Scotch.

"No loot in his pocket, all right. No job, all right. You want to get cheered up, who do you see? Eddie Pierce, that's who. Then—whammo!"

"Whammo?" Fein finished his drink and hiccoughed.

"It all goes bust. You know what?" Hoover grabbed the beefy man's lapels, roughly. "He wanted to be a writer. Like me: I'm a writer. Movies. Anything wrong with movies?"

"I've always liked Claudette Colbert," Fein said.

"Yeah. Well, Eddie could have had it all. But he was going to write novels. And—you want to know something, stupid? He was good. I'm telling you."

"I wonder," Fein said, dreamily, "what ever happened to Laird Cregar. There was a real actor."

"Shut up, Fred. Are you listening to me or not? Eddie, here, was *good* is what I'm trying to get through that hog's head of yours. He would have made it, too. Right on the damn brink. He—what the living *hell* is this?" Hoover was contorted on the couch. His hand reached up to touch the fringe of a greenly floraled lampshade. "Eddie, how come you let her keep such crap in the house?"

"Mr. Pierce," Fein interrupted, cordially. "May I inquire as respects the sort of work you do? I mean your line of business. Do you—"

Hoover howled. "I'll tell you, Jim. He's a goddam butcher. Yah! That's right, all right. His wife's uncle got him a real nice spot in a meat market. Ham hocks and sides of beef—the greatest writer, the sweetest son of a—oh, hell."

Mr. Pierce felt suddenly ill. He could hear the ice cubes rattling in his glass.

"Maybe we ought to leave," Fein said. "Maybe we're keeping people up."

"Then he got married," Hoover went on, his words slurred and indistinct. "A Suth'n belle: very nice, oh my. Course, you can't expect him to spend so much time with the old gang now he's married, right? And, what the hell, you can't expect a wife to get out and work and support her husband while he's slaving over a hot typewriter trying to get ahead, now can you?"

"I understand," Fein said.

"The hell you do, George, the hell you do."

"Lew . . ." Mr. Pierce stepped forward.

"Eddie, listen, remember the party over at Len's where you and me went to sleep in the bathtub? And what's-her-name, Dotty, came in and turned on the water. God damn, we almost drowned!" Hoover chuckled; he was sinking farther down in the couch. "And that trip to Tijuana—huh? How long were we drunk? Was it really a week? Hey, and how about the ball we tossed when you sold your first story—"

"I wonder," Vernon F. Fein said, "if I could please have another drink."

"Damn right," Hoover said. He rose and stumbled into the kitchen.

Mr. Pierce sat remembering it all. His wonderful little bachelor apartment and all his things, just so; the parties; and, most important, his friends. Lew and Jimmy and Len and Paul and Ron . . . the best, the loyalest, closest gang of buddies that ever was.

And then, as Lew had said, Emma. Sweet Emma, who'd caught him when the novel wasn't going right and he was feeling low for no reason, low and—at this he smiled—lonely.

What had made him do it, finally? he wondered for perhaps the first time. Exactly how had it happened? he asked himself. . . .

Things had been strange, that's all he'd known right at the moment.

There had been a wind and it blew city-breath into the branches of the outside elms and made them groan like broken flutes; it plucked up tumbleweeds from empty lots and sent them rolling ponderously down the night-darkened streets like fat brown ghosts; it made the windows and screens of every house quiver together with its small fury—

But it wasn't the wind alone that had made things strange.

Work, perhaps? It hadn't been a heavy day, especially. Oh, sure, he'd caught the tip of his finger in the grinder, but that wasn't anything new. He'd cut and sawed and weighed the meat and hated it no more and no less than ever before.

The apartment? That clump of dust beneath the record cabinet and that half-nibbled melting block of chocolate on the couch arm—

No. Not the wind, not the job, not the apartment. Not singly, anyway.

Then what?

Mr. Pierce got up and picked a cigarette from the coffee-table humidor and eased back into the dust-heavy chair, carefully, uncertainly, as if he half expected someone to strap him in, attach electrodes to his wrists and ankles and throw a switch.

He remembered.

How he had sat just so some hours earlier, and listened to the nasal voice . . .

"Eddie. Sweetheart!"

He had felt his heart come to life, his head begin to throb.

"Eddie, be a lamb and come sit with me."

And he had let the held-in breath rush away, realizing then that the strangeness was not so strange.

"Just a second, honey!" he had called back.

The stubbed-out cigarette uncoiled in the brass ashtray like a dying animal. Mr. Pierce watched it and yielded, while Hoover talked on and on, to the memories . . .

"Eddieeee, baby!"

"Okay; coming."

He had stood up and listened to the splashing sounds. And then walked quickly across the naked living-room floor, past the spit-shine whiteness of ceramic ducks and ceramic geese afloat on the varnished tops of his bookcases; past the tinted Buddha—a gift from Emma's mother—grinning with the ignorance of the ages hidden in that bare white bursting belly, past Emma's gold-framed "Floral Group" and his Matisse "Odalisque," past and through all the freakish unbalance, the mixture of cheap and expensive, her things, and his things, he walked, and into the bathroom.

She was reading.

"Hi."

"Emma, I—"

But—she was reading. How he loved that! No matter what, Donald Duck, Henry Miller, she became hypnotized.

"I hate you," he said.

Her expression remained serene. She turned a page, smiling.

"I think," he said, "of all the females in the world as a vast regatta—full sails, trim white hulls, sleek, frail, swift. Thousands—millions! And there, in the midst of them all, you, my darling, my dearest: a great untidy barge, filled with rotting fruit and the ghosts of fled rats, chugging, straining, sinking; a gross smudge on the clear water . . ."

Emma waved one of her hands. "In a minute, dear," she said. "Just a couple more pages."

"Read on, until you putrefy and have to be gotten up with a vacuum cleaner," Mr. Pierce said in a soft, reedy voice.

"I love you," Emma said.

But even "the game" did no good. Mr. Pierce laid his hornrims on the medicine cabinet and hoisted his trousers and rubbed his eyes. The steam floated like layers of mold in the room. He began to perspire. Coldly.

He watched his wife. In the gray water parts of her rose like little pink islands. She studied the pages of her magazine intensely as always, as a rabbit stares in paralyzed fascination at a cobra.

Then, suddenly, without thinking or questioning or wondering, Mr. Pierce snatched the magazine, hurled it across the small room and stood up.

"Why . . . Eddie!"

He then leaned over, took ahold of Emma's legs and pulled hard. Her massive body shot forward in the tub. Mr. Pierce put one foot on her throat and pushed her head beneath the soapy water: she thrashed and squirmed and bubbled, and splashed, but soon it was quiet.

Then Mr. Pierce shook and trembled for almost half an hour. A full hour had passed before he returned from the kitchen with certain utensils—

"I'm going to clear the air now!" Hoover was weaving uncertainly: his face seemed utterly like warm plastic. "Never had the guts to say it all. But I've got a little under my belt now, and I don't care. Get sore! Get tee'd off! Fein—we were all for him when he married this chick. Really. Hell, she had us all snowed. Pretended to be understanding—see, she loved him just the way he was, no changes. *His* friends? *Her* friends. And that's the way it went—for the first two months. Then it starts. And like magic, kid, like *magic*, this sweet-talking chubby li'l gal turns into a goddam—I don't know what. Shrew, fishwife, harridan: you name it. Any of us, the minute we found out she was what she was, we'd of booted her out on her ear. But that's not Eddie. No-o-o! He wants to do the right thing. So instead, *we* get booted out. And it's all over. His buddies aren't welcome any more. He gives up his ambitions, his friends, and every other goddam thing. Kaput. Schluss."

Listening, Mr. Pierce relived the transformation of his life; all of it, over two years. He relived it in those minutes. How his unconsciously ordered existence had been slowly uprooted and destroyed. How Emma had changed into a new person, one he'd never known. A fat candy-eating movie-magazine-reading dirty-bathrobe-wearing *wife*, with a million nauseating habits. She squeezed his pimples. She made patterns with her feet. She fixed breakfast eggs that glistened with mucus. She threatened to leave—and never did. Refused to, stood adamant. And then, just yesterday, how she had crept up and put her viselike thumbs upon a tender neck-boil and pressed and cooed (her very words!): "Honey, what would you think about having a little stranger in the house?" Oh, how she had murdered him, by inches, centimeters, by days and nights, each time with a new weapon. . . .

Well, it was all right now. He had made it all right. He'd say she ran off with a Turk or an Italian—no one else knew how he had hated her, he'd always been so polite. And if it were done a little at a time, just a little: parts in the freezer, put through the grinder, distributed to a hundred customers over a hundred days . . . who would notice? Who would guess? And without a corpus delicti, of course . . .

Hoover had poured new drinks. He was standing now, weaving like a movie comic. "I'm sorry, Eddie," he said. "Didn't mean to run off at the mouth like that, honest. She'd drive me crazy, personally, but she's your baby. I—well, sorry."

"That's okay, Lew," Mr. Pierce said, graciously.

"Mosey along now. I was a jerk to think we could get it back, I guess."

"No, Lew—" Mr. Pierce hesitated. "It'll come back, some day. You wait and see."

Hoover slapped the face of his companion, who had fallen asleep. "Come on, Max. Let's us go talk about Claudette Colbert."

Mr. Fein opened his eyes. Hoover picked up his white silk scarf and started for the door. He turned, then, and there was an expression of great sorrow on his face. "And you don't even know what tonight is," he said.

"Who—me?" Fein asked.

"Tell him, Eddie. Or have you forgotten?"

Mr. Pierce shook his head. "I don't think I follow you, Lew."

"Like I told you," Hoover said, to Fein; "he's forgotten. Fred, tonight used to be the biggest in the year for us. All Fools Day. For years. And he didn't even remember. It's why I came by in the first place, and I was waiting, just hoping there that he would—but, Eddie, Eddie! You're dead, kid. Dead." He wheeled, snorted and stopped. "Wait. Got to use the bathroom," he said.

Mr. Pierce pulled himself from his regret and from his memories of the parties they had all thrown on this memorable date so many times in the past. He jumped up. "You can't do that, Lew."

"Huh?"

"It's—broken, Lew. Some trouble with the pipes."

Fein had wandered back to the kitchen.

"But," Hoover said, "I've got to."

"It doesn't work. I'm sorry."

Hoover grinned bitterly. "I got people to round up," he muttered. "People that's friends, that remember what the hell tonight is. Time and tide, besides . . ."

"It is out of order," Mr. Pierce said, firmly.

"Okay, then I'll wash my hands. Can I wash my hands?"

"The sink is stopped up."

"Eddie, you're telling me the sink is stopped up?"

"Yes, that's right!" Mr. Pierce almost shouted.

"What are you so jumpy about?"

"I'm not jumpy, Lew: I'm tired. It's all broke, that's all. Can't you understand a simple fact like that?"

Hoover sobered slightly, or seemed to. He looked closely at his friend. "I'm not sure," he said, and pushed forward, stumbling into the bedroom.

"Stop!" Mr. Pierce blenched and threw out his arms. But the tall man in evening dress had already crossed the room.

"Lew, don't spoil everything! It'll be okay. Just leave, will you!"

Hoover paused at the bathroom door. His hand slipped on the knob, crept back upon it and revolved.

Mr. Pierce spoke in a strong, soft voice now. "Don't go in there." He looked terribly small, terribly frail, terribly helpless.

"When you gotta go," Hoover grinned, "you gotta go. If you don't think so, Eddie, you're all wet. Anyway, I feel a little sick. Sick. Verstay?"

As the tall man turned and started in, Mr. Pierce sighed and followed.

Hoover had a glass partially filled with water when he happened to glance at the curtained tub.

His eyes moved to the slit.

"Holy God! Eddie, what—"

Mr. Pierce's arm traveled in a wide arc. The cleaver, which he had plucked off the medicine shelf, sank deep. He wrenched it loose and swung it another time.

Then he pulled open the shower curtain and lifted the now crumpled figure and tumbled it into the tub and did not look at it.

With a soft rag he wiped his hands, thinking: *Lew!* Thinking: Well, that leaves Jimmy, anyway, and Len and . . . It would still be all right.

Trembling, Mr. Pierce surveyed himself in the mirror and returned to the living room.

Mr. Fein was not asleep any more. He was holding a Miró reproduction upside down and making confused sounds.

"How'd it go?" Fein inquired.

"Well," Mr. Pierce said, "Lew isn't feeling so good. He's decided to stay a while."

"I mean about the toilet."

"It's still broken."

Fein got up, staggered, giggled and quickly regained himself. "Take a look at it," he said.

"No—no need. Thanks anyway. I think it'll probably be all right until tomorrow. I've got a plumber coming—"

"Save your money. That's my business, plumbing. Don't have a snake here, do you? What'd she do, back up on you?"

"Who?"

"Toilet."

"Oh. Yes: backed up on me."

"Well, we'll take a look-see."

"Ah—have a drink first."

"All righty. Say, tough about Mr. Hoover."

"Too much liquor."

"Uh-huh. It's okay, though: we came in my car."

Mr. Pierce poured two stiff ones and handed a glass to the red-faced man. "You two just met tonight, is that it?" he asked, hopefully.

"'S right. Fine fella, Hoover. Speaks very high of you. Made a bet you'd remember what tonight was. Well, bottoms up! Over the lips and past the gums, look out, stomach, here it comes!"

"Cheers."

"Shame about it, you ask me. No woman is worth losing your friends over, Mr. Fierst."

"I suppose not. Uh—you just decided on the spur of the moment to visit me? I mean, Lew—he didn't happen to mention to anybody else you were coming over here?"

"Didn't exactly know it myself till we were here. Crazy fella, what he told me was we were goin' to see some broads. I mean, you know, girls. Then," Fein giggled, "we turn up here. I think— say, you got a snake? Take a jiffy if you do. See, I'm on vacation now, otherwise I'd have my tools."

"I think perhaps I do."

"Well, let's get at it. Maybe a plunger would do the trick."

"We'll find something for you," Mr. Pierce said, and led the way.

"Must really be nice," Fein said, "to have buddies. Little town where I hail from, not too many friends. That Hoover fella, he told me you got more buddies than anybody he ever knew."

"I had a lot of friends once, yes," Mr. Pierce said. "I will again."

"Sure you will," Fein said.

He had taken no more than two steps inside the bathroom when he gasped, wheeled, gasped again and fell, clawing, to the pink tile floor.

Mr. Pierce steadied himself, removed from Mr. Fein's neck the long thin knife used for trimming fat, and lifted and pulled and strained and at last managed to get the heavy figure into the bathtub.

Water sloshed over the sides, now, but it was not even like red ink any more, but deeper red, and gummy.

Mr. Pierce sighed, permitted one short spasm to shake his body, sighed two more times, and slipped on the oilcloth apron.

He had it almost tied, when:

There was a knock. Only one, but the glass-squared door shook in its poor-fitting jamb and sent sharp sounds trembling throughout the apartment.

Mr. Pierce froze.

Then there was another sound; a latch opening, a squeak, a voice:

"Happy All Fools Day! Hey—anybody home? Eddie, you old sea-dog, where the devil are you? Hey! It's Len! Just dropped in to say howdy."

"Hi!" Mr. Pierce called out. He removed the apron. "Be with you in a second."

"Jimmy get here yet?"

"No. Not yet."

Mr. Pierce stood erect in the tiny bathroom, looked about, and washed his hands.

Then he walked out with a brand-new sort of smile and a brand-new look in his eyes.

"Good to see you, Len. It's been a long time," he said, wearily.

THE TRAIN

NEELY was the little hand on a clock, he was the mercury in a thermometer: he moved and he didn't move. Hours it had taken just to pull off the bedclothes, because Mother slept quietly and the train had stopped lurching—*hours*—and now he must push his body up and swing his legs over the side of the berth.

He lay barely breathing, his toes strained against the cool hardness of metal. How long since they turned the lights off? From the corner of his eye he looked at Mother and even from the back he could tell she had not yet fallen into a deep sleep. Any little thing woke her up when she was like this. Sometimes she sat right up when the train passed over a rough track section. So he knew he couldn't move any further. Because then she would wake and turn over and ask him what was the matter.

Neely thought of excuses rapidly, rejected rapidly. Say that he had to go to the bathroom? No; she'd want to help him and that would be terrible. Besides, he'd already been—twice, in fact. That he was turning over? No; she'd want to know why the covers were off. Ill, his stomach hurt—no, no, that would spoil everything. There would be the pills that he couldn't swallow and the porters running to telegraph doctors and everything in a mess.

There was no excuse. He'd have to wait, for—something.

Soft light from the moon and moving stars streamed in through the half-shaded windows, making the small bed cool and blue. The heavy green curtains were black now, and the light made the sheets crisp. Neely loved the coolness and the comfort of the berth and he knew that tomorrow night he would sleep. He would slide in between the clean linen, press it tight, watch Mother load up the green net, take one look around him before the overhead lamp snapped off and then relax and let the gentle swaying put him to sleep. He looked forward to tomorrow night. But it had been almost a year since the last time and there was much to do, much

77

to see and feel. . . . So he had gone to bed promptly and without a fuss and waited.

Neely clenched his teeth and tried not to listen to the wheels. He kept his eyes open, fighting all the seductive sensations. He *had* to stay awake! For the Trip.

The train groaned and swayed and rocked and clicked and far ahead it cried mournfully, hot steam rushing out of its iron throat like dragon's breath in the dark unfriendly night.

Clicketa-clicketa-clackata-clicketa . . . Go-to-sleep-go-to-sleep . . . clicketa-clicketa . . .

Neely fought so hard he almost didn't hear the snore. It was a soft snore, but sharp, like a cough, and when he did hear, his heart began to pain him. He waited, praying. The sound came again and now he could tell: it had happened. Mother was really asleep— sound asleep. She wouldn't hear him now. She wouldn't wake and ask him questions and scold him.

He could leave now.

Quickly then, synchronizing each short move with each con- siderable noise or jar, Neely climbed out of the berth. He stopped when his feet touched the rough floor-carpet and watched Mother. She had not stirred. The snores became regular and deeper. Neely smiled and pulled the black suitcase out from under the berth and took from it his old terrycloth bathrobe and leather slippers. Then he carefully pulled the curtains together and buttoned them.

The car was dark and silent: only a dim blue light at the end and the sound of the distant iron wheels. The heavy curtains were all drawn shut, some bulging with the weight of restive bodies, some falling over regularly set shoes. The quiet green hall of sleep.

Neely grinned and thrilled. Things started to come back. It was the same Train he loved and thought about all the time, the same. And he could spend hours going through it, all by himself this time, with no one to direct him or stop him. It was here, right before him, what he'd dreamed about during the long dull days at school and in the ugly house where Mother and Father lived.

He held his robe and slippers and tiptoed past the sealed berths into the narrow rocking hall. He stopped for a moment before the brown-painted case with its ominous brown ax, thought briefly of breaking the glass and grabbing the ax and screaming "Fire! Fire!" and shrugged and went into the room with the curtain for a door.

It glistened with five spotless white sinks and a maze of silver tubes. It was the room Neely loved best, next to the Phantom Car, so he stood on the cold floor for a time, playing with every delicious memory. And thinking, Nothing has changed—it won't ever change!

In the tiny light, he tried out the smells first. The strong smells of iron and soap and stale cigar smoke, of good leather and bright spittoons—more fragrant than the blood of every vanquished giant who ever lived. Then the sign, which started in serious dignity: IT WOULD BE APPRECIATED IF PASSENGERS— He tried out each experience, one by one. . . .

The full-length mirror held the image of the small boy and flattered him. Neely ran a hand through his blond hair and made several hideous faces and then adjusted his robe until it was perfect. He thought of going into the watercloset and reading the sign there, but that took time and there was much to see. There was the Phantom Car, waiting, miles ahead.

He did not see the face peering out from the opening in the corner curtains, the big friendly face with the laughing eyes.

"Hey, young fella, you goin' in or what?"

The voice was an explosion, a rumbling exploded nightmare, before it became familiar.

It was the porter. And he slept where car porters sleep.

"Hello," Neely said, feeling caught.

The man laughed and shook his head. "Boy, your mama know you up this late?"

"Yes sir, she does. . . ."

"Well, okay, all right, get on with what you doin'. Don't let me disturb you!"

The curtains closed again and Neely could hear the chuckling.

He walked out of the room back into the hall and let the air go out of his lungs. Then he went to the heavy door and pushed hard and got it open.

The air was cold between cars: he could feel it blowing through all the hidden openings. He tried to balance between the sections and giggled as he fell and had to grab the rail.

It was all the same! But better, infinitely better, because he was alone, all by himself to see it. The necklace of stars moving slowly out the window, the moaning iron-rubbing-iron and the great wonderful comfort of even the dangerous sliding plates.

He knew he'd have to hurry. It must be very late—hadn't the porter said so? Maybe almost morning. But he had to sort out things and this seemed the best place to get it over with.

Mother had asked him once why he loved the Train and he hadn't been able to answer her. She explained that a train was just a way of getting from one place to another, just like a car or a bus or an airplane, and she said she was worried about him always talking about trains.

Why *did* he feel the way he did? Why did he call the train his World, from the beginning?

Looking out the window at the terrible, desolate and unknown night, with all its lonely fears and terrors, he saw, suddenly, one of the reasons. It was—that he was being safe and in danger, at the same time. All the ugly things were whistling by, and he was going right through them. And none of them touched him. He could laugh at them!

The train went over a soft spot in the bed and the track began another curve. Out the platform window the tiny head of this hollow iron snake could presently be seen, gasping silent orange fire.

Neely balanced himself again and thought about how different it was in an automobile. There you could only sit, and Mother and Father and other people would talk and argue, and you smelled their breath and felt their heavy nearness and you wanted all the time to stretch out your legs, far, always, and you could only sit. And the airplane was no better: just a big automobile in the sky, nothing to do but sit, nothing to see but air. . . .

Neely stopped thinking of reasons. Who cared, anyway? They didn't matter. What mattered was seeing the Train again.

He walked from *Tecumseh* into *Chief Powhatan*, through *Pocahontas* and *Larimee* and *Thundercloud*. And with every step, the other life faded. When he came to *Mt. Rainier* he had forgotten what Mother looked like. At *General Robt. E. Lee* all memories of Father vanished. With each step, the other life peeled away.

When Neely came at last to *Montclair*, there was only the Train. The green walls and the fuzzy rough seat arms and the MEN room and rolling rocking through night. He wasn't a ten-year-old boy any more, but a part—a living part—of the Train.

What was it Mother had said, about everything being different this time—about his growing up and facing life?

Neely pushed hard on the handle, his throat tight, mouth dry, wondering vaguely why the last car was always the hardest to open.

He walked into *Montclair*.

There were no lamps, but he could see clearly now. It was the last thrill. No curtains in this car, no line of shoes or friendly porter sleeping. But strange chairs, unattached to the floor, sitting by tables, silver ashtrays leading to the very end. And everything peculiar, somehow . . . as though nobody had ever, ever been here before. Except, perhaps, ghosts.

The Phantom Car, where he was always—even with Mother—most excited and thrilled and delightfully frightened.

The sounds of the Train were loudest here. The metal ashtrays bobbled on their heavy foundations and the leather-covered magazines shifted slightly. And there was the big glass door at the rear . . .

Neely tiptoed slowly down the hall of chairs, looking forward to every moment and despising every moment that slipped into the past. He walked, sure that the car had some sort of meaning for him—for it was really his destination: he had never wanted to walk toward the engine.

The moon slid behind clouds and it was dark except for small ribbons of glow which fell faintly across the fixtures.

Neely walked.

The door to the observation platform stuck, and for a moment he was terrified, because the moon was still behind clouds. But he tugged and managed to get it open.

Listen, Neely! Listen, to the big sharp wind now, how it screams all around you! And see into the night, into the million fear-filled shadows, the cold and lifeless night. Feel the strong iron wheels bump and pound, carrying you through it all. And most important—he went to the railing and put his small hands about the metal—most important, Neely, let it come true. Let it come true!

"Take him by plane, Dora, for God's sake. Don't let him get disappointed. It's the least we can do."

It was as if he only now heard the words: they whispered deep inside his ears, inside his head.

"Or let me drive you up this time. You know what he's made of this thing. Let the kid have that pleasure!"

Strange words that didn't make any sense. . . . But, Father had used them. Yes. And then, Mother had said:

"If you think I'm going to let my child grow up to be a schizophrene, you're wrong, Jeff Fransen. Any psychologist will tell you—children have got to get out of their dream worlds and the sooner they do, the better. Do you think we'd be able to keep him off trains the rest of his life?"

"But honey, he's only ten!"

"Ten-year-old kids write books on sex these days."

"He'll hate us—I'm telling you. If you take him into his 'train' this time and let him get disappointed, he'll hate us."

"Nonsense. You're—honestly, Jeff, you're talking like a first grade pupil, not a college professor!"

"All right, all right. You'll be taking him; it's you he'll hate most."

Neely shook his head of all the crazy words and let the cindery wind claw at his face. He was alone now, in the Train. Everyone else was sleeping and he had seen the Train again.

He stood, holding the rail, feeling the movement, laughing at the night whirling by.

Time was now the little hand on a clock and the mercury in a thermometer. It almost stopped: Neely stood on the platform, holding it all motionless within himself.

He didn't know how many hours were passing, or days, or minutes, maybe. For he had the thought that was the most wonderful of all: the thought of everything staying just like it was. He could stand forever on the platform of his World and never go back. Mother would sleep forever in the faraway berth and Father would be forever waiting and Time would suspend itself as it was now. . . .

The sudden slowing and jogging and voices filled the air, but not Neely's mind. He had the thought of all eternity in the Train, so for now his mind was filled and there was not room for more.

"Pull 'er on up ahead to the tank," said a voice. "We'll keep this one here."

"Hotbox on 916—I already told MacCready it'd take about half an hour," said another voice.

"Pull 'er up anyways. We're running late," a third voice called.

The buzz of words, close-by. Violet flares. The sound of feet running and then the mile of green cars disconnecting and rumbling ahead, far ahead up the track and out of sight, leaving the last car in the dark, alone.

Then—stillness.

Neely felt the rush of years deliriously and it was not until he knelt his head to swallow that he saw. The moon had come from behind its layer of clouds and he saw—that the ground no longer moved. The cross-ties were not blurred, but stationary, each one distinct. And the wind had ceased.

He rubbed his eyes, turned and ran the length of the car to the door. He opened it savagely, strained to see, looked out into—

The night.

Excitement gathered as he tried to think. He looked again. Nothing. Just a track leading into blackness, nothing else, no train; and around him, the hills and trees and . . .

He remembered. His wish! It—had come true! Now he couldn't go back down the halls of the cars, back to Mother. And he couldn't ever see the other life again. It was a miracle, but the Train itself had been a miracle and this was what he had wished, above all else.

Neely felt his heart about to explode. He raced back to the platform and saw the empty tracks.

The tears rushed up, suddenly. What had happened? His wish had come true: what had happened, *why was he crying?*

He had what he wanted and now he was crying, afraid. He was afraid, afraid. *Why?*

"Please!" Neely screamed. "Please! Make—oh, make it come back. Make it come back. I don't want to be alone here, I don't want to be alone in the Train. Please God!"

He shut his eyes tight, waited and opened them again. Then he stumbled and fell into a corner and sobbed, hysterically, until he realized what he had been saying: That he hated the Train, that he really wanted the other life. No, not that—had to have it. And the strange words began to mold clearly, the words Father had said to Mother. *"Don't let him get disappointed . . ."*

The Train melted, even as Neely understood. The Room of Happiness became a washroom; the Train became iron; the wheels wheels. It all became, slowly, a way to get from one place to another, a machine invented by somebody years and years ago, put together by men, used by people.

Neely screamed out his confusion, sobbed until his throat could make no sound.

Then the black darkness came and entered his mind. . . .

The bridge of black was long—it stretched far across Time. Things happened, they had happened, they were happening: people appeared, talking and exclaiming; and Mother, excited, nervous. Neely felt himself lifted and carried by strong hands, carried through illimitable cars gently while the worried words droned louder, louder in his consciousness. . . . The bridge ascended when he thought of the empty tracks so he stopped thinking and pulled the blackness about him as a quilt to keep out the cold.

But the words came through: he could not cover them over. The important ones came like quick fishes, barbed fishes with big mouths and sharp white teeth.

What's the matter, lady, don't you know better than to leave your kid run all over? . . .

Sorry, ma'am—he probably just got scared is all, maybe just too scared to do anything when he seen we was adding that other car. Thought he was being left behind or something, maybe. . . .

Can you hear us, sonny? You all right? Now now, there's nothing to worry about. It's all over now, all over. See, son, we had what they call a hotbox—that means when something goes wrong, like on a car, you know?—and, see, what we had to do, we had to put on another car. That's all there was to it. . . .

Don't suppose he got sick, do you? . . .

*No, that doctor'd of said so, wouldn't he? Kid just got panicky when he
seen he was alone. . . .*

*You think it's all right now, ma'am? You think we ought to get him
anything? Or just put him to bed; yeah, that's it, best thing in the world
for him. . . .*

Neely waited until the pool was clear and all the words had gone
away; then he let Mother tuck him in and pull down the shades and
pat him with her nervous shaking hands.

"Neely, Neely . . ."

He was tired, so he tried to sleep now. But—the noise disturbed
him. And the berth was too narrow. And all the shaking and rocking hurt his head.

He tried only once to remember.

Then he lay back and began to wonder when they would finally
get to wherever they were going.

THE DARK MUSIC

It was not a path at all but a dry white river of shells, washed clean by the hot summer rain and swept by the winds that came over the gulf from Mexico: a million crushed white shells, spread quietly over the cold earth, for the feet of Miss Lydia Maple.

She'd never seen the place before. She'd never been told of it. It couldn't have been purposeful, her stopping the bus at the unmarked turn, pausing, then inching down the narrow path and stopping again at the tree-formed arch; on the other hand, it certainly was not impulse. She had recognized impulsive actions for what they were years ago: animal actions. And, as she was proud to say, Miss Maple did not choose to think of herself as an animal. Which the residents of Sand Hill might have found a slightly odd attitude for a biology teacher, were it not so characteristic.

Perhaps it was this: that by its virginal nature, the area promised much in the way of specimens. Frogs would be here, and insects, and, if they were lucky, a few garden snakes for the bolder lads.

In any case, Miss Maple was well satisfied. And if one could judge from their excited murmurings, which filtered through the thickness of trees, so were the students.

She smiled. Leaning against the elm, now, with all the forest fragrance rising to her nostrils, and the clean gulf breeze cooling her, she was suddenly very glad indeed that she had selected today for the field trip. Otherwise, she would be at this moment seated in the chalky heat of the classroom. And she would be reminded again of the whole nasty business, made to defend her stand against the clucking tongues, or to pretend there was nothing to defend. The newspapers were not difficult to ignore, but it was impossible to shut away the attitude of her colleagues; and—no: one must not think about it.

She looked at the shredded lace of sunlight.

It was a lovely spot! Not a single beer can, not a bottle nor a cellophane wrapper nor even a cigarette to suggest that human beings had ever been here before. It was—*pure*.

In a way, Miss Maple liked to think of herself in similar terms. She believed in purity, and had her own definition of the word. Of course she realized—how could she doubt it now?—she might be an outmoded and slightly incongruous figure in this day and age; but that was all right. She took pride in the distinction. And to Mr. Owen Tracy's famous remark that hers was the only biology class in the world where one would hear nothing to discourage the idea of the stork, she had responded as though to a great compliment. The Lord could testify, it hadn't been easy! How many, she wondered, would have fought as valiantly as she to protect the town's children from that most pernicious and evil encroachment of them all?

Sex education, indeed!

By all means, let us kill every last lovely dream; let us destroy the only trace of goodness and innocence in this wretched, guilty world!

Miss Maple twitched, vaguely aware that she was dozing. The word *sex* jarred her toward wakefulness, but *purity* pulled her back again. What a pity, in a way, she thought, that I was born so late. . . .

She had no idea what the thought meant; only that, for all the force of good she might be in Sand Hill, her battle was probably a losing one; and she was something of a dinosaur. In earlier, unquestionably better times, how different it would have been! Her purity would then have served a very real and necessary function, and would not have called down charges from the magazines that she was "hindering education." She might have been born in pre-Dynastian Egypt, for instance, and marched at the forefront of the court maidens toward some enormously important sacrifice. Or in the early Virginia, when the ladies were ladies and wore fifteen petticoats and were cherished because of it. Or in New England. In any time but this!

A sound brushed her ear.

She opened her eyes, watched a fat wren on a pipestem twig, and settled back to the half-sleep, deciding to dream a while now about

Mr. Hennig and Sally Barnes. They had been meeting secretly after three o'clock, Miss Maple knew. She'd waited, though, and taken her time, and then struck. And she'd caught them, in the basement, doing those unspeakable things.

Mr. Hennig would not be teaching school for a while now.

She stretched, almost invisible against the forest floor. The mouse-colored dress covered her like an embarrassed hand, concealing, not too successfully, the rounded hills of her breasts, keeping the secret of her slender waist and full hips, trailing down below the legs she hated because they were so smooth and white and shapely, down to the plain black leather shoes. Her face was pale and naked as a nun's, but the lips were large and moist, and the cheekbones high, and it did not look very much like a nun's face. Miss Maple fought her body and her face every morning, but she was not victorious. In spite of it all, and to her eternal dismay, she was an attractive woman.

The sound came again, and woke her.

It was not the fat bird and it was not the children. It was music. Like the music of flutes, very high-pitched and mellow, yet sharp; and though there was a melody, she could not recognize it.

Miss Maple shook her head, and listened.

The sound was real. It was coming from the forest, distant and far off and if you did not shut out the other noises, you could scarcely hear it. But it was there.

Miss Maple rose, instantly alert, and brushed the leaves and pine needles away. For some reason, she felt a chill.

Why should there be music in a lost place like this?

She listened. The wind cooled through the trees and the piping sound seemed to be carried along with it, light as shadows. Three quick high notes; a pause; then a trill, like an infant's weeping; and a pause. Miss Maple shivered and started back to the field where the children were. She took three steps and did not take any more in that direction.

The music changed. Now it did not weep, and the notes were not so high-pitched. They were slow and sinuous, lower to the ground.

Imploring. Beckoning. . . .

Miss Maple turned and, without having the slightest notion why, began to walk into the thickness. The foliage was wet, glistening dark green, and it was not long before her thin dress was soaked in many places, but she understood that she must go on. She must find the person who was making such beautiful sounds.

In minutes she was surrounded by bushes, and the trail had vanished. She pushed branches aside, walked, listened.

The music grew louder. It grew nearer. But now it was fast, yelping and crying, and there was great urgency in it. Once, to Miss Maple's terror, it sounded, for a brief moment, like chuckling; still, there was no note that was not lonely, and sad.

She walked, marveling at her foolishness. It was, of course, not proper for a school teacher to go tumbling through the shrubbery, and she was a proper person. Besides—she stopped, and heard the beating of her heart—what if it were one of those horrid men who live on the banks of rivers and in woods and wait for women? She'd heard of such men.

The music became plaintive. It soothed her, told her not to be afraid; and some of the fear drained away.

She was coming closer, she knew. It had seemed vague and elusive before, now it thrummed in the air and encircled her.

Was there ever such lonely music?

She walked carefully across a webwork of stones. They protruded like small islands from the rushing brook, and the silver water looked very cold, but when her foot slipped and sank, she did not flinch.

The music grew impossibly loud. Miss Maple covered her ears with her hands, and could not still it. She listened and tried to run.

The notes rolled and danced in her mind: shrill screams and soft whispers and silences that pulsed and roared.

Beyond the trees.

Beyond the trees; another step; one more—

Miss Maple threw her hands out and parted the heavy green curtain.

The music stopped.

There was only the sound of the brook, and the wind, and her heart.

She swallowed and let the breath come out of her lungs. Then, slowly, she went through the shrubs and bushes, and rubbed her eyes.

She was standing in a grove. Slender saplings, spotted brown, undulated about her like the necks of restless giraffes, and beneath her feet there was soft golden grass, high and wild. The branches of the trees came together at the top to form a green dome. Sunlight speared the ground.

Miss Maple looked in every direction. Across the grove to the surrounding dark and shadowed woods, and to all sides. And saw nothing. Only the grass and the trees and the sunlight.

Then she sank to the earth and lay still, wondering why she felt such heat and such fear.

It was at this moment that she became conscious of it: one thing which her vision might deny, and her senses, but which she knew nonetheless to be.

She was not alone.

"Yes?" The word rushed up and then died before it could ever leave her mouth.

A rustle of leaves: tiny hands applauding.

"Who is it?"

A drum in her chest.

"Yes, *please*—who is it? Who's here?"

And silence.

Miss Maple put fisted fingers to her chin and stopped breathing. I'm not alone, she thought. I'm not alone.

No.

Did someone say that?

The terror built, and then she felt something else entirely that wasn't terror and wasn't fear, either. Something that started her trembling. She lay on the grass, trembling, while this new sensation washed over her, catching her up in great tides and filling her.

What was it? She tried to think. She'd known this feeling before, a very long time ago; years ago on a summer night when the moon was a round, unblinking, huge and watchful eye, and that boy—John?—had stopped talking and touched her. And how strange it was then, wondering what his hands were going to do next. John!

There's a big eye watching us; take me home, I'm afraid! I'm afraid, John.

If you don't take me home, I'll tell.

I'll tell them the things you tried to do.

Miss Maple stiffened when she felt the nearness, and heard the laughter. Her eyes arced over the grove.

"Who's laughing?"

She rose to her feet. There was a new smell in the air. A coarse animal smell, like wet fur: hot and fetid, thick, heavy, rolling toward her, covering her.

Miss Maple screamed.

Then the pipes began, and the music was frenzied this time. In front of her, in back, to the sides of her; growing louder, growing faster, and faster. She heard it deep in her blood and when her body began to sway, rhythmically, she closed her eyes and fought and found she could do nothing.

Almost of their own volition, her legs moved in quick, graceful steps. She felt herself being carried over the grass, swiftly, light as a blown leaf—

"Stop!"

—swiftly, leaping and turning, to the shaded dell at the end of the grove.

Here, consumed with heat, she dropped to the softness, and breathed the animal air.

The music ceased.

A hand touched her, roughly.

She threw her arms over her face: "No. Please—"

"Miss Maple!"

She felt her hands reaching toward the top button of her dress.

"Miss Maple! What's the matter?"

An infinite moment; then, everything sliding, melting, like a vivid dream you will not remember. Miss Maple shook her head from side to side and stared up at a young boy with straw hair and wide eyes.

She pulled reality about her.

"You all right, Miss Maple?"

"Of course, William," she said. The smell was gone. The music was gone. It was a dream. "I was following a snake, you see—a chicken snake, to be exact: and a nice, long one, too—and I almost had it, but I twisted my ankle on one of the stones in the brook. That's why I called."

The boy said, "Wow."

"Unfortunately," Miss Maple continued, getting to her feet, "it escaped me. You don't happen to see it, do you, William?"

William said no, and she pretended to hobble back to the field.

At 4:19, after grading three groups of tests, Miss Lydia Maple put on her gray cotton coat and flat black hat and started for home. She was not exactly thinking about the incident in the forest, but Owen Tracy had to speak twice. He had been waiting.

"Miss Maple. Over here!"

She stopped, turned, and approached the blue car. The principal of Overton High was smiling: he was too handsome for his job, too tall and too young, and Miss Maple resented his eyes. They traveled. "Yes, Mr. Tracy?"

"Thought maybe you'd like a lift home."

"That is very nice of you," she said, "but I enjoy walking. It isn't far."

"Well, then, how about my walking along with you?"

Miss Maple flushed. "I—"

"Like to talk with you, off the record." The tall man got out of his car, locked it.

"Not, I hope, about the same subject."

"Yes."

"I'm sorry. I have nothing further to add."

Owen Tracy fell into step. His face was still pleasant, and it was obvious that he intended to retain his good humor, his charm. "I suppose you read Ben Sugrue's piece in the *Sun-Mirror* yesterday?"

Miss Maple said, "No," perfunctorily. Sugrue was a monster, a libertine: it was he who had started the campaign, whose gross libidinous whispers had first swept the town.

"It refers to Overton High as a medieval fortress."

"Indeed? Well," Miss Maple said, "perhaps that's so." She smiled, delicately. "It was, I believe, a medieval fortress that saved the lives of four hundred people during the time of the Black Plague."

Tracy stopped a moment to light a cigarette. "Very good," he conceded. "You're an intelligent person, Lydia. Intelligent and sharp."

"Thank you."

"And that's what puzzles me. This mess over the sex-education program isn't intelligent and it isn't sharp. It's foolish. As a biology teacher you ought to know that."

Miss Maple was silent.

"If we were an elementary school," Tracy said, "well, maybe your idea would make sense. I personally don't think so, but at least you'd have a case. In a high school, though, it's silly; and it's making a laughingstock out of us. If I know Sugrue, he'll keep hammering until one of the national magazines picks it up. And that will be bad."

Miss Maple did not change her expression. "My stand," she said, "ought to be perfectly clear by now, Mr. Tracy. In the event it isn't, let me tell you again. There will be no sex-education program at Overton so long as I am in charge of the biology department. I consider the suggestion vile and unspeakable—and quite impractical—and am not to be persuaded otherwise: neither by yourself, nor by that journalist, nor by the combined efforts of the faculty. Because, Mr. Tracy, I feel a responsibility toward my students. Not only to fill their minds with biological data, but to protect them, also." Her voice was even. "If you wish to take action, of course, you are at liberty to do so—"

"I wouldn't want to do that," Owen Tracy said. He seemed to be struggling with his calm.

"I think that's wise," Miss Maple said. She paused and stared at the principal.

"And what is that supposed to mean?"

"Simply that any measures to interrupt or impede my work, or force changes upon the present curriculum, will prove embarrassing, Mr. Tracy, both to yourself and to Overton." She noticed his fingers and how they were curling.

"Go on."

"I hardly think that's necessary."

"I do. Go on, please."

"I may be . . . old-fashioned," she said, "but I am not stupid. Nor am I unobservant. I happen to have learned some of the facts concerning yourself and Miss Bond . . ."

Owen Tracy's calm fled like a released animal. Anger began to twitch along his temples. "I see."

They looked at one another for a while; then the principal turned and started back in the opposite direction. The fire had gone out of his eyes. After a few steps, he turned again and said, "It may interest you to know that Miss Bond and I are going to be married at the end of the term."

"I wonder why," Miss Maple said, and left the tall man standing in the bloody twilight.

She felt a surge of exultation as she went up the stairs of her apartment. Of course she'd known nothing about them, only guessed: but when you think the worst of people, you're seldom disappointed. It had been true, after all. And now her position was absolutely unassailable.

She opened cans and bottles and packages and prepared her usual supper. Then, when the dishes were done, she read Richards' *Practical Criticism* until nine o'clock. At nine-thirty she tested the doors to see that they were securely locked, drew the curtains, fastened the windows and removed her clothes, hanging them carefully in the one small closet.

The gown she chose was white cotton, chin-high and ankle-low, faintly figured with tiny fleur-de-lis. For a brief moment her naked body was exposed; then, at once, covered up again, wrapped, encased, sealed.

Miss Maple lay in the bed, her mind untroubled.

But sleep would not come.

She got up after a while and warmed some milk; still she could not sleep. Unidentifiable thoughts came, disturbing her. Unnormal sensations. A feeling that was not proper. . . .

Then she heard the music.

The pipes: the high-pitched, dancing pipes of the afternoon, so distant now that she felt perhaps she was imagining them, so real she knew that couldn't be true. They were real.

She became frightened, when the music did not stop, and reached for the telephone. But what person would she call? And what would she say?

Miss Maple decided to ignore the sounds, and the hot strange feeling that was creeping upon her alone in her bed.

She pressed the pillow tight against her ears, and held it there, and almost screamed when she saw that her legs were moving apart slowly, beyond her will.

The heat in her body grew. It was a flame, the heat of high fevers, moist and interior: not a warmth.

And it would not abate.

She threw the covers off and began to pace the room, hands clenched. The music came through the locked windows.

Miss Maple!

She remembered things, without remembering them.

She fought another minute, very hard; then surrendered. Without knowing why, she ran to the closet and removed her gray coat and put it on over the nightgown; then she opened a bureau drawer and pocketed a ring of keys, ran out the front door, down the hall, her naked feet silent upon the thick-piled carpet, and into the garage where it was dark. The music played fast, her heart beat fast, and she moaned softly when the seldom-used automobile sat cold and unresponding to her touch.

At last it came to life, when she thought she must go out of her mind; and Miss Maple shuddered at the dry coughs and violent starts and black explosions.

In moments she was out of town, driving faster than she had ever driven, pointed toward the wine-dark waters of the gulf. The highway turned beneath her in a blur and sometimes, on the curves, she heard the shocked and painful cry of the tires, and felt the car slide; but it didn't matter. Nothing mattered, except the music.

Though her eyes were blind, she found the turn-off, and soon she was hurtling across the white path of shells, so fast that there was a wake behind her; then, scant yards from the restless stream, she brought her foot down hard upon the brake pedal, and the car danced to a stop.

Miss Maple rushed out because now the piping was inside her, and ran across the path into the field and across the field into the trees and through the trees, stumbling and falling and getting up again, not feeling the cold sharp fingers of brush tearing at her and the high wet grass soaking her and the thousand stones daggering her flesh, feeling only the pumping of her heart and the music, calling and calling.

There! The brook was cold, but she was across it, and past the wall of foliage. And there! The grove, moon-silvered and waiting.

Miss Maple tried to pause and rest; but the music would not let her do this. Heat enveloped her: she removed the coat; ate her: she tore the tiny pearl buttons of her gown and pulled the gown over her head and threw it to the ground.

It did no good. Proper Miss Lydia Maple stood there, while the wind lifted her hair and sent it billowing like shreds of amber silk, and felt the burning and listened to the pipes.

Dance! they told her. Dance tonight, Miss Maple: now. It's easy. You remember. Dance!

She began to sway then, and her legs moved, and soon she was leaping over the tall grass, whirling and pirouetting.

Like this?

Like that, Miss Maple. Yes, like that!

She danced until she could dance no more, then she stopped by the first tree by the end of the grove, and waited for the music to stop as she knew it would.

The forest became silent.

Miss Maple smelled the goaty animal smell and felt it coming closer; she lay against the tree and squinted her eyes, but there was nothing to see, only shadows.

She waited.

There was a laugh, a wild shriek of amusement; bull-like and heavily masculine it was, but wild as no man's laugh ever could be. And then the sweaty fur odor was upon her, and she experienced a strength about her, and there was breath against her face, hot as steam.

"Yes," she said, and hands touched her, hurting with fierce pain.

"Yes!" and she felt glistening muscles beneath her fingers, and a weight upon her, a shaggy, tawny weight that was neither ghost nor human nor animal, but with much heat; hot as the fires that blazed inside her.

"Yes," said Miss Maple, parting her lips. "Yes! *Yes!*"

The change in Lydia Maple thenceforth was noticed by some but not marked, for she hid it well. Owen Tracy would stare at her sometimes, and sometimes the other teachers would wonder to themselves why she should be looking so tired so much of the time; but since she did not say or do anything specifically different, it was left a small mystery.

When some of the older boys said that they had seen Miss Maple driving like a bat out of hell down the gulf highway at two in the morning, they were quickly silenced: for such a thing was, on the face of it, too absurd for consideration.

The girls of her classes were of the opinion that Miss Maple looked happier than she had ever been, but this was attributed to her victory over the press and the principal's wishes on the matter of sex-education.

To Mr. Owen Tracy, it seemed to be a distasteful subject for conversation all the way around. He was in full agreement with the members of the school board that progress at Overton would begin only when Miss Maple was removed: but in order to remove her, one would have to have grounds. Sufficient grounds, at that, for there was the business of himself and Lorraine Bond. . . .

As for Miss Maple, she developed the facility of detachment to a fine degree. A week went by and she answered the call of the pipes without fail—though going about it in a more orderly manner— and still, wondering vaguely about the spattered mud on her legs, about the grass stains and bits of leaves and fresh twigs, she did not actually believe that any of it was happening. It was fantastic, and fantasy had no place in Miss Maple's life.

She would awaken each morning satisfied that she had had another unusual dream; then she would forget it, and go about her business.

It was on a Monday—the night of the day that she had assembled positive proof that Willie Hammacher and Rosalia Forbes were cutting classes together and stealing away to Dauphin Park; and submitted this proof; and had Willie and Rosalia threatened with expulsion from school—that Miss Maple scented her body with perfumes, lay down and waited, again, for the music.

She waited, tremulous as usual, aching beneath the temporary sheets; but the air was still.

He's late, she thought, and tried to sleep. Often she would sit up, though, certain that she had heard it, and once she got halfway across the room toward the closet; and sleep was impossible.

She stared at the ceiling until three A.M., listening.

Then she rose and dressed and got into her car.

She went to the grove.

She stood under the crescent moon, under the bruised sky.

And heard the wind; her heart; owls high in the trees; the shifting currents of the stream; the stony rustle of the brook; and heard the forest quiet.

Tentatively, she took off her clothes, and stacked them in a neat pile.

She raised her arms from her sides and tried a few steps. They were awkward. She stopped, embarrassed.

"Where are you?" she whispered.

Silence.

"I'm here," she whispered.

Then, she heard the chuckling: it was cruel and hearty, but not mirthless.

Over here, Miss Maple.

She smiled and ran to the middle of the grove. Here?

No, Miss Maple: over here! You're looking beautiful tonight. And hungry. Why don't you dance?

The laughter came from the trees, to the right. She ran to it. It disappeared. It appeared again, from the trees to the left.

What can you be after, madame? It's hardly proper, you know. Miss Maple, where are your clothes?

She covered her breasts with her hands, and knew fear. "Don't," she said. "Please, don't." The aching and the awful heat were in her. "Come out! I want—"

"You want—?"

Miss Maple went from tree to tree, blindly. She ran until pain clutched at her legs, and, by the shadowed dell, she sank exhausted.

There was one more sound. A laugh. It faded.

And everything became suddenly very still and quiet.

Miss Maple looked down and saw that she was naked. It shocked her. It shocked her, also, to become aware that she was Lydia Maple, thirty-seven, teacher of biology at Overton.

"Where are you?" she cried.

The wind felt cold upon her body. Her feet were cold among the grasses. She knew a hunger and a longing that were unbearable.

"Come to me," she said, but her voice was soft and hopeless.

She was alone in the wood now.

And this was the way it had been meant.

She put her face against the rough bark of the tree and wept for the first time in her life. Because she knew that there was no more music for her, there would never be any music for her again.

Miss Maple went to the grove a few more times, late at night, desperately hoping it was not true. But her blood thought for her: What it was, or who it was, that played the pipes so sweetly in the wooded place would play no more; of that she was sure. She did not know why. And it gave her much pain for many hours, and sleep was difficult, but there was nothing to be done.

Her body considered seeking out someone in the town, and rejected the notion. For what good was a man when one had been loved by a god?

In time she forgot everything, because she had to forget.

The music, the dancing, the fire, the feel of strong arms about her: everything.

And she might have gone on living quietly, applauding purity, battling the impure, and holding the Beast of Worldliness outside the gates of Sand Hill forever—if a strange thing had not happened.

It happened in a small way.

During dinner one evening Miss Maple found herself craving things. It had been a good day, she had found proof that the rumors about Mr. Etlin, the English I teacher, were true—he did indeed subscribe to that dreadful magazine; and Owen Tracy was thinking of transferring to another school; yet, as she sat there in her apartment, alone, content, she was hungry for things.

First it was ice cream. Big plates of strawberry ice cream topped with marshmallow sauce.

Then it was wine.

And then Miss Maple began to crave grass—

Nobody ever did find out why she moved away from Sand Hill in such a hurry, or where she went, or what happened to her.

But then, nobody cared.

THE CUSTOMERS

THE room was quiet and the old woman sat in the room looking out the window, out into the steel-gray afternoon. At the
cheddar-sharp little fingers of wind playing with icy bits of weeds
and leaves; at the sickly rays of sunlight tumbling to the ashen
earth; at the soft clean fragrance of moist grass and moldering
pine needles; the gray wind, the gray sunlight.

She fretted the neck of the brown tomcat asleep in her lap, and
watched. Then she leaned forward, squinted and rubbed away
some window-frost with her hand.

"Henry," the old woman said.

The old man's hand fell from the arm of his chair. He made a
small noise.

"*Henry.*"

His head bobbled. His lips moved.

"Wake up."

The old man's eyes opened. "All right," he said. "Just give me a
second."

"Second nothing. Wake up now."

"Well, what is it? What is it?"

The old woman's voice sounded filled with fear. "It's Him," she
said. "He's coming."

The old man sat up and yawned and wiped the sleep from his
face. He smiled. "Didn't I tell you to quit staring out that blamed
window? Didn't I say that you'd go imagining things?"

"Henry Ludlow, nobody's imagining nothing. Get up from
there and come look."

Mr. Ludlow braced his fingers on the chair. He walked to the
window, patted his wife upon her wrists and parted the curtains.
He squinted.

"Hmm!" Mr. Ludlow said.

"Mr. Know-it-all. You see or don't you see?"

"I see," the old man said, dropping the curtains again. "But we can't be sure, Myrtle. Not actually."

Mrs. Ludlow turned her head. "Just look at him," she said. "*You* ever see such an elegant person around these parts? Black suit, briefcase, even a little bitty old mustache. Now who in thunder else could it be?"

Mr. Ludlow laid a finger alongside his nose and shook his head. "I ain't saying it don't look like Him."

"Of *course* it's Him." Mrs. Ludlow removed a lace handkerchief from her sleeve.

"You said that about them others too, remember. That last feller, what was he? A census taker, that's what. I'm only saying you don't want to go jumping to conclusions."

"Jump, jump—*tsk*! Aunt Lucia said we'd get fooled the first few times, didn't she? Said He'd be everywhere inside and out, a feeling of Him in the air. We never was right certain *sure* the last times—just sort of hoped or feared, like. Besides, the sun was shining them times. And my bones didn't ache neither."

Mr. Ludlow caressed a small amulet shaped like an elk's tooth. "Myrtle, your bones—they feeling pretty shipshape now?"

"Ache like the dickens. Feel just right, they do: conditions is right everywhere. Watch at how He walks—mincey-like, like He don't even touch the ground."

Mr. Ludlow sighed. "Well," he said. "Well—guess maybe you're right this time, my dear. Come to think about it, I got the feeling myself."

The old woman clutched suddenly at her husband's arm. She searched his face. "You don't suppose—I mean, He wouldn't want just one of us, would He? It wouldn't happen like that."

"Shh. Still now. You want Him to see you all broke up and whiny?" Mr. Ludlow paused. "Either way, it wouldn't be for long."

The brown tomcat put its head to one side and stood with arched back, listening. Steps on the outside porch sounded briskly, then stopped.

Mrs. Ludlow held to her husband's hand.

"Henry— Oh, tarnation! Go and answer the blame door. Said I wouldn't act like this and I ain't. Go on now."

Mr. Ludlow brushed the tops of his shoes along the backs of his legs and walked out into the hall. He looked at the old woman sitting in the chair by the window, paused a moment and then unlatched the door.

A man in black stood smiling. "How do you do, sir. Do I have the pleasure of addressing Mr. Henry L. Ludlow?"

Mr. Ludlow wet his lips and looked at the man, at the man's tailored suit, gray homburg hat, briefcase, small waxed mustache. "Yes, sir, you do."

"*Ex*cellent. Now, my name is—"

"Come on in."

The man stepped lightly into the hall and took the homburg hat carefully from his head so that no single hair was disturbed.

"Thank you. Thank you very much. My goodness, sir, such a charming house! And so secluded—I tell you, I had the devil's own time finding it. Yes indeedy." The man examined a wooden hat rack briefly before depositing his homburg thereupon. "Exquisite," he said.

Mr. Ludlow looked curious. "Had trouble finding us, you say?"

"Well, a slight exaggeration. Although, well, I *did* get a little bit lost once or twice."

"*You* got lost?"

"I certainly did. In fact, I called on two other homes by mistake."

"Say, I'll have to tell Myrtle that one! The wrong house—twice!"

The man looked sheepish. "But now then," he said, "I imagine you're wondering who I am and why I'm here."

"Well, wouldn't exactly say that, no."

"No?" The man furled his brows. "Oh, the print on the briefcase, eh? Ha ha, now that's very perspicacious of you, sir. I mean, for a man of your age—what I mean is—"

"Never mind, son. That's all right."

"Most folks getting along in years," the man said, "why, they never give us a second thought. You might not believe it, but they wait right up to the last minute, wait until it's too late."

"You don't mean to tell me!"

The man looked sad. "Yes. You'd be amazed. No perception, no acceptance of reality. Why, if we'd known you were thinking of us, we would never have troubled you in this way. Most people, you see, somehow don't take to the idea. Can you countenance it, sir: eighty-seven per cent of people above age seventy must be sought out by us!"

"Huh!"

"Oh yes. Those that do call are pretty generally goaded into it by others. Therefore, if I may, I'd like to congratulate you, Mr. Ludlow, on your down-to-earth common-sense attitude."

Mr. Ludlow scratched his head.

The man in black went through some papers. "Now let's see," he said. "According to our records, we understand you have a wife—Myrtle Louisa Ludlow. May I ask if she is present?"

"Will you be wanting her, too?"

"By all means, sir. By all means! This is something for all of us to talk over. I—that is, I take it you have something definite in mind?"

"Something definite . . ."

"What I mean to say is, I gather from what you've said that you've been considering us?"

"Oh. Yes—we've had you in mind, all right. For quite a spell. Ever since Myrtle—that's my wife—well, since she had that heart attack about four, five months back. We've been sort of sitting around waiting, you might say."

"Good! I can't tell you how pleased that makes me. For your sake as well as my own. You simply would not believe it: I usually have to plead with people, beg them."

"That a fact?"

"Yes indeedy. They're that stubborn."

"Well," Mr. Ludlow said, "I guess you ain't been turned down by nobody."

The man in black brightened and smoothed his mustache. "No sir, I am glad to say that that has not happened yet. I take a certain pride in the fact."

"I imagine you do."

"Oh yes, they all come around in time. But I've always said, why drag it out—when all the details can be taken care of in an afternoon?"

Mr. Ludlow hooked his thumbs in his vest and began to walk

toward the big living-room doors. "The wife's in here," he said. "She's probably wondering what we've been up to."

They went in.

Mrs. Ludlow looked up and sighed deeply. "Henry, you gave me a scare. I couldn't even move I was so scared."

"Just a little preliminary talk, Myrtle. My dear, this here is—"

"I know who it is. How do, young man?"

Mrs. Ludlow stared at the man and a faint pink flushed her thin cheeks. She turned her eyes to her husband and whispered: "Henry—something happened while you was in the hall talking. No mistake about it now. I—had it."

Mr. Ludlow answered in a loud voice full of admiration. "The vision? You had the vision, like Aunt Lucia said?"

"Clear as creekwater. There she was, tapping her foot, smiling away. 'That's Him,' she says, 'that's Him.'"

The young man bowed uncertainly and sat down. "Very happy to meet you, Mrs. Ludlow," he said.

"Expect you are."

The man in black opened his mouth and then closed it. He put the briefcase on his lap. "Now then, folks, shall we get down to business?"

Mrs. Ludlow put a hand to her throat and the sternness went from her face. "So soon?" She looked about the room, at the pictures, at the walls, at the big brown tomcat. She looked at her husband.

"Oh, all right. Go ahead then."

"Thank you. My!" The man's face lost its look of annoyed confusion. "You can't even guess what a pleasure it is to deal with you folks. My job isn't as easy as some might think."

"No," Mr. Ludlow said. "Can't say I'd want to swap with you."

"Not easy work," the man went on. "But it does have its reward. I like to think that I—one should say, 'we'—are giving a lot of people a lot of happiness. Even if some of them won't admit it at the time."

"You look terrible young," Mrs. Ludlow said. "You been at this here kind of work long?"

"Not actually—at least, not in this particular section. I've only been in Martinburg for, oh, two years. Before that I was with the army."

Mrs. Ludlow gasped. "Then it was *you*—all them poor boys— you hear that, Henry?"

"No," Mr. Ludlow said, "can't say I'd swap places with you."

The young man was working his fingers through papers, swiftly, meticulously. "As I was saying to your husband, Mrs. L., if you folks had anything special in mind—?"

"Well sir, to tell the truth, we ain't give the matter much thought. Didn't rightly know we had anything to say about it."

"Why, but you have everything to say about it!"

"We do?"

"Certainly! Indeedy yes, you do!"

Frost was forming heavily on the windows; the room was going dark.

"Now Henry," Mrs. Ludlow said, "that's right thoughtful of them, ain't it."

Mr. Ludlow didn't seem to hear. "I think," he said, "we ought to get one thing die-straight right off the bat here. Is this for certain for both of us, my wife and I?"

"Mr. Ludlow, there are innumerable fine things about Murmuring Everglades, but the finest, possibly, is this policy. *Definitely* for both of you."

Mr. Ludlow walked to his wife and stroked her head. He waited a long moment, then he said: "This Murmuring Everglades, that there's a good spot you say?"

The young man looked momentarily confused. "A good spot? Why, it is, if I may say so, sir, the very best. Did you happen to have any other cemeter—no, but of course you didn't."

Mrs. Ludlow shook her head. The brown tomcat leapt into her lap, purring, stretching.

"Very well. Now then, as I say, to business. Did you folks prefer a vault, the regular mausoleum or something a bit less expensive?"

Mr. Ludlow bit off the end of a cigar. "You handle all that, too?" he said.

"Oh, yes indeedy."

"Well, I'll be darned. What do you think of that, Myrtle?

Well—for myself, I can't say I much relish the idea of six foot of
dirt on top of me."

Mrs. Ludlow shuddered and looked out the window.

"But then again, I don't reckon it'd make much difference one
way or the other. What say, my dear?"

"You take care of it, Henry. Ain't my place to."

The man in black produced a sheet of paper and held it before
his eyes. "If you think the vault is too expensive," he said, "let me
say, *there* is where you're off on the wrong track. Yes indeedy. For
a fine vault on selected property, the cost to you is negligible—in
comparison with the rates of other similar establishments. For
example—Mr. Ludlow, you see on this table I have—for a twelve-
by-eighteen, completely air-tight, guaranteed Italian marble and
imported granite vault—or Rest Haven—you pay only one thousand dollars down and—how old did you say you were, sir?"

"Eighty-four."

"And the Missus?"

"Same."

"Serious illnesses—tuberculosis, et cetera?"

"Well, not exactly. Just those heart attacks of Myrtle's."

"Oh yes, of course—*those*." The young man scribbled on a
piece of paper, consulted columns of figures. "Well," he said at
last, "that would come to twelve-hundred down with the balance
insured. Can you beat that?"

"I don't quite understand," Mr. Ludlow said.

"Well, sir, it only means that Murmuring Everglades bets that
you will live the two years necessary to pay up the balance."

"And you let them do that?"

"I beg your pardon?" the young man said. "You see, Murmuring
Everglades sets up this guarantee so that if anything *should* happen
to you, the vault will still be yours. No risk that way, on your part.
I think you'll find it all quite in order."

"Sounds all right to me," Mrs. Ludlow said. "Henry?"

The old man nodded.

"The vault, then?" the man in black said.

"Yes, the vault."

"Good. A splendid choice. So many people—well, you know,

they simply don't care *how* they're put to their peace. The intelligent ones—like yourselves—always, I have found, *always* make adequate provisions. Now, there's a Rest Haven on one half of an acre, overlooking the town. I've a picture—there, you see?"

Mr. and Mrs. Ludlow gazed thoughtfully at the brightly tinted photograph. Centered at the crest of a knoll was a large whitewash-white crypt, clean lined, solemn despite the colors around it.

"As you might guess," the man was saying, "that construction is A-1. Completely impregnable to atom bombs, excepting direct hits. The statue, by the way, is a perfect reproduction of Rodin's 'The Kiss.'"

Mr. Ludlow showed the photograph again to his wife.

"Well," she said, "it's right pretty, but I *have* seen prettier places in my time. We'll take it—you can tell them so."

The man in black beamed. He extracted two other forms and wrote things upon these. "Yes indeedy," he smiled, "a real pleasure to do business with you folks. Don't often run up against such co-operation."

Mr. Ludlow touched his wife's shoulder. "It's nice of you to say, my boy."

"Tah!" The young man busied himself. "Most of the others feel it's sort of looking on the dark side of things, and, well, that makes me feel bad. It's a reality everyone has to face; but they don't seem to understand."

Mrs. Ludlow pulled her chair around quickly and stared into the frost. The voices and the talk and the papers faded into gray silence; time began to gather up like a hurricane, time and memory and presence. The old woman stroked the back of the brown tomcat and held the delicate lace handkerchief to her eyes. Minutes went by unheard.

Mrs. Ludlow started at the gentle pressure. She looked up and smiled, took the pen in her thin fingers and signed her name on five black lines.

Then the young man in black took all the papers and returned them to his briefcase. He rose, smiled. "May I congratulate you both? A great burden has been lifted from your minds; and in these twilight moments of your life, you can know that the best possible thing has been done, the best possible resting place chosen for your final peace. No trouble, no more bother—all arrangements waiting for you."

Mrs. Ludlow put her hands about the arms of her chair. "How—how long will it be?" she said.

"How long? Before—" The young man straightened his suit. "Well, Murmuring Everglades will have all preparations completed by next week, I should say."

"Just—a week?"

"We try to be prompt."

Mrs. Ludlow held to the chair. "Only a week . . ."

"Yes indeedy, folks. But that old vault might stand empty for ten more years!"

Mr. Ludlow unhanded his elk's tooth. "What was that?"

"Um? Oh, merely that you might not see the inside of your property—unless on routine inspection, of course—for ten years or longer. It's entirely possible. Just because we look at reality doesn't mean we ought to be pessimists, no indeedy. You may both have many wonderful years ahead of you. And that's the beauty of it! You can spend them now without worries and heartaches about the Afterwards."

Mr. Ludlow stared at the young man. "I don't understand."

"Who does?" the young man said. "Who does? Just for an example: I called on a gentleman of ninety-two a year and a half ago. He purchased his property—a modest but very pleasant plot very near the Kirche by the Heide—and I haven't seen him since. Understand he's in excellent health, all things considered—a little weak but the doctors aren't particularly concerned."

"Is that so?" Mr. Ludlow's mouth was open. "You really—you really mean all that?"

The man in black walked toward the hall. "I do indeed, I do."

"And you came here—only to make these arrangements for later on?"

"That's right."

"And—" Mr. Ludlow was gasping. "And we can stay here, right here, stay on for ten more years? We won't have to sit waiting for you and looking for you, scared all the time, scared you'll come?"

"Not unless some question arises about your property. But I don't think that's very likely, heh? You both look in fine shape to me and, well, I see no reason whatever to believe an estimate of ten years is anything but skimpy." The man grinned. "After all, you know," he said, "Murmuring Everglades is betting on it."

Mrs. Ludlow picked up the tomcat and held it to her breast. Her body trembled slightly.

The young man stood silently, looking at the two old people. "And, of course, if anything should come up, if you should ever need me for anything, don't hesitate to call. Yes indeedy."

Mr. Ludlow took his hand gently from his wife's cheek. His face glistened. He switched off the light. "I don't think we'll be needing you for anything, young feller."

"Fine." The young man walked into the hall. "Don't bother," he called. "I can find my way."

The house waited for the crisp sharp steps to disappear and then it was silent.

Mr. Ludlow went to the door and watched the figure walk down the little path, on past the twin gates; watched the figure turn and wave, standing tall against the sulphurous sky; then he closed the door, leaned against it for a moment, and returned to the living room.

"Henry, now what's happened to the air? Ain't it warm, all of a sudden? Warm like honey!"

Mr. Ludlow took off his jacket and tie-pin and replaced them in the closet. He sat down in his chair and scooted it nearer his wife.

"And look at the window," Mrs. Ludlow said. "The frost is going away. It's melting."

Mr. Ludlow leaned back in the chair.

"Henry, look! The moon's come out!"

"That so?"

"It's big, and yellow; it's lighting up the whole yard. You can see every tree!"

The old man smiled and put his head on his chest.

In moments he was asleep, and his wife was asleep, and there was only the sound of the brown cat, purring.

LAST NIGHT THE RAIN

WE'D been clear out to the cemetery and we'd climbed the hill and now it was getting dark—or seemed to be, it had been gray since morning, and wet—but Amy had that look. She said, "Josh," in her quiet way, and I knew what she wanted to do.

I said, "Let's go home."

She shook her head. We were on the road that goes by the Lindamood farm, six miles from town and a mile from the river. Across the farm you could see the brush that went all the way to the bank, thick wild raspberry bushes and stingweeds and grass as high as your waist. Amy was smiling and looking that way.

"It's late," I said.

"No it isn't," she said, and shook her head again. "Josh, listen!"

I did, but there wasn't anything to listen to. The cows were frozen solid, it seemed like, and there was no wind to speak of.

"Do you hear it?" she said.

"No," I said. "Hear what?"

But I knew. One time up in the attic of my folks' place when it was raining and she'd been sitting at the window for I can't remember how long—hours—she pulled the same trick. I asked her then what she thought she heard and she said she heard the grass drinking!

I squeezed the horn on my bike, hard, and said, "Amy, come on, let's go home." But she didn't answer or make a move to tell she knew who I was.

"It's the river," she said finally, in a whisper.

I got turned around fast and pedaled a few feet and stopped. "Amy, listen, it's all soaking wet and muddy down there and you've got on a good dress."

She moved her head and looked at me. Sometimes she gave me this look. "I want to see Beckman," she said.

I wasn't surprised. It had been in her mind all day and that was why we were here, on this road.

"What makes you think he's home? He could be anywhere."

"He's there," she said, "and you don't want to go because you're afraid of him."

"That's a lie," I said, but it wasn't, exactly. Beckman always had made me a little afraid. Like the way you'd be afraid of a wild animal that's behind bars and can't get at you only sometimes its eyes turn your way. But I wasn't the only one. Whether they'd admit it or not, most of the people in town were at least nervous of him. He was Indian-old and almost helpless, but there was something about him that wasn't right. Not just the ragged clothes he wore, or the smell of him, or the way he had of following you around, watching, even; it was just *something*.

Amy said, "It isn't for Beckman, anyway. I want to go down to the river."

"Goddamn it, Amy. I'm not going."

Her face relaxed. "Then you wait for me, Josh." She didn't look like a fourteen-year-old girl at all, but more like a woman who'd gotten her way in spite of everything. I didn't know what to say. I only knew that it had all gone like she wanted. It didn't give me much choice.

"Fine," I yelled. "But you go down there and I'll let your pa know."

"Please wait for me."

I wondered what to do. There wasn't anything actually *wrong* with going to the river, of course. Only, I was scared. I remembered seeing Beckman just that morning and the thought of it sent a little chill down my back. He'd been watching one of the railroad men root a pack of hoboes out of the jungle, standing there to himself on the other side of the track, dirtier than any of the bums, watching. Later on when I was coming back from the grocery store I saw him again. This time he had found one of those great big rocks of his and he was pulling it down the road. They all looked the same, ordinary rocks, so you could never tell unless you went down to the river which tower they were for. Now I guessed it was for Sin, because the railroad man had been sort of rough. I didn't know, though: Beckman had his own ideas on the subject.

That was about all he ever did, too—hang around town and study you. My Uncle Rand remarked to me, on Beckman's two towers there on the sand, that the old man simply had a Jehovah complex, in addition to being nutty as a squirrel, and was to be pitied. But somehow that didn't come so easy. Not to me, anyway. Or to anybody, for that matter, except Amy . . . And she pitied just about everything that wasn't quite right. Dogs, cats, snakes, it didn't matter.

I liked her, though. All the people, up to and including her father, who was all she had, thought she was queer, and I did, too, a little—but I liked her. At least I did when she was what you could call normal and I was with her then and could listen to her voice. It was the softest voice a girl ever owned, and her eyes were the biggest.

I guess I felt sorry for her because of her father. He was in politics or something, I don't know exactly what, but they say he wasn't strictly honest and it's certain he was blood-mean. To Amy especially. I don't care how queer she was, he didn't have any business keeping her shut up for days at a time like he did. Everybody talked about it. Beckman must have dragged a hundred stones down to the river on that score alone—but that doesn't prove anything. According to him, my bagging up a lot of kittens, like I did once, and throwing them in the slew was sinful. I got a regular boulder for that.

But Amy wasn't scared of Beckman at all. Even though he reeked something fierce, she'd run after him on the street and walked with him as far as Five Points; and sometimes she'd help him lug one of his damn rocks. That was a picture. It made me feel awful, just like I'd feel when she'd start on one of her peculiar talking sprees. We'd be riding along or coming back from school or something and all of a sudden she'd start. What did I suppose that dogs dreamed about when they were asleep? Did I think there were really people on the moon? How long did a tree live? I never knew what to say, but getting mad at Amy and not seeing her was even worse than putting up with her, so I invented answers. It didn't make much difference, because she never listened to me, anyhow.

I think it was the funny way she made me want to sort of look out for her that kept us going together. It's what my Uncle Rand called "super-stupid" all right, since she had more courage than any two grown men; but at the same time you felt that if you let her go, she'd just blow away, or break.

That's why I was so mad when she went down to the river by herself. I watched her drop her bicycle and go into the bushes without even so much as a look back in my direction, and I sat there, scared and mad.

Finally I decided I'd better go after her.

I rode as far as I could on the bike and laid it next to hers. Then I went into the brush. The quiet got heavier, all soaked and heavy, now. Most of the wet was dew and leftover rain and there wasn't a wind to start it dripping, so it just hung there. With some sun it would have been pretty. Amy and I had gone down to one of the sandbars a few weeks back and then it was sunshine and she compared the water drops on the brush to diamonds and the spider webs to strands of jewelry, which was all right, they did look like that a little; but then she got the idea we were surrounded by chandeliers and you couldn't stop her after that.

Now I was close enough to hear the river, but it was a soft kind of sound that you had to hang on to, and I *know* Amy couldn't have heard it from all the way out to the road. I went the only way you could, trying not to make any noise, for about a hundred feet. The brush thinned out a bit and I could see the edge of the river below. Then, because I was nervous, I walked faster, right to the rim.

The first thing I saw was Beckman's houseboat. It was exactly like an old woodshed, without any windows or anything, and square as a box.

I looked for Beckman. Why it was, I can't say, but I began to despise him. He was the cause of a lot of what was wrong with Amy, after all. Every time she saw him she'd start in with the silly things, every time, right afterwards. Then it wouldn't be the same: I'd be a stranger.

They weren't anywhere on the sand. Over to the right, almost directly down, were the towers. Side by side.

They'd grown quite a lot since I'd seen them last, which was a long time ago when a bunch of us kids did it on a dare. Now they looked like regular fortresses or castles—or, at least, the one on the left did. That was Beckman's Sin Tower. It went up for fifteen feet or more, and the weight of all those rocks had pushed the bottom foundation rocks clear into the sand until you could just barely see the tops of them. How he managed to get anything up there is a question that I couldn't begin to answer, because those were stones of all different sizes, not flat or anything, and they were just piled up, one on top of the other. I know he didn't have a derrick or the right equipment, and I couldn't see where he could lean a ladder against that stack because it looked like a deep breath would topple the whole thing over.

The Sin Tower was leaning, I saw, to the left. Below it, about a third as big, was the other one, the Tower of Good. It was a scrubby-looking thing. Not even a tower, exactly. I thought: By God, it's pretty clear what Beckman thinks of our town, all right.

The wet soaked clear through to my chest and I got up. Just as I did, I heard a laugh, and I knew it was Amy. You couldn't mistake a thing like Amy's laugh.

It was coming from inside the houseboat.

I cussed and climbed down the side of the cutaway. When I jumped, I didn't stop to think what I was going to say or do but walked catty corner around the towers, where I couldn't be seen from the door, which was open, and walked until I heard good.

Amy's voice was going. It sounded sad. "I could get it from Daddy," she was saying. "He carries an awful lot of money in his pockets and I could get it all."

The next voice was Beckman's. All dry and squeezed, like kindling snapping across somebody's knee a mile off. Nobody had ever heard him talk that I knew of; Uncle Rand had figured he was dumb. "It won't do," he said.

"Why not?" Amy said.

"Because, now, it wouldn't. Just so."

"I don't care," Amy said. "We could go clear to wherever the river ends and then into the ocean and maybe India. I bet you didn't know the Earth is practically all water!"

Beckman did something, laugh I guess; I bit off a slice of finger skin. It was the kind of sound that people with no teeth make, a lot of air going in and out.

I edged closer and scrunched down to see in without them seeing me.

"Amy, now—"

"You don't want to go away."

"Can't."

"Can, too. Beckman, we could sail all over, just us, and nobody to poke fun. Sleep all day and stay up nights, if we were of a mind, and catch flying fish for food." Her voice got that well-it's-all-settled tone. "I'll get the money from Daddy and you'll buy the boat and we'll go."

I could see now. Beckman was sitting on the floor of the shack, cross-legged. There was dirt everywhere. His clothes seemed to have all melted from sweat and years and glued together; and looking at them, you couldn't imagine that they had once been ordinary clothes in a store window. His beard was even whiter than usual, stubby white, like a fox terrier's coat. It was clean-looking, and the only thing connected with him that was, too. His face was all grooved and rutted and streaked with grime, eyes night-dark and hard as marbles.

"Got work to do," he said, after a while. "You oughtn't to of come here."

Amy was leaning against the wall, her hands behind her. The difference between them was something to see! Her frock had dried so it looked as fresh and clean as it had in the early morning, her hair fell over her shoulders like cornsilk, as fine and gold as that, and she was staring down at her feet.

Beckman said he had to stay and build the towers because he had been commanded to by God Almighty, and when God Almighty commands you to do something, you can't turn your back.

Amy didn't say a word. She was real disappointed, I could tell, and hurt.

Beckman said, "Go on home, now. You oughtn't to come here."

What Amy said then made me catch fire inside. She said, "I had to. No one else understands." She said, "Just you, Beckman. We're the same. They don't have any use for us, and they laugh, but—I know. When the wind sings you hear it, I know you do."

He sat there.

"And you know all the rest I do, too. I found out that the river is a woman, but that wasn't news to you, and even if you can't understand them, you hear the birds talking to each other. Don't you?"

He sighed. Then he said, "You're crazy," and stopped. "Get home," he said.

Amy's voice trembled. "I don't want to," she said. "I'm scared, Beckman."

"What of?" Beckman said, looking at her.

"I don't know," she said, "I get ideas."

"What kind?"

"I'm not sure," Amy said. "Nothing seems right to me now, though. Daddy says if I don't improve he's going to send me away to the city. He hardly even talks to me any more because I make him nervous, he says. When the sun goes red at night now, I want to cry."

Beckman was still.

"Yesterday I slipped out," Amy said, "and walked through Mr. Jackson's garden, like I used to, but it wasn't the same—it was so quiet. I laid down to watch the ladybugs. They didn't come, and it was quiet, and I just wanted to stay there on the grass forever and never leave. I thought if I left I wouldn't come back. Everything is so goodbye!" She dropped onto the floor, then, and grabbed Beckman's hand and put her cheek against it. "Please," she said, "let's go away. Tonight. Please."

Beckman stroked her head a couple of times and then shook away from her. "I got work to do," he said. Then he yelled it at her. "Goddamn it, now, I got work. We can't go anywhere, you can't and I can't, there isn't anywhere to go. I don't know why. Just get on home, now, and don't come back."

She wouldn't move and he slapped her, and I could see that he was shaking, too. It was the craziest thing I'd ever seen. I felt like

I was watching something that I wasn't supposed to, and I could hear my heart balled up and knocking a hole in my chest. I tried to move. In my head there was just that picture of this filthy old man hitting Amy, and everything they said.

I got up and stood in front of the doorway. "Amy!" I said, and maybe more, I don't know. I stood there.

Amy jumped and ran and threw her arms around me.

I held on to her tight. Beckman was still sitting on the floor, but he was staring, too, and his mouth was open.

"Come on, Amy," I said.

She didn't move. She hung on there, crying. I don't know what I wanted to do, then—kiss her, I think. Hold her and squeeze until she was broken and get her inside of me so I'd know she was safe. I thought stuff like that.

Then she stopped crying. Except for one thing, the sound of birds back in the brush, it was dead quiet.

Amy pulled away from me.

I never saw anyone's face like hers. It was white and wet, and her eyes were big as saucers.

"What's the matter?" I said.

She took three steps backwards and started to run.

I went after her, but she was faster than I was. She seemed to glide over the sand, her feet hardly even touching. She was running and looking back over her shoulder at me, and maybe it sounds funny, but I never knew anyone to look so *afraid* as she did.

I stopped running when I saw where she was headed.

I put out my hand. "Amy!" I called at her over and over, but she ran on.

She ran right up on to the tall pile of rocks there by the cutaway.

It all went very slow, but I saw every bit of it. I can see it now when I close my eyes. Her running and bumping the base of the Sin Tower and the stone at the top tipping and tipping and falling and the whole thing breaking loose.

"Amy!"

It didn't bury her completely. But eight or nine of the big rocks came down over her.

I must have gone crazy then because I didn't do anything. I just stood there. Even when I saw the blood and saw that she wasn't moving, even then I didn't do anything.

Beckman crossed the sand slowly.

He went to the broken tower and lifted the rocks off of Amy and put his head on her chest for a while; then he looked back at me.

I wished to God I could have cried. I wished a thousand things, and stood there.

Beckman knelt down more and got his arms under Amy. He was gentle. He picked her up and managed to pull himself to his feet, and started back. Amy's head leaned back across his dirty sleeve, the wind caught her hair, and I noticed one thing, I noticed that the ribbon was still on.

I watched them. It was like it made sense only I didn't understand, like it was a sensible thing. Beckman walked straight. He walked past the rim of the cutaway, and didn't look back at me any more.

Everything got crowded in my head. Amy's dead, I thought— but who killed her?

"Who killed Amy?" I yelled at Beckman. "You goddamn old fool, you filthy old crazy fool!"

The rocks did, was what came into my mind. And the town did. And I did. I was to blame, by God I was: she'd been running away from me, hadn't she?

I got dizzy, and I knew I was going to be sick. I wanted to stop Beckman and hit him, but instead I kept thinking about the tower. About how if it had been smaller, and the other one bigger, then Amy would be alive.

"Did I do it?" I cried.

He was almost to the river. There weren't any bones in him or Amy, there wasn't any weight in them. She was light in his arms and his arms were light. When they got a ways off I knew it had got dark because they turned into shadows, moving toward that river, getting smaller.

I got panicky then. Even though I don't remember doing any of it, I ran back to the cutaway—I must have—and got my bike and went home.

Mom didn't believe me, at first. But then she did and she called Amy's father at his office and told him about it. He made her let me go back with him so he'd know where to go, but when we got to the rim, there wasn't anything to see. Not Beckman or Amy, anyway. Just the tumbled-down tower of rocks and the little one next to it.

And the river.

They dragged it for a good month. They sent out bulletins and calls and organized search parties and had police all over the county, only it wasn't any use, and finally they gave up. Things simmered down to normal after a while, and you hardly heard anybody talking much about the accident—that's what they called it.

I guess they're right. My Uncle Rand says it was a simple case of two crazy people coming together, he says that whenever that happens there's bound to be trouble, or worse, and that nobody is to blame. And I guess that's right, too.

But at night, when things are quiet, I still get a funny feeling on my neck. And every now and then I have a dream that wakes me up.

And sometimes, when it's raining, I go up to the attic, and I listen and wonder what it really was that Amy heard.

I only hear the rain.

THE CROOKED MAN

*"Professing themselves to be wise, they became fools . . . who
changed the truth of God into a lie . . . for even their women
did change the natural use into that which is against nature:
and likewise also the men, leaving the natural use of the
woman, burned in their lust one toward another; men with
men working that which is unseemly . . ."*
                                        —St. Paul: Romans, I

HE slipped into a corner booth away from the dancing men,
where it was quietest, where the odors of musk and frangipani
hung less heavy on the air. A slender lamp glowed softly in the
booth. He turned it down: down to where only the club's blue
overheads filtered through the beaded curtain, diffusing, blurring
the image thrown back by the mirrored walls of his light, thin-
boned handsomeness.

"Yes sir?" The barboy stepped through the beads and stood
smiling. Clad in gold-sequined trunks, his greased muscles seemed
to roll in independent motion, like fat snakes beneath his naked
skin.

"Whiskey," Jesse said. He caught the insouciant grin, the broad
white-tooth crescent that formed on the young man's face. Jesse
looked away, tried to control the flow of blood to his cheeks.

"Yes sir," the barboy said, running his thick tanned fingers over
his solar plexus, tapping the fingers, making them hop in a sinuous
dance. He hesitated, still smiling, this time questioningly, hopefully, a smile deep drenched in admiration and desire. The Finger
Dance, the accepted symbol, stopped: the pudgy brown digits
curled into angry fists. "Right away, sir."

Jesse watched him turn; before the beads had tinkled together
he watched the handsome athlete make his way imperiously
through the crowd, shaking off the tentative hands of single men

at the tables, ignoring the many desire symbols directed toward him.

That shouldn't have happened. Now the fellow's feelings were hurt. If hurt enough, he would start thinking, wondering—and that would ruin everything. No. It must be put right.

Jesse thought of Mina, of the beautiful Mina— It was such a rotten chance. It *had* to go right!

"Your whiskey, sir," the young man said. His face looked like a dog's face, large, sad; his lips were a pouting bloat of line.

Jesse reached into his pocket for some change. He started to say something, something nice.

"It's been paid for," the barboy said. He scowled and laid a card on the table and left.

The card carried the name E. J. Two Hobart, embossed, in lavender ink. Jesse heard the curtains tinkle.

"Well, hello. I hope you don't mind my barging in like this, but—you didn't seem to be with anyone . . ."

The man was small, chubby, bald; his face had a dirty growth of beard and he looked out of tiny eyes encased in bulging contacts. He was bare to the waist. His white hairless chest drooped and turned in folds at the stomach. Softly, more subtly than the barboy had done, he put his porky stubs of fingers into a suggestive rhythm.

Jesse smiled. "Thanks for the drink," he said. "But I really am expecting someone."

"Oh?" the man said. "Someone—special?"

"Pretty special," Jesse said smoothly, now that the words had become automatic. "He's my fiancée."

"I see." The man frowned momentarily and then brightened. "Well, I thought to myself, I said: E. J., a beauty like that couldn't very well be unattached. But—well, it was certainly worth a try. Sorry."

"Perfectly all right," Jesse said. The predatory little eyes were rolling, the fingers dancing in one last-ditch attempt. "Good evening, Mr. Hobart."

Bluey veins showed under the whiteness of the man's nearly female mammae. Jesse felt slightly amused this time: it was the

other kind, the intent ones, the humorless ones like—like the
barboy—that repulsed him, turned him ill, made him want to take
a knife and carve unspeakable ugliness into his own smooth ascetic
face.

The man turned and waddled away crabwise. The club was
becoming more crowded. It was getting later and heads full of
liquor shook away the inhibitions of the earlier hours. Jesse tried
not to watch, but he had long ago given up trying to rid himself
of his fascination. So he watched the men together. The pair over
in the far corner, pressed close together, dancing with their bodies,
never moving their feet, swaying in slow lissome movements
to the music, their tongues twisting in the air, jerking, like pink
snakes, contracting to points and curling invitingly, barely making
touch, then snapping back. The Tongue Dance . . . The couple
seated by the bar. One a Beast, the other a Hunter, the Beast old,
his cheeks caked hard and cracking with powder and liniments,
the perfume rising from his body like steam; the Hunter, young
but unhandsome, the fury evident in his eyes, the hurt anger at
having to make do with a Beast—from time to time he would look
around, wetting his lips in shame. . . . And those two just coming
in, dressed in Mother's uniforms, tanned, mustached, proud of
their station. . . .

Jesse held the beads apart. *Mina must come soon.* He wanted to
run from this place, out into the air, into the darkness and silence.

No. He just wanted Mina. To see her, touch her, listen to the
music of her voice. . . .

Two women came in, arm in arm, Beast and Hunter, drunk.
They were stopped at the door. Angrily, shrilly, told to leave. The
manager swept by Jesse's booth, muttering about them, asking
why they should want to come dirtying up The Phallus with their
presence when they had their own section, their own clubs—

Jesse pulled his head back inside. He'd gotten used to the light
by now, so he closed his eyes against his multiplied image. The dis-
organized sounds of love got louder, the singsong syrup of voices:
deep, throaty, baritone, falsetto. It was crowded now. The Orgies
would begin before long and the couples would pair off for the
cubicles. He hated the place. But close to Orgy-time you didn't

get noticed here—and where else was there to go? Outside, where every inch of pavement was patrolled electronically, every word of conversation, every movement recorded, catalogued, filed?

Damn Knudson! Damn the little man! Thanks to him, to the Senator, Jesse was now a criminal. Before, it wasn't so bad—not this bad, anyway. You were laughed at and shunned and fired from your job, sometimes kids lobbed stones at you, but at least you weren't hunted. Now—it was a crime. A sickness.

He remembered when Knudson had taken over. It had been one of the little man's first telecasts; in fact, it was the platform that got him the majority vote:

> "Vice is on the upswing in our city. In the dark corners of every Unit perversion blossoms like an evil flower. Our children are exposed to its stink, and they wonder— *our children wonder*—why nothing is done to put a halt to this disgrace. We have ignored it long enough! The time has come for *action*, not mere words. The perverts who infest our land must be flushed out, eliminated *completely*, as a threat not only to public morals but to society at large. These sick people must be cured and made normal. The disease that throws men and women together in this dreadful abnormal relationship and leads to acts of retrogression—retrogression that will, unless it is stopped and stopped fast, push us inevitably back to the status of animals—this is to be considered as any other disease. It must be conquered as heart trouble, cancer, polio, schizophrenia, paranoia, all other diseases have been conquered. . . ."

The Women's Senator had taken Knudson's lead and issued a similar pronunciamento and then the bill became a law and the law was carried out.

Jesse sipped at the whiskey, remembering the Hunts. How the frenzied mobs had gone through the city at first, chanting, yelling, bearing placards with slogans: WIPE OUT THE HETEROS! KILL THE QUEERS! MAKE OUR CITY CLEAN AGAIN! And how they'd lost interest finally after the passion had worn down and the novelty had ended. But they had killed many and they had sent many more to the hospitals. . . .

He remembered the nights of running and hiding, choked dry breath glued to his throat, heart rattling loose. He had been lucky. He didn't look like a hetero. They said you could tell one just by watching him walk—Jesse walked correctly. He fooled them. He was lucky.

And he was a criminal. He, Jesse Four Martin, no different from the rest, tube-born and machine-nursed, raised in the Character Schools like everyone else—was terribly different from the rest.

It had happened—his awful suspicions had crystallized—on his first formal date. The man had been a Rocketeer, the best high quality, even out of the Hunter class. Mother had arranged it carefully. There was the dance. And then the ride in the space-sled. The big man had put an arm about Jesse and—Jesse knew. He knew for certain and it made him very angry and very sad.

He remembered the days that came after the knowledge: bad days, days fallen upon evil, black desires, deep-cored frustrations. He had tried to find a friend at the Crooked Clubs that flourished then, but it was no use. There was a sensationalism, a bravura to these people, that he could not love. The sight of men and women together, too, shocked the parts of him he could not change, and repulsed him. Then the vice squads had come and closed up the clubs and the heteros were forced underground and he never sought them out again or saw them. He was alone.

The beads tinkled.

"Jesse—" He looked up quickly, afraid. It was Mina. She wore a loose man's shirt, an old hat that hid her golden hair: her face was shadowed by the turned-up collar. Through the shirt the rise and fall of her breasts could be faintly detected. She smiled once, nervously.

Jesse looked out the curtain. Without speaking, he put his hands about her soft thin shoulders and held her like this for a long minute.

"Mina—" She looked away. He pulled her chin forward and ran a finger along her lips. Then he pressed her body to his, tightly, touching her neck, her back, kissing her forehead, her eyes, kissing her mouth. They sat down.

They sought for words. The curtains parted.

"Beer," Jesse said, winking at the barboy, who tried to come closer, to see the one loved by this thin handsome man.

"Yes sir."

The barboy looked at Mina very hard, but she had turned and he could see only the back. Jesse held his breath. The barboy smiled contemptuously then, a smile that said: You're insane—I was hired for my beauty. See my chest, look—a pectoral vision. My arms, strong; my lips—come, were there ever such sensuous ones? And you turn me down for this bag of bones. . . .

Jesse winked again, shrugged suggestively and danced his fingers: *Tomorrow, my friend, I'm stuck tonight. Can't help it. Tomorrow.*

The barboy grinned and left. In a few moments he returned with the beer. "On the house," he said, for Mina's benefit. She turned only when Jesse said, softly:

"It's all right. He's gone now."

Jesse looked at her. Then he reached over and took off the hat. Blond hair rushed out and over the rough shirt.

She grabbed for the hat. "We mustn't," she said. "Please—what if somebody should come in?"

"No one will come in. I told you that."

"But what if? I don't know—I don't like it here. That man at the door—he almost recognized me."

"But he didn't."

"Almost though. And then what?"

"Forget it. Mina, for God's sake. Let's not quarrel."

She calmed. "I'm sorry, Jesse. It's only that—this place makes me feel—"

"—what?"

"Dirty." She said it defiantly.

"You don't really believe that, do you?"

"No. I don't know. I just want to be alone with you."

Jesse took out a cigarette and started to use the lighter. Then he cursed and threw the vulgarly shaped object under the table and crushed the cigarette. "You know that's impossible," he said. The idea of separate Units for homes had disappeared, to be replaced by giant dormitories. There were no more parks, no country lanes. There was no place to hide at all now, thanks to Senator Knudson, to the little bald crest of this new sociological wave. "This is all we have," Jesse said, throwing a sardonic look around the booth, with its carved symbols and framed pictures of entertainment stars—all naked and leering.

They were silent for a time, hands interlocked on the table top. Then the girl began to cry. "I—I can't go on like this," she said.

"I know. It's hard. But what else can we do?" Jesse tried to keep the hopelessness out of his voice.

"Maybe," the girl said, "we ought to go underground with the rest."

"And hide there, like rats?" Jesse said.

"We're hiding here," Mina said, "like rats."

"Besides, Parner is getting ready to crack down. I know, Mina—I work at Centraldome, after all. In a little while there won't be any underground."

"I love you," the girl said, leaning forward, parting her lips for a kiss. "Jesse, I do." She closed her eyes. "Oh, why won't they leave us alone? Why? Just because we're que—"

"Mina! I've told you—don't ever use that word. It isn't true! *We're* not the queers. You've got to believe that. Years ago it was *normal* for men and women to love each other: they married and had children together; that's the way it was. Don't you remember anything of what I've told you?"

The girl sobbed. "Of course I do. I do. But, darling, that was a long time ago."

"Not so long! Where I work—listen to me—they have books. You know, I told you about books? I've read them, Mina. I learned what the words meant from other books. It's only been since the use of artificial insemination—not even five hundred years ago."

"Yes dear," the girl said. "I'm sure, dear."

"Mina, stop that! We are not the unnatural ones, no matter what they say. I don't know exactly how it happened—maybe, maybe as women gradually became equal to men in every way—or maybe solely because of the way we're born—I don't know. But the point is, darling, the whole world was like us, once. Even now, look at the animals—"

"Jesse! Don't you dare talk as if we're like those horrid little dogs and cats and things!"

Jesse sighed. He had tried so often to tell her, show her. But he knew, actually, what she thought. That she felt she was exactly what the authorities told her she was—God, maybe that's how they all thought, all the Crooked People, all the "unnormal" ones. . . .

The girl's hands caressed his arms and the touch became suddenly repugnant to him. Unnatural. Terribly unnatural.

Jesse shook his head. Forget it, he thought. Never mind. She's a woman and you love her and there's nothing wrong nothing wrong nothing wrong in that . . . or am I the insane person of old days who was insane because he was so sure he wasn't insane because—

"Disgusting!"

It was the fat little man, the smiling masher, E. J. Two Hobart. But he wasn't smiling now.

Jesse got up quickly and stepped in front of Mina. "What do you want? I thought I told you—"

The man pulled a metal disk from his trunks. "Vice squad, friend," he said. "Better sit down." The disk was pointed at Jesse's belly.

The man's arm went out the curtain and two other men came in, holding disks.

"I've been watching you quite a while, mister," the man said. "Quite a while."

"Look," Jesse said, "I don't know what you're talking about. I work at Centraldome and I'm seeing Miss Smith here on some business."

"We know all about that kind of business," the man said.

"All right—I'll tell you the truth. I forced her to come here. I—"

"Mister—didn't you hear me? I said I've been watching you. All evening. Let's go."

One man took Mina's arm, roughly; the other two began to

propel Jesse out through the club. Heads turned. Tangled bodies moved embarrassedly.

"It's all right," the little fat man said, his white skin glistening with perspiration. "It's all right, folks. Go on back to whatever you were doing." He grinned and tightened his grasp on Jesse's arm.

Mina didn't struggle. There was something in her eyes—it took Jesse a long time to recognize it. Then he knew. He knew what she had come to tell him tonight: that even if they hadn't been caught—she would have submitted to the Cure voluntarily. No more worries then, no more guilt. No more meeting at midnight dives, feeling shame, feeling dirt. . . .

Mina didn't meet Jesse's look as they took her out into the street.

"You'll be okay," the fat man was saying. He opened the wagon's doors. "They've got it down pat now—couple days in the ward, one short session with the doctors; take out a few glands, make a few injections, attach a few wires to your head, turn on a machine: presto! You'll be surprised."

The fat officer leaned close. His sausage fingers danced wildly near Jesse's face.

"It'll make a new man of you," he said.

Then they closed the doors and locked them.

NURSERY RHYME

"I HEAR him," the old woman said, leaning forward. "I hear Carlie." Her fingers paused in their flight and she sat very still, listening.

The old man looked up from his newspaper. "I don't think so," he said. Then he sighed. "You want me to go see?"

"No!" The old woman's cheeks trembled. "He's calling for me. Can't you hear? He's calling Mother."

She gathered up the rug she had been hooking and held it in front of her. There was a barn, brown, with a red roof; and a sun with a smiling face; and a cow; and a bird that looked like a robin only the bird was many times larger than the barn on which it perched. She dropped the rug to the floor.

"You don't suppose he's sick," she said. "You don't think that, do you?"

"Who—Carlie? Our Carlie?"

"But he cries so pitiful—listen, you can hear him. Is that the cry of a well child?"

"Most likely he wants a glass of water."

"Then I must bring him one."

She walked into the kitchen where the floor was pocked black from the rubber tips of her canes. She drew a glass of water from the chipped enamel sink.

"Randolph!" she called.

The old man came in.

"You'll have to help me."

He took the glass and walked behind her as she limped on the canes. Through the living room piled high with black mahogany pieces they went, past the corroded face of the grandfather clock, past the tapestries of Venice and Pisa.

"Listen," she said, moving her head to the door.

"Don't hear nothing. He's asleep by this time. Maybe just tossing in his sleep was all."

130

"No; *listen.*"

The house was filled with quiet, the quiet that comes when the boards are too old to squeak, when the clocks have all stopped ticking, when the air is clear and still outside.

"I hear him," the old woman said, turning to look at her husband.

He nodded.

They opened the door slowly and went into the room.

"Carlie?" the old woman said, stretching out her arm. "Carlie child, don't you feel well?"

The room glowed soft in the April moonlight, the cool silver light that came in through the open window. It took out shadows and left everything dim, as if seen from a great distance.

"Carlie, you don't want to talk to Mother?"

"He's asleep, Agnes. Don't wake him up."

"He is not asleep. He just won't talk."

The old woman came forward and sat on the edge of the bed. The pain made her sigh.

"Now then," she said. "Would you like a nice glass of water? See—Daddy has it already. Wouldn't that be nice?"

A sudden silent wind came up, not a big one, but it rustled the gaily tinted curtains and scattered the moonlight in the room.

"Daddy, give our little boy some water."

The old man set the glass on the nightstand. His hand shook so that some of the water spilled out onto the painted elephant.

There were many elephants in the room: red ones, yellow ones, purple ones; and orange-and-black-striped tigers tracked the elephants along the walls. Books made out of linen instead of paper and showing pictures of hens and rabbits and monkeys lay on the floor.

There were also toys on the floor. Wooden Easter eggs, hand-painted; little boats with candles inside them; a red horse that didn't look like a horse; and dolls—there were many dolls. Mostly of cloth stuffed with cotton. Raggedy Ann was there. And Humpty-Dumpty. And The Old Woman Who Lived in a Shoe. Punch lay on the window sill, his head split at the seams and the stained cotton trailing down over his sewn smile.

On the far wall was a single picture, night-darkened, indistinct, framed in heavy gold.

"See—he's gone back to sleep," the man said.

"Quiet! Randolph, don't beller so!" The woman bent down and moved her hand slowly. "Well, he doesn't have a fever. We can be thankful for that."

"Let's leave him alone. Let's let him sleep."

"All right," the woman said, rising carefully so that the bed-springs would not creak. "But if he wakes again, I'm going to call a doctor."

The man merely stared, a weak tired stare.

They went out of the room. It became quiet again.

Quiet, and as empty as before.

He ran across the drenched field, stumbling and falling, picking himself up from the mud, running on.

A young man wearing strapped overalls and a colorless shirt, sleeves rolled up over the gray underwear. Tall, unhandsome: the nose was too large; it had been broken so that now it mashed against his face. Eyes small, set well apart, but small and gray. Mouth twisted, thin-lipped. And hair like a Zulu native's, black and kinky; though the young man's skin beneath the week-old beard was fair, fish-belly pale and smooth.

He ran.

When he came to a silo, he fell beside it and lay gasping, forcing the air into his lungs. He lay there until his breathing became regular. Then he squatted and sat without moving.

There was the smell of wet hay in the air. From inside the long field, deep inside where they could not be seen, small creatures put heavy music out over the night-still land: over the young forests, the useless rivulets now white in the moon's brightness, over the dark quiet silos and silent corrals and sleeping farmhouses.

But there was another sound, and the young man stiffened when he heard it.

The sound of dogs—far away, but getting closer. Yelping dogs and heavy boots tramping through the mire, and men's voices.

The young man pulled himself up and began to run again.

He stopped many times to listen.

His shoes clattered over a rotted bridge and the noise made him yell and the yelling snapped something because he kept on yelling long after he had passed the bridge. But that took even more of his breath. So he stopped yelling.

He fell and rolled on the ground and looked for a place to hide. There was no place. No place they wouldn't look.

He went on.

When he came to a tiny dirt road marked by a mailbox and a sign that you could no longer read, he halted. No light was on in the house up this road.

The young man began to laugh, and as suddenly stopped. His hands went about his face, as if to cover it, as he weaved up the road and fell against the door.

He tried to say something, but each time the words caught short.

"Open," he said, finally. "It's me. It's Carlie."

The man in the house stared. He wore a nightshirt and a cap. He peered into the darkness through the crack he'd made in the door.

"Quiet," he said. "Who is it?"

Then the door was forced, and the young man came in and slammed it closed again.

"Go away," the old man said, looking over his shoulder toward the hallway. "Get on out of here. She'll hear you!"

"I don't care," the young man said. He was leaning against a wall, his face on his arm. "Let her find out. I don't care."

The old man transferred the flashlight to his left hand. With his right hand he struck the back of the boy's neck.

The boy sank to the floor. "Pa, Jesus Christ. Don't do that, Pa."

The old man walked to the hall and pulled the door to. Then he walked back slowly, hesitating by the young man, walked to the window and pulled down the shade.

"What'd you do?" he said.

The boy shook his head.

"They don't chase a man who never did nothing to cause trouble. What'd you do?"

The boy rubbed the knees of his overalls with his hands. "God, I didn't even know such a girl," he said.

The old man sat down.

"Told you I don't know. They found a girl out in the fields, dead. Now, you got to believe me—"

"Why do I got to?"

The boy ran a hand through his kinky hair. "Look—it was Joey. I'll tell you the truth now, Pa. It was Joey Neisen. I didn't want nothing to do with it, but Joey's older than me and he made me drink all that beer— Will you back me up? Please, will you say I was home all night, here, with you?"

"No," the old man said.

"Come on, Pa. They're out there looking for me. Please say that. Please tell them. If you do, I swear to God I'll straighten out. Help you. I *will*." He paused. "You know what they'll do? They'll hang me."

The old man said nothing. He stared ahead.

"I didn't know what I was doing, Pa—you know that. I ain't mean, like some of them. Honest. Don't let them put a rope around my neck, please, God, Pa."

The sound of dogs suddenly came into the room. Their frenzied yelping could be heard clearly.

The dogs were close. They were coming.

"If you wake up your ma," the old man said, slowly, "I'll kill you before they get a chance to."

The young man walked to the door, listened, then walked in a perfect circle, moving his lips. He said, calmly: "It was the Withers girl, Pa. Now, you know her. Flirts with everything in pants. She always had a hankering for me—you *know* that. Well, sir, she got me drunk and pretty soon we were out in the field. Then she played the high lady. *After* we got to the field, do you see? What would you do? You'd get hopping mad, just like I did. So mad you couldn't see. So mad you wouldn't know what you was doing." He breathed hard and fast. "I guess—maybe—I hit her or something. Next thing I knew I was running. She was bellering."

The old man was a quiet clay statue.

"Pa? Can't you hear them?"

The old man nodded.

"You going to let them take me, without moving your little finger?"

The young man suddenly straightened. His face became red. He vaulted across the room and gathered the old man's nightshirt in his hands. "Well, let me tell you, you just listen. I don't aim to get hung just on account of some cheap little no-account whore. You just *better* tell them fellas I was home. You know what I'm talking about? You better tell them."

"What would you do, son?" the old man said.

"I'd—just listen to that 'son' talk. Don't it sound pretty, though." The boy released his grip, coughed violently.

The old man dropped his flashlight, after a long moment. He looked confused. "Why did you leave us, Carlie?" he said.

"Why?" The boy laughed. "You crazy? Should I of stayed around here when she wouldn't even look at me? Wouldn't even touch me or talk to me, like I didn't exist on earth—my own ma? You tell me—you tell me why. What'd I do to make her take on like that, hate me so?"

The old man shrugged. "You—growed up, boy."

"They something sinful in that? What'd she expect me to do, stay a baby my whole life?"

"Your ma was a sick woman. I tried to tell you that! Does things to you to lose four young'uns—I don't know. How would I know? I ain't a woman. It was just like as if she wasn't going to lose you any way, any way at all."

"You think that was right? Fair?"

The old man bristled. "She's a sick woman. *Sick*—can't you get that through your brain!"

The boy smiled. "That why you treated me thataway, too? Like you wished I'd go on and get, sooner the better? And now you want to know why I left you. Pa, that's a honest-to-God laugh. That's a genuine laugh."

The dogs' howls pierced the air.

"They got to quit that," the old man murmured. "It'll wake Agnes. She got all upset tonight. Heard you crying."

"Stop it! Pa, you're going as crazy as her! Look—" The boy

reached under his shirt and took out a Colt .45 pistol. He held it in front of him. "You tell them fellas I was here all evening with you."

"I'll tell them," the old man said. The confusion was mostly in his eyes, like excited bugs of light. His mouth was slightly open.

Neither the old man nor his son was aware of the presence of the woman until she spoke.

"Who you going to tell what, Randolph?"

She stood in the hallway, the doorknob in her hand. "Who's this?" she said.

The old man looked at her, then at the boy.

"Who are you, young Mister?" she said, coming forward on her canes. The yelps issued from the direction of the farthest cowshed now.

The boy's mouth twitched.

"Carlie!" he screamed. "Carlie, Carlie, Carlie. Are you all blind?"

The old woman looked suspiciously at her husband.

The dogs were on the porch now, their claws scratching furiously at the wood.

There was a polite knock at the door.

"Tell her what to say, Pa," the young man whispered. "Go on, tell her." He gestured with the gun.

The old man tried to speak. His mouth moved.

"Yes, who is it?" the old woman called. "Who's there? Please be quiet," she said, "or you'll wake my baby."

"It's Joe Barton," the voice answered. "Like to come in, if I can. Important."

"Ma!"

The knocks got louder and quicker, and the dogs thrashed and scratched and whined.

The young man took the old woman by the shoulders. He shook her; gently, though, not hard. "Look at me! Hey. Hey, Ma."

"Randolph, go see who's at the door. They're making so much noise. Randolph—"

The young man looked into cool green eyes, eyes that seemed to pass through him; then he threw his head back and yelled, one time.

The doorknob began to twirl, turned and rattled from the outside.

"Mr. Phillips! We know the boy's there. Why don't you—"

The young man pointed his gun at the door and pulled the trigger.

A big jagged hole appeared in the wood and there was a shout on the other side, a shout of pain, and the sound of something heavy dropping.

"Randolph, tell them to be quiet. Can't you hear them? What are they doing to make so much noise?"

The young man ran out of the living room, through the hall-way. As he did so, the front door was pushed suddenly inward.

Faces appeared at the windows.

The young man stopped in the hall. Then he chose a door, opened it quickly and stepped inside.

The room was dark and quiet.

There were toys on the floor, pictures on the walls. And also on the wall, an oval portrait in a square gilt frame. A portrait of a woman holding a small child. The child was smiling; so was the woman. She wore a dark dress—it had been tinted blue with oils in the picture—and her hair hung in tubular curls. The child was dressed in a playsuit: it had a colored stipple effect, retouched so that the short pants and shirt seemed one. The child wore a little round cap, carefully cocked to one side to permit the dark kinky twists of his hair to show.

The young man in the room looked at the portrait. His hand, the one that did not hold the gun, reached out and gripped the edge of the frame harshly.

Then the hand dropped.

There were loud voices in the house now.

He aimed the gun at the picture and fired. Smoke curled from a wide slash in the portrait. He fired again, and again, until the faces were completely obliterated.

Then he hurled the emptied pistol at the door.

A woman's voice rose above the others: "Let me go in. Let me see to him. I know my Carlie."

And the voices turned into a soft mumble.

The young man looked out the window and pulled his head back sharply. Three men stood outside.

He struck something with his foot. It was a book. A large book. The light from the moon was strong and the words could be read, the words on the very first page.

This book belongs to Carlie Lee Phillips.

He held the book. Went to a corner, holding the book.

The door opened, flooding light.

A woman stood in the doorway, balanced on canes.

There were men behind the woman.

They had guns.

"Carlie," the woman said.

The young man in the corner stood up, questioningly.

"Carlie," she said, and walked into the room.

"Be careful . . ."

The young man stared.

"What's she doing?" a voice came. "Where's she going?"

The woman walked to the bed, kept her eyes on the bed. She sat down. "Carlie," she said. "Are you upset? Is there anything Mother can do?"

The men watched the woman on the bed, watched her make stroking motions in the empty air with her hand, watched the expression on her face.

Then they came into the room.

They stepped over the books and the boats and the elephants, past the red horse and the doll with the bleeding head.

They went to the young man and led him outside and took him away from the house.

THE MURDERERS

The pale young man in the bright red vest leaned back, sucked reflectively at a Russian candy pellet—the kind with real Jamaican rum inside—and said, yawning: "Let's kill somebody tonight."

"Herbie, *please!*" the other man said. He re-adjusted his fingers on the strings of the large guitar and plucked out a few loose chords.

> *"Come listen, all you boys 'n girls,"* he sang,
> *"I'se jest from Tuckyhoe;*
> *I'm gwine'a sing a little song:*
> *My name's Jim Crow.*
> *Weel about 'n turn about and do jes' so,*
> *Ebry time I weel about I jump Jim Crow.*
> *Ohhh, arter I been—"*

"Stop!" Herbert Foss put his hands to his ears. "You depress me. Besides, you're off key—utterly, hopelessly."

"Liar!" Ronald Raphael flung the guitar clear across the room. "I despise you," he said. "You know that, of course?"

"Of course."

They sat quietly for a while. That is, Herbert did; his younger friend lay belly-down on the rug, outstretched legs encased in chartreuse slacks, quite still but for the slow motion of his several toes, which waggled in their straw-thonged sandals like small snakes.

The room had grown dark. A little moonlight sifted through the dense foliage of the outside garden and through the heavy leaded French window, making shadows where the African masks and imitation shrunken heads hung on the walls. From the bathroom a fresco of a naked green woman without a face glowed; otherwise, the room was dark.

Herbert got up from his chair and walked over to one of the

many bookcases. Upon a copy of *Les Fleurs du Mal* was a clay-colored skull, and upon the skull was a candle. Herbert lit the candle. It flickered.

"Why not?" he said.

"Why not what?"

"Murder somebody."

Ronald gathered himself into a squatting position. "Anyone particular you have in mind?"

"Don't be foolish. No—I've given the matter some thought and it's really quite priceless. Though I ought to warn you: it involves courage."

"How extremely *roman policier*. But, Herbie, are you serious?"

"Deadly. You're for it?"

"Sounds all right. When?"

Herbert walked to the center of the big high-ceilinged room and blew at a mobile. "Tonight," he said, lowering his voice. "I mean, after all. I mean, damn it, why not?"

Ronald picked at the tendriled frieze which protruded from his carelessly buttoned shirt, and smiled inscrutably. He went to the phonograph and put on some minor Bartók; then he turned, a remarkably thin figure in the moonlight window, and whipped off his heavy black horn-rimmed spectacles.

"Go on," he said.

Herbert had been tamping down the tobacco in a long, hand-carved pipe. "Well, the way I see it, we've got to be methodical," he said. "Too many crimes are done clumsily, without discretion, without grace and forethought, you know? In the case of the *crime passionel*, it's always a simple matter for the police; with a planned murder, the criminal gets panicky at the last minute and ruins everything. A poor lot, Ronnie: their motives are so base, so unbearably bourgeois. Don't you agree?"

"One hundred per cent."

"Well then, don't you see, we fall into neither category. We aren't going to commit a *crime passionel*, and as for the plan—why, we don't even know the identity of our victim yet!"

Ronald clapped his hands together once, rushed into the kitchen and returned bearing a bottle and two long-stemmed glasses.

"A toast!" he said, delightedly. "A toast, to our nameless friend, wherever he may be."

They drank in solemn silence, concluding by flinging their glasses against the fireplace.

Herbert's close-cropped blond hair was haloed in the guttering candlelight. "How invigorating!" he exclaimed. "It's the first time in three months that I haven't been bored. Not since that Javanese girl—what *was* her name? I've forgotten. It's unimportant: she bored me, anyway. But this—"

Ronald fairly shook with excitement. "I must give you credit. It *has* all been so infernally dull—dull, *dull*."

The candle sputtered out in a soft wind from the open window.

"Then," Herbert said, "you'll go through with it?"

"I simply can't wait, old man."

"Tonight?"

"Immediately!"

"All right. I've mapped out a little schedule, a working plan. Please listen carefully."

Herbert leaned close to his friend's ear and began to whisper, in soft, conspiratorial tones. . . .

"Bughouse Square" was not thickly populated, for the hour was late. There were no speakers, no huddled groups. Only the old men and women who sit on the hard benches. A young girl glued to the side of a sailor swung her hips against his as they meandered across the lawn; a woman in many shredded silk dresses, many scarves and handkerchiefs, hobbled haltingly, moving her lips; a lithe Negro man pranced by the rim of a stone fountain. There were no others and the night was empty of human sounds, except for the traffic far away and the city's distant hum.

Ronald shifted uncomfortably. "Don't you think," he said, grinding out another cigarette, "that we should go somewhere? Like home, maybe? Damn it, I'm freezing to death—we've been here for two hours, for Chrissake." His chartreuse slacks had been replaced by faded levis; he had on a cheap windbreaker and his face was dirty.

Herbert had on a peajacket and looked more disreputable: his hair was blackened with shoe polish and he wasn't wearing his glasses. "Whine, whine, whine," he said. "After all this trouble, you . want to give up?"

"But we've been here *two hours*, I'm telling you. What's wrong with killing one of these guys?"

"Not so loud! They offend me, that's what's wrong with it. Besides, they look like they belong here; they'd be missed. We want someone completely anonymous—a nobody, a nothing, without friends or relatives. That was the plan."

Ronald sighed loudly. "All right. But it *is* getting late."

"Be *still*. Go, if you choose; leave me, leave and live your coward's life. Or, staying, shut up."

"There is no call for getting rude."

They sat and watched the Bughouse Square people break up slowly, only the bench sitters remaining, the old people.

"Very well," Herbert said, finally, "perhaps tonight is unlucky for us. I'll give it another ten minutes."

Ten minutes passed and the night grew colder and later and the two youths fidgeted.

Then they got up. And they were clear past the stone fountain before they saw the figure moving toward them.

"*Shhh. Wait!*" said Herbert.

The figure drew closer. It was a man: an old man, but not old like the bench sitters: his eyes were alive, and his beard was the color of Georgia mud. He was smoking the butt of a peeling cigar whose tip glowed red against his wrinkled leather skin. And his clothes were rags.

Herbert looked around quickly and saw that they were alone.

"Good evening, sir," he said softly, and the old man glanced up.

"Evening, boys."

"Late, isn't it?"

"Reckon so," the old man said, scratching his nose. "Late for some, early for others, hey?"

"Ha ha," Herbert said. "That's very good."

The old man cocked his head to one side and studied the two young men with casual intensity. "Say," he said, "you boys wouldn't happen to have the price of a flop on you, now would you?"

Herbert looked astonished. "Why, surely you don't mean that you haven't a place to sleep tonight!"

"Ain't tromping the sidewalks for my health, young fella. Tell you what— for two bits I could get me a fine old place."

"But, don't you have friends?" Ronald said.

"No," the old man said. "Them as I had is all under the ground. They found *them* a place to sleep, anyways."

Herbert took the old man's arm. "This is terrible! What a comment upon our society!"

"Since you're placing blame, laddie buck, place her on a blondined woman long gone . . ."

"A relative?" Ronald said quickly.

"No, no. My wife. Or pretty nearly, leastwise. See, I was a traveling salesman, supporting my dear mother at the time, when—but that there is a long old story. Now about that two bits—"

Herbert and Ronald exchanged short but highly meaningful looks.

"See here," Herbert said, "we don't have any money with us right now, but if you'd care to share our quarters for the evening, we'd be only too happy to oblige. Permit me to introduce us, Mr.—"

They had begun walking automatically in the general direction of the car, headed for the darkest, emptiest streets.

"Fogarty," the old man said, "James Oliver Fogarty." He said it with a certain wonderment, as if surprised to recall it so exactly.

Herbert said, "I am Artur Schopenhauer. And this is my good friend, Fred Nietzsche."

"Proud to know you, boys."

They passed many dark stores, many dirty gray brick apartments and hotels of clapboard and they didn't encounter a soul.

"We wouldn't be able to sleep, thinking of you wandering the cold night, Mr. Fogarty. I can only regret that we can't accommodate *all* the lonely, the sad of heart, the homeless of the world," Herbert said, digging Ronald in the ribs.

"Now there is a Christian thought," the old man said, "if I ever heard one: a fine Christian thought. Say, you wouldn't by chance have a bite to eat at your place?"

"Oh yes," Ronald said. "We'll fix you up just fine. Wait and see!"

They walked to the blackest section of the blackness, and when they caught sight of the car—a long, low, foreign make—Ronald halted and said: "Would you excuse us, Mr. Fogarty? I'd like to have a word with my friend."

The old man looked slightly bewildered. "Sure thing," he said.

"I just happened to think," Ronald whispered, having stepped into an odorous doorway, "what if someone sees him in the car?"

Herbert rubbed his chin thoughtfully. "You think we should do it now," he said, "right here and now, is that what you mean?"

"Well, no, not exactly."

They thought a moment. "We'll put the top up," Herbert said, brightening. "And place him between us. And I'll go through side streets. All right?"

"Well . . ."

"*Come* now; have you ever seen such a fatted calf? Sans friends, sans relatives—*exactly* what we wanted!"

The old man smiled at them from the corner.

Herbert smiled back. "We'll take him to the place, give him a few drinks, and then . . ."

"By the way, who's going to do it?"

"Does it matter?"

They walked back to the corner and helped the ragged old man into the automobile; fastened the top securely, looked around, roared away.

"Hey now, this is sure a funny place," the old man said, as they propelled him up the curving stone ramp. It was a small walkway, bounded on either side by tropical growths, spiny fronds and thick leaves with tips as sharp as needles.

"You like it?" Herbert said. "It used to belong to a religious sect—now defunct—and this was known as the 'death walk.' People brought their lately departed relatives to be resuscitated."

"You don't mean to tell me!"

"It suits our modest wants."

A curve in the ramp brought them to a large oak door topped

by an octagonal window of glass stained with curious symbols: from this promontory, the city's tiny lights could be clearly seen. They continued down the hall past the door, past several smaller doors, to one no different from the rest except that it was painted bright red.

"Home," Ronald said.

"By golly!" the old man said, and they went in.

Suffused light softened the rather startling effect of the gold walls and black ceiling; however, the fish-net drapes, colored orange, stood out in bold relief. The old man studied the room, or seemed to: his eyes darted from point to point, subtly.

"What will it be, sir," Ronald said, taking the double coat and hat, "Martini? Manhattan? Scotch-on-the-rocks?"

"Welsir, boys, those all sound mighty appetizing—but, now, if you have a sandwich of something—"

"Of course." Herbert motioned to Ronald and they went into the kitchen.

"Did you see anybody?" Herbert whispered.

"No."

"What about when I parked the car—anybody, in the windows or anything?"

"No. We weren't seen. I was watching."

"Doesn't it excite you! There's something so terribly *existential* in committing the perfect crime. Here—you fix the sandwiches, I'll see to it he has enough to drink."

The old man was sitting in the chair quite still, his hands folded across his stomach. He smelt somewhat rancid.

"Thank you, laddie." He took the drink and downed it at a single gulp. "Ahhh!"

"Another? Help yourself."

"*Thank* you, laddie!"

Ronald came out with the tray, and set it on the purple ottoman before the old man. "This ought to make you feel better, Mr. Fogarty," he said.

As the old man began to eat, Herbert said: "We've a bit of straightening up to do in the kitchen, so if you'll excuse us?" and they went back into the kitchen and closed the door.

"First, another toast!" Ronald said. A bottle was taken from the cupboard. "To James Oliver Fogarty: R. I. P.!"

Herbert smiled, and they chug-a-lugged the gin.

"By the bye, old man," Ronald said, grimacing, "you haven't yet told me how we're going to do it."

Looking somewhat blank, Herbert sat on the drainboard and replaced his glasses. "Well," he said, "let's give it some thought. It's actually an embarrassment of riches, you know. We *could* shoot him, I suppose."

"Oh *no*, Herbie—*everybody* shoots *everybody* these days. Also, it would make too much noise. I mean, you know Mrs. Fitzsimmons."

"You're right. Dear Mrs. Fitzsimmons. But *dear* Mrs. Fitz-simmons! Well . . . what about poison? Silent, fast, effective, its praises sung in lyric and in epic. . . . I rather fancy poison. Do we have any in the apartment?"

"I don't think so. Unless you refer to that wine you bought yesterday."

"At a time like this, levity seems grotesquely out of place, Ronnie. Do control yourself and not be such an ass."

"Sorry."

"Now let's see. Odd I didn't work this part of it out . . . I know! It's too perfect!" Herbert pulled open a drawer and withdrew a large butcher knife spotted with cake frosting.

Ronald shuddered slightly.

"Well?"

"It's all right, I guess. But—"

"But? *But?*"

"I'm just thinking of all that blood. It's supposed to be hard to clean up, and the police find things in it."

Herbert made a face and put down the knife. He poured two more glasses, and they listened for a time to the eating sounds from the living room.

"Herbie! I've got it!"

"*Quietly!* Yes?"

Ronald was smiling slyly. "Do you remember that statue we picked up a few months ago?"

"Which? 'The Forbidden Embrace'?"

"And do you remember how heavy it was . . . ?"

Herbert's face broke into a beam. "Of course! We'll club him!"

Ronald blushed. "Club him to death with an *objet d'art*—how excruciatingly *cloche!*"

They shook hands solemnly and went back into the living room.

"Hey-o!" The old man belched mildly, and settled back in the chair. "This here was mighty white of you, boys. Accept an old man's humble thanks. Would you—well, dagnab it, what for a drink on it?"

"Splendid!"

"Here's to a couple of red-blooded American boys!"

They drank.

"Ahhh," the old man said again, refilling the glasses. "Been a time since I tasted lappings good as that. Say, you have got a real nice place here! All them pictures and things, them draperies—real expensive."

Herbert sniffed. "If you find yourself on the stage," he drawled, "then I say, act the part. My parents *epit*omize the American capitalistic fallacy. Filthy rich, and all that. They throw me a bone from time to time."

"Do tell! Bet you're right fond of them for that, hey?"

"He loathes them," Ronald said, chewing at an olive.

The old man threw down his drink and pointed at a picture of a man with both eyes on one side of his face and no hair. "There's a funny one!"

"Picasso. Original, of course. Should have taken it down *weeks* ago: Picasso doesn't wear well, you know. Have another drink."

They drank again. And the glasses filled again. And another bottle came out of the cupboard.

"Mr. Fogarty," Herbert said, eying a heavy statue which resembled a squashed turnip, "for conversation's sake, would you mind telling us your views on life? We might as well confess to you: we're social directors for the Y. M. C. A."

"I kind of took me a notion that's what you was," the old man said, chuckling. "Life, hey? Well; she's a hard old go. Full of grief for some and joy for others, reckon. Never have rightly figgered her out."

"I imagine," Ronald said, "one must get desperately tired of it all, when one is as advanced in years as yourself."

"Well, no: not exactly," the old man said.

"Then—you fear death?"

"Don't everybody?"

Herbert sipped at his highball. "'Tis a consummation devoutly to be wish'd,'" he said. "Would you excuse our rudeness another time? The dishes want drying. No, no—please stay right where you are. It won't take a jiffy, then we'll show you to your bed."

Back in the kitchen, Herbert whispered: "Well?"

"Well what?"

"I mean, what are we waiting for?"

"Oh." Ronald poured out another three fingers of gin with unsteady hands. "You want to do it now?"

"Why not?" Herbert tried to hop up onto the drainboard, but, in hiccuping, didn't quite make it. "He's loaded," he said, confidentially. "Never know what happened."

From the living room came the old man's voice, thick and unclear, in an off key rendition of "That Little Old Red Shawl My Mother Wore."

"Okay," Ronald said, "but let's have just one more toast."

"One more. To the imminent demise of James Oliver Curwood. I mean Fogarty."

The gin was gone, however, so they made recourse to the Scotch.

"Getting along all right, are you, Mr. Fogarty?" Herbert called.

"—it was tatter'd, it was torn, it showed signs of being worn—" the old man sang.

"Poor old schmoe. He doesn't know what he's got coming, huh!"

"Ronnie, stop giggling obscenely. After all, you're about to kill a man."

Ronald stopped giggling. "Who is?" he said, faintly.

"You are, of course."

The younger man stumbled slightly and downed his glass of Scotch. "Now wait, just a minute—"

"What's this, what's this? Don't tell me you don't want to go through with it!"

"Who's telling you that?"

"He'll *hear* us, you silly ape, if you don't quiet down! It's only fair that you should finish the job; after all, I did every bit of the groundwork, didn't I? Are you not my *compagnon de voyage?* I mean, do you or do you not intend to be fair?"

"Certainly, certainly I do. It isn't that."

"Well then?"

"Don't you think we ought to wait a little while first?"

"Impossible. It's almost four o'clock in the morning now. We've got to allow time for disposing of the body, you idiot."

"All right, all right. One more drink!"

Herbert poured out some more Scotch, went into the living room and replenished the old man's drink.

Ronald was weaving a bit, and his glass was empty. "What's the matter?" he said, suddenly. "I don't hear him singing."

Herbert smiled. He had "The Forbidden Embrace" in his hand. "Passed out. *Sic transit gloria mundi!*"

"Did—did you do it?"

"Ronnie, my friend! Am I the sort who would cheat you?"

"Herbert, I have something to tell you."

"Yes, old man?"

"I refuse to rob you of the experience—no, no, I insist: *You* kill him."

"Such self-sacrifice does not fail to move me. Yet, fair is fair. It's quite settled—here's the statue. If you hit him hard, it shouldn't take more than one blow."

Ronald gulped loudly. "A toast, then!"

"To the Well of Experience!"

"To the Well of Experience!"

The Scotch dropped several inches in the bottle.

Ronald grasped "The Forbidden Embrace" in his hand and made a couple of tentative swipes in the air with it. His balance was disturbed and, sitting on the kitchen floor, he said: "Herbie, I just happened to think. I *can't* kill him."

"What do you mean?"

"I'm not twenty-one yet."

"Coward!" Herbert shrieked, and snatched up the statue. "Sniveling, groveling *petite bourgeois poupon!*"

He dashed through the door into the living room and advanced upon the old man, whose breathing was regular now.

"Farewell!" Herbert cried, raising the statue.

Then he lowered it. But, not on the old man's head.

"The Forbidden Embrace" crashed resoundingly through a stack of buckram-bound esoterica and fell to the floor. As did Herbert.

He said *"Shhh!"* to no one in particular, saw that James Oliver Fogarty still slept undisturbed and crawled back into the kitchen, where Ronald was forcing the cork of a bottle of vin rosé.

"I was assailed suddenly," Herbert said, dribbling the wine into his half-glass of Scotch, tossing it off and grimacing thereafter, "with a thought. May I explain? Though the risk is infinitesimal, nay, minuscule, still we ought to be intelligent about this."

Ronald nodded without enthusiasm.

"Now whereas I am of legal age and therefore subject to punishment as meted out by our savage and pagan society—*you* aren't. We've got to cover ourselves, you know."

"Absolutely."

"Very well: you must administer the *coup d'état* to our victim; it's air-tight then. On the off chance of something's going wrong, you merely plead juvenile delinquency."

Ronald stared at Herbert for a time. He sloshed some more wine into the glasses. "No," he said.

"No? *No?* Oh yes, I begin to get it now. You want to see me, *Herbie*, your oldest, dearest friend, fry in the chair! That's what you want."

"No, Herbie, I don't want that. Honest."

They were quiet, but for the staccato hiccup Ronald had developed.

Herbert was scratching his head madly. "Look here," he said, "we're behaving like children. Like *children!* Let us be mature. Do we have *weltanschauung,* or don't we? Are we ridden with the cheap morality of the herd, or aren't we?"

"Certainly."

"All right! Oh, Ronnie, we've reached a critical stage in our development as thinking people. An *impasse*, as it were. If we falter now, fail in our mission—*think!*—how then face ourselves? How exist with the awful knowledge?"

"How?"

"We would be worse than bourgeois; we would be *common*. We must have the courage of our lack of convictions! To the one side, intellectual freedom; to the other, slavery and eternal subjugation."

"Subjugation."

"Well—which is it, friend of four long years? When the balance hangs on the mere cracking of an old man's skull, which will you have: freedom or slavery?"

"More wine," Ronald said.

"Decide! The hour grows late, you must decide!"

"Sure. Okay. But—*you* do it, Herbie: I'm nervous."

Herbert Foss summoned a glance of profound contempt. "Weakling!" he yelled. "You may consider our relationship at a *finis*. I will do the deed myself, and if I am caught, then I shall sit in the electric chair a far, far freer man than you, Ronald Raphael. And so shall I die: free, content in my own company. *Drink your filthy wine!*"

Herbert's face glowed a deep, burning red; tiny balls of sweat speckled his forehead, and some of the shoe polish had run from his hair in thin dirty lines down his sallow cheeks. His eyes were large, the pupils bloated and black: he trembled as he snapped his fingers under Ronald's nose. Then he went back into the living room where the old man slept and he stopped trembling completely, for the first time.

He walked over to the fallen statue, picked it up and tested it against his palm. It was very heavy. Heavy enough to crush the bone of any man's skull, however thick, crush and drive the splinters of bone deep down; heavy enough to summon death quickly.

Herbert didn't tremble. He circled the snoring elder, then he sat down in the white campaign chair and reached for one of the glasses. The Scotch within had retained its unwatered light-gold lethal dignity.

Herbert gasped and coughed. From the half-open door he could see Ronald, slumped on the floor like a wet cotton doll.

He rolled the bright-beaded glass against his brow and stared at the old man. . . .

Daylight limped into the big room and thrashed, sullenly. The gold walls, the black ceiling, the piles of books and records, the whole vast high-timbered, many-leveled apartment looked tremendously different in the cold morning rays.

Sticky glasses littered the soiled rug, and several bottles lay overturned and empty: there was an oversweet smell pervasive, too, settled over everything like a heavy mildew.

"I've gone blind!" Herbert Foss cried, but this was not so: his eyes had stuck together with sleep. He pried the lids apart.

The blood on his hands had almost dried. But not quite.

"Oh, God!"

Ronald was curled up where he had fallen. At the outcry he raised his head and clamped his hands onto his ears. He moaned, softly.

"Ronnie—" Herbert held up his crimsoned hands, then made a sudden leap from the chair: The cloth blazed white around the spots of dark red.

He made a series of short animal noises, put his fingers to his temples, threw his head back and walked in a small circle twice around the room, eyes tightly clenched.

"No," Herbert said. "No. No. No."

At the fourth *No* his foot encountered the broken bottle by the fireplace: a square Scotch bottle, quite empty, splintered at the top, the shards and needles of glass brilliantly covered with wet red. A little trail of glass and blood led to the campaign chair.

"Good God," Herbert cried. "It's all over the place!"

Ronald was staring at the large overstuffed chair, however. He was seized, from time to time, by violent but short spasms.

"Herbie—did we? I mean, did you?"

"I don't know. Don't shout. If we did, you did it. I fell asleep—I remember distinctly."

"What about that blood all over you?"

Herbert shuddered. Then he saw the broken Scotch bottle and rattled out a sigh of high relief. He examined the small cuts on his palm. "I tripped on that glass; I recall."

Ronald covered his eyes. "Oh, my head!" he wailed. "Don't you understand—my *head!* Are you sure you didn't club *me* by mistake?"

The sentence had a sobering effect.

Herbert began to shake with fair regularity, as they stood there, huddled, in the middle of the room.

"Did you—did you see him?" he whispered.

"Who?"

"You know who."

"When?"

"Just now. I'm having a bit of trouble with my eyes. Is he—here, with us—?"

"I don't think so."

"Well, *look.*"

"I can't seem to focus my eyes—Herbie, *you* look. You're the leader, you're—"

Herbert made fists of his hands, swallowed dryly and opened one eye, revolving his head at the same time.

Then he opened the other eye.

"*Ronnie!*"

Ronald jumped at the sudden sound. He opened his eyes, and together they looked.

Then, they went upstairs to the shelf that served as a bedroom and looked on the bed and under the bed and in the closet. They looked in the kitchen and in the pantry; in the hall closet; in the bathroom and, after some delay, behind the shower curtain.

"Herbie, you don't suppose—I mean, you couldn't have done it and disposed of . . . the . . ."

Herbert's face, already white, turned whiter. "No," he said. "No. No."

"Let's check the car. Let's check the car. I said, let's—"

"Shhh! All right."

They rushed out the back door and through the garden, peering behind palm trees as they hurried, until they had reached the garage.

Whereat they stared, first at the open garage, immaculate, dark and empty; then at themselves, and back at the garage.

"My Jaguar," Herbert said, with immense simplicity, "is gone."

They rushed back to the apartment and stood still, except for the trembling.

"The pictures!" Herbert said. "The Picasso! The Motherwell! The Mondrian!"

"The Kuniyoshi," Ronald said.

"Where are they?"

"Look!"

The hall chiffonier sat disarrayed, the drawers, for the most part, empty, pulled out, some of them sprawled on the floor.

"Oh, *not* Mother's silver!" Herbert said.

Slowly then, a bit like somnambulists, they marched through the apartment.

And their words were full of wonder and disbelief.

"Our clothes—*all* our clothes!"

"Dad's luggage!"

"My ring—my *emerald* cuff links!"

A large complacent Buddha smiled above its unlocked belly. The camouflaged strongbox lay open and empty.

"Herbie, my shorts! My shorts are gone, the ones Carmencita gave me!"

And then Herbert Foss and Ronald Raphael stopped looking. They sat down in the living room, the quiet, cold living room, and put their heads on their arms and stayed this way for a very long time.

THE HUNGER

Now, with the sun almost gone, the sky looked wounded—as if a gigantic razor had been drawn across it, slicing deep. It bled richly. And the wind, which came down from High Mountain, cool as rain, sounded a little like children crying: a soft, unhappy kind of sound, rising and falling.

Afraid, somehow, it seemed to Julia. Terribly afraid.

She quickened her step. I'm an idiot, she thought, looking away from the sky. A complete idiot. That's why I'm frightened now; and if anything happens—which it won't, and can't—then I'll have no one to blame but myself.

She shifted the bag of groceries to her other arm and turned, slightly. There was no one in sight, except old Mr. Hannaford, pulling in his newspaper stands, preparing to close up the drugstore, and Jake Spiker, barely moving across to the Blue Haven for a glass of beer: no one else. The rippling red brick streets were silent.

But even if she got nearly all the way home, she could scream and someone would hear her. Who would be fool enough to try anything right out in the open? Not even a lunatic. Besides, it wasn't dark yet, not technically, anyway.

Still, as she passed the vacant lots, all shoulder-high in wild grass, Julia could not help thinking, He might be hiding there, right now. It was possible. Hiding there, all crouched up, waiting. And he'd only have to grab her, and—she wouldn't scream. She knew that suddenly, and the thought terrified her. Sometimes you *can't* scream. . . .

If only she'd not bothered to get that spool of yellow thread over at Younger's, it would be bright daylight now, bright clear daylight. And—

Nonsense! This was the middle of the town. She was surrounded by houses full of people. People all around. Everywhere.

(*He was a hunger; a need; a force. Dark emptiness filled him. He* moved, when he moved, like a leaf caught in some dark and secret river, rushing. But mostly he slept now, an animal, always ready to wake and leap and be gone . . .)

The shadows came to life, dancing where Julia walked. Now the sky was ugly and festered, and the wind had become stronger, colder. She clicked along the sidewalk, looking straight ahead, wondering, Why, why am I so infernally stupid? What's the matter with me?

Then she was home, and it was all over. The trip had taken not more than half an hour. And here was Maud, running. Julia felt her sister's arms fly around her, hugging. "God, my God."

And Louise's voice: "We were just about to call Mick to go after you."

Julia pulled free and went into the kitchen and put down the bag of groceries.

"Where in the world have you been?" Maud demanded.

"I had to get something at Younger's." Julia took off her coat. "They had to go look for it, and—I didn't keep track of the time."

Maud shook her head. "Well, I don't know," she said, wearily. "You're just lucky you're alive, that's all."

"Now—"

"You listen! He's out there somewhere. Don't you understand that? It's a fact. They haven't even come close to catching him yet."

"They will," Julia said, not knowing why: she wasn't entirely convinced of it.

"Of course they will. Meantime, how many more is he going to murder? Can you answer me that?"

"I'm going to put my coat away." Julia brushed past her sister. Then she turned and said, "I'm sorry you were worried. It won't happen again." She went to the closet, feeling strangely upset. They would talk about it tonight. All night. Analyzing, hinting, questioning. They would talk of nothing else, as from the very first. And they would not be able to conceal their delight.

"Wasn't it awful about poor Eva Schillings?"

No, Julia had thought: from her sisters' point of view it was not awful at all. It was wonderful. It was priceless.

It was news.

Julia's sisters . . . Sometimes she thought of them as mice. Giant gray mice, in high white collars: groaning a little, panting a little, working about the house. Endlessly, untiringly: they would squint at pictures, knock them crooked, then straighten them again; they swept invisible dust from clean carpets and took the invisible dust outside in shining pans and dumped it carefully into spotless apple-baskets; they stood by beds whose sheets shone gleaming white and tight, and clucked in soft disgust, and replaced the sheets with others. All day, every day, from six in the morning until most definite dusk. Never questioning, never doubting that the work had to be done.

They ran like arteries through the old house, keeping it alive. For it had become now a part of them, and they part of it—like the handcrank mahogany Victrola in the hall, or the lion-pelted sofa, or the Boutelle piano (ten years silent, its keys yellowed and decayed and ferocious, like the teeth of an aged mule).

Nights, they spoke of sin. Also of other times and better days: Maud and Louise—sitting there in the bellying heat of the obsolete but steadfast stove, hooking rugs, crocheting doilies, sewing linen, chatting, chatting.

Occasionally Julia listened, because she was there and there was nothing else to do; but mostly she didn't. It had become a simple thing to rock and nod and think of nothing at all, while *they* traded dreams of dead husbands, constantly relishing their mutual widowhood—relishing it!—pitching these fragile ghosts into moral combat. "Ernie, God rest him, was an honorable man." (So were they all, Julia would think, all honorable men; but we are here to praise Caesar, not to bury him . . .) "Jack would be alive today if it hadn't been for that trunk lid slamming down on his head: that's what started it all." Poor Ernie! Poor Jack!

(*He walked along the railroad tracks, blending with the night. He could have been young, or old: an age-hiding beard dirtied his face and throat. He wore a blue sweater, ripped in a dozen places. On the front of the sweater was sewn a large felt letter: E. Also sewn there was a small design showing a football and calipers. His gray trousers were dark with stain where he had fouled them. He walked along the tracks, seeing*

and not seeing the pulse of light far ahead; thinking and not thinking,
Perhaps I'll find it there, Perhaps they won't catch me, Perhaps I won't be
hungry any more . . .)

"You forgot the margarine," Louise said, holding the large sack
upside down.

"Did I? I'm sorry." Julia took her place at the table. The food
immediately began to make her ill: the sight of it, the smell of
it. Great bowls of beans, crisp-skinned chunks of turkey, mashed
potatoes. She put some on her plate, and watched her sisters. They
ate earnestly; and now, for no reason, this, too, was upsetting.

She looked away. What was it? What was wrong?

"Mick says that fellow didn't die," Maud announced. "Julia—"

"What fellow?"

"At the asylum, that got choked. He's going to be all right."

"That's good."

Louise broke a square of toast. She addressed Maud: "What else
did he say, when you talked to him? Are they making any progress?"

"Some. I understand there's a bunch of police coming down
from Seattle. If they don't get him in a few days, they'll bring in
some bloodhounds from out-of-state. Of course, you can imagine
how much Mick likes *that!*"

"Well, it's his own fault. If he was any kind of a sheriff, he'd
of caught that fellow a long time before this. I mean, after all,
Burlington just isn't that big." Louise dismembered a turkey leg,
ripped little shreds of the meat off, put them into her mouth.

Maud shook her head. "I don't know. Mick claims it isn't like
catching an ordinary criminal. With this one, you never can guess
what he's going to do, or where he'll be. Nobody has figured out
how he stays alive, for instance."

"Probably," Louise said, "he eats bugs and things."

Julia folded her napkin quickly and pressed it onto the table.

Maud said, "No. Most likely he finds stray dogs and cats."

They finished the meal in silence. Not, Julia knew, because there
was any lull in thought: merely so the rest could be savored in the
living room, next to the fire. A proper place for everything.

They moved out of the kitchen. Louise insisted on doing the
dishes, while Maud settled at the radio and tried to find a local

news broadcast. Finally she snapped the radio off, angrily. "You'd think they'd at least keep us informed! Isn't that the least they could do?"

Louise materialized in her favorite chair. The kitchen was dark. The stove warmed noisily, its metal sides undulating.

And it was time.

"Where do you suppose he is right now?" Maud asked.

Louise shrugged. "Out there somewhere. If they'd got him, Mick would of called us. He's out there somewhere."

"Yes. Laughing at all of us, too, I'll wager. Trying to figure out who'll be next."

Julia sat in the rocker and tried not to listen. Outside, there was a wind. A cold wind, biting; the kind that slips right through window putty, that you can feel on the glass. Was there ever such a cold wind? she wondered.

Then Louise's words started to echo. "He's out there somewhere. . . ."

Julia looked away from the window, and attempted to take an interest in the lacework in her lap.

Louise was talking. Her fingers flashed long silver needles. ". . . spoke to Mrs. Schillings today."

"I don't want to hear about it." Maud's eyes flashed like the needles.

"God love her heart, she's about crazy. Could barely talk."

"God, God."

"I tried to comfort her, of course, but it didn't do any good."

Julia was glad she had been spared that conversation. It sent a shudder across her, even to think about it. Mrs. Schillings was Eva's mother, and Eva—only seventeen . . . The thoughts she vowed not to think, came back. She remembered Mick's description of the body, and his words: ". . . she'd got through with work over at the telephone office around about nine. Carl Jasperson offered to see her home, but he says she said not to bother, it was only a few blocks. Our boy must have been hiding around the other side of the cannery. Just as Eva passed, he jumped. Raped her and then strangled her. I figure he's a pretty man-sized bugger. Thumbs like to went clean through the throat—"

In two weeks, three women had died. First, Charlotte Adams, the librarian. She had been taking her usual shortcut across the school playground, about 9:15 P.M. They found her by the slide, her clothes ripped from her body, her throat raw and bruised.

Julia tried very hard not to think of it, but when her mind would clear, there were her sisters' voices, droning, pulling her back, deeper.

She remembered how the town had reacted. It was the first murder Burlington had had in fifteen years. It was the very first mystery. Who was the sex-crazed killer? Who could have done this terrible thing to Charlotte Adams? One of her gentleman friends, perhaps. Or a hobo, from one of the nearby jungles. Or . . .

Mick Daniels and his tiny force of deputies had swung into action immediately. Everyone in town took up the topic, chewed it, talked it, chewed it, until it lost its shape completely. The air became electrically charged. And a grim gaiety swept Burlington, reminding Julia of a circus where everyone is forbidden to smile.

Days passed, uneventfully. Vagrants were pulled in and released. People were questioned. A few were booked, temporarily.

Then, when the hum of it had begun to die, it happened again. Mrs. Dovie Samuelson, member of the local P.T.A., mother of two, moderately attractive and moderately young, was found in her garden, sprawled across a rhododendron bush, dead. She was naked, and it was established that she had been attacked. Of the killer, once again, there was no trace.

Then the State Hospital for the Criminally Insane released the information that one of its inmates—a Robert Oakes—had escaped. Mick, and many others, had known this all along. Oakes had originally been placed in the asylum on a charge of raping and murdering his cousin, a girl named Patsy Blair.

After he had broken into his former home and stolen some old school clothes, he had disappeared, totally.

Now he was loose.

Burlington, population 3,000, went into a state of ecstasy: delicious fear gripped the town. The men foraged out at night with torches and weapons; the women squeaked and looked under their beds and . . . chatted.

But still no progress was made. The maniac eluded hundreds of searchers. They knew he was near, perhaps at times only a few feet away, hidden; but always they returned home, defeated.

They looked in the forests and in the fields and along the river banks. They covered High Mountain—a miniature hill at the south end of town—like ants, poking at every clump of brush, investigating every abandoned tunnel and water tank. They broke into deserted houses, searched barns, silos, haystacks, tree-tops. They looked everywhere, everywhere. And found nothing.

When they decided for sure that their killer had gone far away, that he couldn't conceivably be within fifty miles of Burlington, a third crime was committed. Young Eva Schillings' body had been found, less than a hundred yards from her home.

And that was three days ago. . . .

". . . they get him," Louise was saying, "they ought to kill him by little pieces, for what he's done."

Maud nodded. "Yes; but they won't."

"Of course they—"

"No! You wait. They'll shake his hand and lead him back to the bughouse and wait on him hand and foot—till he gets a notion to bust out again."

"Well, I'm of a mind the people will have something to say about that."

"Anyway," Maud continued, never lifting her eyes from her knitting, "what makes you so sure they *will* catch him? Supposing he just drops out of sight for six months, and—"

"You stop that! They'll get him. Even if he *is* a maniac, he's still human."

"I really doubt that. I doubt that a human could have done these awful things." Maud sniffed. Suddenly, like small rivers, tears began to course down her snowbound cheeks, cutting and melting the hard white-packed powder, revealing flesh underneath even paler. Her hair was shot with gray, and her dress was the color of rocks and moths; yet, she did not succeed in looking either old or frail. There was nothing whatever frail about Maud.

"He's a man," she said. Her lips seemed to curl at the word. Louise nodded, and they were quiet.

(*His ragged tennis shoes padded softly on the gravel bed. Now his heart*

*was trying to tear loose from his chest. The men, the men . . . They had
almost stepped on him, they were that close. But he had been silent. They
had gone past him, and away. He could see their flares back in the distance. And far ahead, the pulsing light. Also a square building: the depot,
yes. He must be careful. He must walk in the shadows. He must be very
still.*

The fury burned him, and he fought it.

Soon.

It would be all right, soon . . .)

". . . think about it, this here maniac is only doing what every
man would *like* to do but can't."

"Maud!"

"I mean it. It's a man's natural instinct—it's all they ever think
about." Maud smiled. She looked up. "Julia, you're feeling sick.
Don't tell me you're not."

"I'm all right," Julia said, tightening her grip on the chair-arms
slightly. She thought, They've been married! They talk this way
about men, as they always have, and yet soft words have been
spoken to them, and strong arms placed around their shoulders. . . .

Maud made tiny circles with her fingers. "Well, I can't force
you to take care of yourself. Except, when you land in the hospital
again, I suppose you know who'll be doing the worrying and staying up nights—as per usual."

"I'll . . . go on to bed in a minute." But, why was she hesitating?
Didn't she want to be alone?

Why didn't she want to be alone?

Louise was testing the door. She rattled the knob vigorously,
and returned to her chair.

"What would he want, anyway," Maud said, "with two old bid-
dies like us?"

"We're not so old," Louise said, saying, actually: "That's true;
we're old."

But it wasn't true, not at all. Looking at them, studying them,
it suddenly occurred to Julia that her sisters were ashamed of their
essential attractiveness. Beneath the 'twenties hair-dos, the ill-used
cosmetics, the ancient dresses (which did not quite succeed in concealing their still voluptuous physiques), Maud and Louise were

youthfully full and pretty. They were. Not even the birch-twig toothbrushes and traditional snuff could hide it.

Yet, Julia thought, they envy me.

They envy my plainness.

"What kind of a man would do such heinous things?" Louise said, pronouncing the word, carefully, heen-ious.

And Julia, without calling or forming the thought, discovered an answer grown in her mind: an impression, a feeling.

What kind of a man?

A lonely man.

It came upon her like a chill. She rose from the pillowed chair, lightly. "I think," she said, "I'll go on to my room."

"Are your windows good and locked?"

"Yes."

"You'd better make sure. All he'd have to do is climb up the drainpipe." Maud's expression was peculiar. Was she really saying, "This is only to comfort you, dear. Of the three of us, it's unlikely he'd pick on you"?

"I'll make sure." Julia walked to the hallway. "Good night."

"Try to get some sleep." Louise smiled. "And don't think about him, hear? We're perfectly safe. He couldn't possibly get in, even if he tried. Besides," she said, "I'll be awake."

(*He stopped and leaned against a pole and looked up at the deaf and swollen sky. It was a movement of dark shapes, a hurrying, a running.*

He closed his eyes.

> "*The moon is the shepherd,*
>   *The clouds are his sheep . . ."*

He tried to hold the words, tried very hard, but they scattered and were gone.

"*No.*"

He pushed away from the pole, turned, and walked back to the gravel bed.

The hunger grew: with every step it grew. He thought that it had died, that he had killed it at last and now he could rest, but it had not died. It sat inside him, inside his mind, gnawing, calling, howling to be released. Stronger than before. Stronger than ever before.

"The moon is the shepherd . . ."

A cold wind raced across the surrounding fields of wild grass, turning the land into a heaving dark-green ocean. It sighed up through the branches of cherry trees and rattled the thick leaves. Sometimes a cherry would break loose, tumble in the gale, fall and split, filling the night with its fragrance. The air was iron and loam and growth.

He walked and tried to pull these things into his lungs, the silence and coolness of them.

But someone was screaming, deep inside him. Someone was talking.

"What are you going to do—"

He balled his fingers into fists.

"Get away from me! Get away!"

"Don't—"

The scream faded.

The girl's face remained. Her lips and her smooth white skin and her eyes, her eyes . . .

He shook the vision away.

The hunger continued to grow. It wrapped his body in sheets of living fire. It got inside his mind and bubbled in hot acids, filling and filling him.

He stumbled, fell, plunged his hands deep into the gravel, withdrew fists full of the grit and sharp stones and squeezed them until blood trailed down his wrists.

He groaned, softly.

Ahead, the light glowed and pulsed and whispered, Here, Here, Here, Here, Here.

He dropped the stones and opened his mouth to the wind and walked on . . .)

Julia closed the door and slipped the lock noiselessly. She could no longer hear the drone of voices: it was quiet, still, but for the sighing breeze.

What kind of a man . . .

She did not move, waiting for her heart to stop throbbing. But it would not stop.

She went to the bed and sat down. Her eyes traveled to the window, held there.

"He's out there somewhere . . ."

Julia felt her hands move along her dress. It was an old dress, once purple, now gray with faded gray flowers. The cloth was tissue-thin. Her fingers touched it and moved upward to her throat. They undid the top button.

For some reason, her body trembled. The chill had turned to heat, tiny needles of heat, puncturing her all over.

She threw the dress over a chair and removed the underclothing. Then she walked to the bureau and took from the top drawer a flannel nightdress, and turned.

What she saw in the tall mirror caused her to stop and make a small sound.

Julia Landon stared back at her from the polished glass.

Julia Landon, thirty-eight, neither young nor old, attractive nor unattractive, a woman so plain she was almost invisible. All angles and sharpnesses, and flesh that would once have been called "milky" but was now only white, pale white. A little too tall. A little too thin. And faded.

Only the eyes had softness. Only the eyes burned with life and youth and—

Julia moved away from the mirror. She snapped off the light. She touched the window shade, pulled it slightly, guided it soundlessly upward.

Then she unfastened the window latch.

Night came into the room and filled it. Outside, giant clouds roved across the moon, obscuring it, revealing it, obscuring it again.

It was cold. Soon there would be rain.

Julia looked out beyond the yard, in the direction of the depot, dark and silent now, and the tracks and the jungles beyond the tracks where lost people lived.

"I wonder if he can see me."

She thought of the man who had brought terror and excitement to the town. She thought of him openly, for the first time, trying to imagine his features.

He was probably miles away.

Or, perhaps he was nearby. Behind the tree, there, or under the hedge. . . .

"I'm afraid of you, Robert Oakes," she whispered to the night.

"You're insane, and a killer. You would frighten the wits out of me."

The fresh smell swept into Julia's mind. She wished she were surrounded by it, in it, just for a little while.

Just for a few minutes.

A walk. A short walk in the evening.

She felt the urge strengthening.

"You're dirty, young man. And heartless—ask Mick, if you don't believe me. You want love so badly you must kill for it—but nevertheless, you're heartless. Understand? And you're not terribly bright, either, they say. Have you read Shakespeare's Sonnets? Herrick? How about Shelley, then? There, you see! I'd detest you on sight. Just look at your fingernails!"

She said these things silently, but as she said them she moved toward her clothes.

She paused, went to the closet.

The green dress. It was warmer.

A warm dress and a short walk—that will clear my head. Then I'll come back and sleep.

It's perfectly safe.

She started for the door, stopped, returned to the window. Maud and Louise would still be up, talking.

She slid one leg over the sill; then the other leg.

Softly she dropped to the frosted lawn.

The gate did not creak.

She walked into the darkness.

Better! So much better. Good clean air that you can breathe!

The town was a silence. A few lights gleamed in distant houses, up ahead; behind, there was only blackness. And the wind.

In the heavy green frock, which was still too light to keep out the cold—though she felt no cold; only the needled heat—she walked away from the house and toward the depot.

It was a small structure, unchanged by passing years, like the Landon home and most of the homes in Burlington. There were tracks on either side of it.

Now it was deserted. Perhaps Mr. Gaffey was inside, making insect sounds on the wireless. Perhaps he was not.

Julia stepped over the first track, and stood, wondering what had happened and why she was here. Vaguely she understood something. Something about the yellow thread that had made her late and forced her to return home through the gathering dusk. And this dress—had she chosen it because it was warmer than the others . . . or because it was prettier?

Beyond this point there was wilderness, for miles. Marshes and fields overgrown with weeds and thick foliage. The hobo jungles: some tents, dead campfires, empty tins of canned heat.

She stepped over the second rail, and began to follow the gravel bed. Heat consumed her. She could not keep her hands still.

In a dim way, she realized—with a tiny part of her—why she had come out tonight.

She was looking for someone.

The words formed in her mind, unwilled: "Robert Oakes, listen, listen to me. You're not the only one who is lonely. But you can't steal what we're lonely for, you can't take it by force. Don't you know that? Haven't you learned that yet?"

I'll talk to him, she thought, and he'll go along with me and give himself up . . .

No.

That isn't why you're out tonight. You don't care whether he gives himself up or not. You . . . only want him to know that you understand. Isn't that it?

You couldn't have any other reason.

It isn't possible that you're seeking out a lunatic for any other reason.

Certainly you don't want him to touch you.

Assuredly you don't want him to put his arms around you and kiss you, because no man has ever done that—assuredly, assuredly.

It isn't you he wants. It isn't love. He wouldn't be taking Julia Landon. . . .

"But what if he doesn't!" The words spilled out in a small choked cry. "What if he sees me and runs away! Or I don't find him. Others have been looking. What makes me think I'll—"

Now the air swelled with sounds of life: frogs and birds and locusts, moving; and the wind, running across the trees and reeds and foliage at immense speed, whining, sighing.

Everywhere there was this loudness, and a dark like none Julia had ever known. The moon was gone entirely. Shadowless, the surrounding fields were great pools of liquid black, stretching infinitely, without horizon.

Fear came up in her chest, clutching.

She tried to scream.

She stood paralyzed, moveless, a pale terror drying into her throat and into her heart.

Then, from far away, indistinctly, there came a sound. A sound like footsteps on gravel.

Julia listened, and tried to pierce the darkness. The sounds grew louder. And louder. Someone was on the tracks. Coming closer.

She waited. Years passed, slowly. Her breath turned into a ball of expanding ice in her lungs.

Now she could see, just a bit.

It was a man. A black man-form. Perhaps—the thought increased her fear—a hobo. It mustn't be one of the hobos.

No. It was a young man. Mick! Mick, come to tell her, "Well, we got the bastard!" and to ask, narrowly, "What the devil you doing out here, Julie?" Was it?

She saw the sweater. The ball of ice in her lungs began to melt, a little. A sweater. And shoes that seemed almost white.

Not a hobo. Not Mick. Not anyone she knew.

She waited an instant longer. Then, at once, she knew without question who the young man was.

And she knew that he had seen her.

The fear went away. She moved to the center of the tracks.

"I've been looking for you," she said, soundlessly. "Every night I've thought of you. I have." She walked toward the man. "Don't be afraid, Mr. Oakes. Please don't be afraid. I'm not."

The young man stopped. He seemed to freeze, like an animal, prepared for flight.

He did not move, for several seconds.

Then he began to walk toward Julia, lightly, hesitantly, rubbing his hands along his trousers.

When Julia was close enough to see his eyes, she relaxed, and smiled.

Perhaps, she thought, feeling the first drops of rain upon her face, perhaps if I don't scream he'll let me live.

That would be nice.

TEARS OF THE MADONNA

THE man in the American suit smiled and pressed the perspiration from his mustache. "It is much too hot," he said, "for death. Even in the shade, too hot." He unwrapped his handkerchief from a cold-beaded beer bottle and placed the handkerchief across his forehead. "The bulls will be sluggish," he said.

"Perhaps not," Ramon said. The stranger was trying very hard to take his money away.

"Believe me, young friend, it will be no contest. Did you travel these many miles to watch a slaughter?"

Ramon frowned. Why had he permitted this stranger to sit at his table? Go away, he wanted to say: You are spoiling my pleasure; I have waited a long time for this and now you are spoiling it. Go away!

"You must take the word of one who knows. I have gone to the fights and come away sick on just such days as this one. The bulls sweat out their strength before the first banderillo is placed: after that, it is butcher's work." The man wiped the handkerchief all over his wet brown face.

"I will take the chance," Ramon said.

"Chance? There is none. Look: this is your first time, isn't it?"

Ramon nodded sorrowfully.

"Then I *beg* you. On bended knee. Save your money or throw it away, but do not waste it like this. A good fight you will never forget: it will live with you and fill your heart with pride: it will show you better than any book that there are the animals and then, there is Man—"

Yes, yes, Ramon thought, that is true!

"—but this is a good fight that I speak of, sir. A bad fight—like what you would see today—is something else. It is the saddest thing in all the world! For the spirit is not there, and without the

170

spirit this beauty is degraded. Courage is gone. Symbol is gone. Suddenly you are at a cheap show where you watch a dumb brute killed by a trained man. You leave ashamed. You never come back."

"All right. I'll go tomorrow," Ramon said.

"Tomorrow? No. Not for two weeks is there another."

Ramon drank the rest of his beer without answering the stranger. You are lying, he thought: I know this. But what if you are right even so? What if the fight is not a good one? Certainly it was hot, hot enough to make even the mightiest of all bulls sweat. . . .

"What is the name of this girl?" Ramon said.

The man seemed to sigh. He hunched forward and extended his effeminate-fingered hand. "You are smart," he said. "Any young fool from the country can see a bad bullfight, but Ramon de Castro! Not many are so fortunate as to enjoy the favors of the flower of all Mexico."

"What is her name?" Ramon said, still holding his money. "What does she look like?"

The man grinned. "Like nothing you have ever seen. She is not of this world."

"In that case," Ramon said, "she will have no use for my money."

The man laughed loudly. "More to drink!" he called and paid the waiter. "Shall I describe her, lucky Ramon? Shall I describe with poor crippled words a perfection that goes beyond even dreams? Speak to you of her softness which is softer than—what? a swan? the petal of a white rose? a robin's breast? Or say, look! her hair is more black and shining with diamond-light than the clearest, darkest night sky and her lips redder than this sky when the darkness is gone and—"

"Show me a photograph," Ramon said, "of this girl."

The man pulled a glossy snapshot from the pocket of his American suit. He held it in his palm for a moment.

"What is the difference, young friend," he said musically, "between love and a bullfight, when they are good, when the spirit is there? They involve courage equally, dear Ramon. Look at it this way: today you will enter an arena exactly as you had planned to do. But you will not merely watch. You will *be* the fine torero, and is this not better any time than watching, even from the shady side?" The man winked.

Ramon finished the beer again. "But how do I know," he asked, "that this bull will not also be tired and sweaty? How do I know that I won't come away sick from this fight as from the other because it is hot and the spirit is not there?"

"There are some bulls," the man said, "who never lose the spirit. These are the finest bulls. They aren't many; and they're expensive."

"How expensive?" Ramon said.

"Ah!" the man said.

"First I must see the photograph."

The man placed it carefully in front of Ramon. "Her name is Dolores. You can meet her tonight, if you wish."

"How expensive?" Ramon said.

"Little more than you would pay for a seat in the shade to watch the sticking of a pig."

Ramon looked at the picture. The woman was older than he by several years. Her long black hair was brushed over her shoulders, which seemed to Ramon the whitest shoulders he had ever looked at. Her mouth was large and painted and her breasts strained against the soft cloth of her blouse. Her eyes were closed. She was beautiful.

"It is important," the man was saying, "that you be as discriminating and thoughtful in entering one arena as the other. Especially when it is for the first time."

"It is not the first time!" Ramon lied. The confidence he had felt in his mustache and sideburns and pinstripe suit crumbled, because the stranger saw his seventeen years and laughed at them. The stranger shrugged, smiling.

"Still," he said, "you may count this as the first. Dolores will show you. It is one of her values: she shows a man that he is more of a man than he has ever thought. You will come away proud. Believe me."

"She has a large nose."

"The fault of the photographer. Her nose is perfect."

Ramon studied the picture. Oh, he had not dreamed of this . . . no; *Ramon, lie to others, not to yourself*; he had dreamed of it. Yes.

Was that not why he had let the man sit down and was that not why he had listened, so carefully, to him?

She was very beautiful, this Dolores. More beautiful than the bulls. More beautiful than any other woman on earth.

"All right," Ramon said, boredly. "Where? What time?"

"I must have a deposit," the man said, the poetry suddenly gone from his voice.

Ramon began to count his money. The man laughed and reached over and took half. "The rest tonight," he said. He gave Ramon directions. "Eleven o'clock. Be on time."

"Why so late?"

"Dolores works elsewhere. She is not what you might think." The man rose to leave. "I do this for you only because you are a nice boy, Ramon de Castro."

Ramon ordered tequila. For the first time. But it made him sick so he bought whiskey.

—*Ramon, did you have a good time?*

—*Yes, my mother.*

—*Was the city big? Did it frighten you alone? Were you afraid?*

—*The city was big, my mother.*

—*And did you go to the bullfights, Ramon?*

—*Yes, my mother, I went to the bullfights.*

Ramon recounted his money and smiled because the pain of it was over and out of him and even if he wanted to he could not change his mind now and go instead to watch the running of the bulls.

He looked at the picture and began to be afraid.

He was not afraid when it was dark and the sun had stopped baking the smooth streets. He was not even worried, for had he not been to a barber? and had he not bathed carefully and perfumed under his arms? and did he not look fine and grown now tonight, more fine and grown than ever Manuel or Jesus with their filthy lying mouths!

—*Little Ramon, tend to your cows and don't bother us; come around again when you've seen more than the flesh of your sister in the morning; then we'll talk. . . .*

He looked at himself, tall in the store window. Was this Señor de Castro's best son who saved his pesos and begged and was permitted to go to the city to see the fights?

He giggled and looked at his watch. Only nine-thirty.

He went into the bar with the big paintings of beautiful big women and sat down.

"Whiskey."

He belched hotly and took out the now crumpled and sticky photograph. A white webwork of cracks ran across the face of the flower of Mexico, soft and light as the moon, and old enough to teach you and kind enough to understand. . . .

Ramon felt something heavy thump against his back. "Ha! my friend," a voice said, "and I was wondering if the fine young fellow was old enough to drink!"

An old man leaned across and tapped the snapshot.

"I should not worry so much, eh? You are old enough. See, isn't she lovely!"

The man had long yellow teeth that crept down over his lip. He looked greenish in the bar light. His eyes were deep holes like the holes you make in dirty clay with a round stick.

"Don't look at me with your mouth open, my little. We are brothers."

"You know the lady?" Ramon thought of what the man in the American suit had told him.

"Know her? *Dolores?* I?" The man laughed until the whiskey made him choke. "I have . . . spoken to her, eh, Carmen? Haven't I spoken with Dolores?"

The man called Carmen nodded sadly.

"I am to be with her tonight," Ramon said, his chest swelling with pride.

"No! You? With the flower of our land? How lucky you are. You must drink the next with me—I am Garcia; remember me to the mother, will you?"

"I will," Ramon said. He sat straight on the stool and drank the whiskey and then more and presently he did not sit so straight any more and this annoyed him. He started to leave.

"Wait," the man Garcia called. "When do you see her?"

"Eleven."

"Then you must watch her act. She is last, so there is time."

Ramon stopped.

"What, what? Don Alvarado didn't tell you about her act?"

"No. What do you speak of?"

Some of the men turned. The bartender smiled pensively.

Garcia walked over and put his arm about Ramon. He whispered in a low smelly voice. "You have seen nothing until you see this. Some say it is better than what follows: I say so myself, and I have had both. Say, you've seen these shows where the women dance and take off their clothes, eh, my little?"

Ramon nodded quickly.

"Dolores is to them what a blooded mare is to a burro: worse, beside her they are all pigs. What, my friends? Do I lie?"

"No." The men grumbled and snickered.

"Nowhere else on earth can one see such a sight, my brother, my little. To watch Dolores perform and know that afterwards, ah, afterwards . . ."

"Where is this place," Ramon said, "where she is at?"

"The corner where you are to meet—one block and then another to the right. It is a theatre, do you understand? It costs little. They do not have pictures on the outside and it is small, almost as small as this place. But it is a theatre. You will see the lights."

The man talked on and Ramon's head danced.

"Watch yourself, my brother, or your blood will boil over on the floor!"

Ramon hurried out into the coolness and breathed the air and walked away fast.

He did not hear the laughter.

The theatre was small, as the man Garcia had said: a cube of heat-bulged boards painted with colors which had once been bright. The sign was solemnly lettered: TEATRO DE LA ALEGORIA.

Ramon paid. He went in wondering about the sign. Alegoria: a strange word, one you did not find in the country—otherwise he would have found it and learned its meaning.

There were mostly very old people and very young. Few the age of Ramon. They were a thick crowd; the smell of breath and sweat was heavy in the closeness; it was enough to make you sick at the stomach.

He sat down, not looking yet at the lighted stage. The woman he sat next to was fat. She was staring with big white chicken eyes and mumbling softly to herself as Mama de Castro did when her blood was up.

He put away the snapshot. He would think only about tonight. Tonight, in an hour; in less time, even!

Ramon tasted the whiskey inside him and was suddenly afraid all over again. His knees were water, he could feel his heart beating too swiftly. The city was very big and he was very young and this woman—

The stage was small, lit by spotlights that came from somewhere in the back. There was a crude burlap curtain sewn and resewn so many times you could see the fists of stitching from any seat. The curtain had been dropped. And now there was applause from the old and young people.

Ramon settled. He was tall, so he did not need to squint as the fat woman did.

Soon the curtain pulled up slowly and Ramon trembled in his dream of naked women. He had lied to Garcia. He had seen only skinny hags who had embarrassed him. Never had he seen beautiful women unclothed. Never had he seen anything.

The stage was empty now. The earth floor had been combed and tamped; but there was nothing, only the tense waiting of the people.

Then a figure walked out upon the floor. A figure clad in the heaviest white robe Ramon had ever seen: its folds trailed in the dirt. The face was hidden.

A voice from a microphone, high-pitched and hurtful to the ears: "Ladies, Gentlemen, Number Twelve: She looks upon her children and is grieved!"

The figure walked to the center of the stage and then turned and walked to the black curtain and then turned again.

Ramon blinked his eyes.

The figure parted the hood that had covered the face.

Ramon got to his feet.

It was the most beautiful face he had ever seen; but that was not what tore him from the chair. It was that this face, so white against even the snow-white cloth, was exactly like the painted pictures of the Madonna that hung in his bedroom.

Slowly the face lifted and the closed eyes opened and the eyes of the woman looked into the rays of the spotlights, the hot white spotlights filled with smoke and dust and the stink of the room, the brightnesses that stung Ramon's eyes even when he did not look at them. The robed woman, whose hands were crossed upon her bosom, looked directly into the light.

Ramon felt the sickness start to come up. The yellow face of Garcia floated in front of him. Then, as hands pulled him down again, he looked and there was movement on the stage.

A man covered in bandages and in the uniform of the Mexican army. White bandages red with blood over his forehead and over his heart. The man had no legs, or seemed to have none.

"My God, my God, they have made it so real!" the fat woman whispered.

The man lay in a crude field wheelbarrow crusted with tan dirt and the wheelbarrow was pushed slowly—slowly—by another man without bandages but on crutches, and blind.

"It represents war," someone said.

"No: just suffering," someone else said.

The figures moved across the stage like the people of a dream, so slowly. There was only the music of the iron wheel turning.

"Simple: War is bad!"

The figures moved on in the path of the robed Madonna, and then Ramon looked at this face he had been afraid to look at, and he saw the shining tears that coursed down the pale cheeks slowly and into the cloth of the robes.

Never had he seen such pain in the eyes of a human, such pain and pity and kindness and—

Ramon stiffened. He shook his head and felt his heart stop.

It was the girl in the snapshot! The White Madonna, the Mother of Pain who wept now for all the evil and wrong in her children's hearts—*Dolores*.

She works elsewhere . . . She is not what you might think . . . I do this for you only because you are a nice boy, Ramon de Castro. . . .

The curtain had not yet begun to fall. Ramon bit his underlip and turned and pushed the old and young people aside.

"She looks and she is grieved!"

He ran into the night air and stopped and let the sickness run out of him and into the street.

"Ha, Ramon! Too much to drink. Now you will feel better."

The man in the American suit lit a cigarette and blew the smoke away. He looked at Ramon, then in the direction of the theatre. People were coming out. The man smiled.

"You have been to see her?" He laughed. "Well, did I lie to you then? *Is* she of this world? And do you wonder she is called the Flower of Mexico?"

Ramon leaned against the building, waiting for the sourness to leave his throat.

"In all the world they could not find one whose face was perfect enough for the part of the Virgin. Except for Dolores. It was my work: I introduced her to the owner: he took one look, one look only. 'She has come, at last!' I did not tell him where I found her." The man seemed to be talking to himself. "Ironic? Perhaps. But did not the one who modeled Michelangelo's Infant Christ, did he not come back one day to the master and sit for the portrait of Judas Iscariot? That is far more ironic."

The man took out his wallet and held it in his hand.

"I saw you in the crowd, Ramon," he said. "I saw you sitting there. I go every night to watch her, did you know? Then the allegory is over and the theatre is closed and—I remember. Every night I do this!" The man did not look happy: he tapped the wallet and straightened. "Well, but it is over now. Alas, for her beauty they cannot pay her enough to live. These theatres make so little. . . . Would you believe me if I told you something? Before she met me, she passed her blessings to the rich and poor alike and did not charge! I told her, even the Church charges! You have the money?"

Ramon pushed his fist out and dropped its contents into the man's hand.

"She will do you much good, little friend. But be careful: she lifts misery from many hearts, with others she leaves a different kind of misery. It is the worst. Can you understand me?"

The sound of snapping castanets rose from the shadows. The big brown man put his wallet away and turned. Ramon turned.

A woman came toward them, smiling. She wore a white blouse of thin cloth and her bosom pressed against the cloth. Her black hair was lustrous against the pale shoulders. She wore stockings and very high thin black heels that snapped along the sidewalk, louder and louder. Her face was encased in powder: the contrast of red cheeks and scarlet lips glowed even in the darkness.

The man in the American suit frowned at the woman, whose smile was directed at Ramon. He frowned at the movement of her hips, at the sound of her bracelets, at the smell of cheap musk perfume: but without anger; his frown was not easy to read, for it was hidden well.

"Dolores, my dear," the man said, "I would like you to meet Ramon. He has come a great distance—for the first time. If he leaves full of pride, perhaps he will return."

The woman winked and moved her head.

Ramon came close and saw her eyes.

"They make her stare into the lights," the man said. "Otherwise, she cannot cry. The redness will go away."

The woman's eyes were swollen and puffy and the tears still gleamed beneath the heavy blue lids.

Ramon backed away from the man and the woman. The sickness churned in his stomach and he fought for his breath.

"Where are you going, little brother?"

Ramon stumbled on the curb and got up and then walked fast through the dark streets, fast; then he ran.

He ran from the soft white robes that rustled behind him; from the tears and the lights; from the laughter of giant hot bulls dying in their sweat.

He did not stop running for a very long time.

THE INFERNAL BOUILLABAISSE

"I LIKE to think of our stomachs," Mr. Frenchaboy said, in conclusion, "as small but select museums, to which a new treasure should be added at least once a day. We are all curators, gentlemen; and I believe that we ought to be careful to maintain our gastronomic establishments in the best possible taste. No cheap reproductions! No penny-a-lot artifacts of dubious origin! But, instead, only the finest, the *crème de la crème: shared one with all.*" He sent a sharp look in the direction of Mr. Edmund Peskin and adjusted his bifocals. "The exhibits themselves," he said, "may not linger long in our museums. But the memory of them is a lasting pleasure. Thank you."

Mr. Frenchaboy nodded to gloved and spiritless applause and made his way to the dinner table. Once he had seated himself, a hundred napkins flew listlessly into a hundred laps and seven expressionless men in velvet jackets entered the hall bearing trays.

The meal, if it mattered, which it didn't, was a masterpiece. Mr. Frenchaboy had begun preparations five weeks previous and worked himself into a nervous tic over the selection. Why? He could not say. Force of habit, perhaps, a blind refusal to admit that there was no point to the Gourmet's Club any more. Honeycomb Tripe à la Creole had been the first thought. It might have been a good thought, too, except that Peskin had written a monograph on the subject—damn and damn him! Braised Pigeons on Croutons followed, but this was a rather pedestrian choice, and where could one get the right sort of mushrooms these days? Rapidly, he'd hit upon and rejected Roasted Saddle of Young Boar, Steamed Chicken Mère Fillioux, Sweetbreads à la Napolitaine, Cock in Vintage Wine, Chicken in Half Mourning, and Escargots à la Frenchaboy; all unworthy. As time had grown shorter, he'd become desperate—almost as in the old, pre-Peskin days!—wandering the house in a half-daze, muttering recipes aloud: Sauté of Baby Armadillo, Gizzards of Lizards in Sauce Bearnaise, Pie of Bull's Cojones, minced, Brain of Veal à la Mustafa, Sucking Pig with Eels—but when he would hit upon something pleasant, he would remember Peskin's Bouillabaisse, and then he would turn the color of a broiled lobster.

At last, ill with weakness—for in preparing the feast he had neglected to eat—he sent a cable to a friend in South America, requesting immediate delivery of two healthy young llamas. The llamas arrived and were carefully slaughtered by Mr. Frenchaboy himself and put on ice. On the day of the semi-annual meeting of the Gourmet's Club, of which he was president, he placed the animals in a Mexican pot of hard wattle and allowed them to simmer for five hours.

Fricasee of Llama; Truffles de Chambéry; Gazpacho of Malaga: a chef d'oeuvre, indeed, to the most exacting! Mr. Frenchaboy had blended the tastes, the sharp and the mellow, as a fine artist blends colors; and the result was an addling mixture of dark and light, overwhelming as a late Goya, exotic as Gauguin, humbling as Tintoretto. But Mr. Frenchaboy did it all automatically, with less than half a heart. The spirit was not in him. It was not in any of them.

Even as he sat discreetly spooning the last traces of Sorbet d'Champagne, he knew; and the knowledge made him sadder than if he had been ordered onto a lifetime diet of enchiladas and bottled pop.

"Magnificent, Frenchaboy," they said, when the meal was over; and, "Frenchaboy, really, you know, you have outdone yourself!" but he knew what they were thinking.

They were thinking, It was all very excellent, old man, but how can we be genuinely enthusiastic over anything after having tasted Peskin's Bouillabaisse? Don't fret, though: he has reduced all of our best efforts to second rate. One must, after all, go on, mustn't one?

No, Mr. Frenchaboy thought, suddenly: one mustn't. Because one can't. For two years, ever since the blasted meal was first served up, I've been at him. I've made every appeal to the man's sense of good sportsmanship, even going to the length of *asking* him, in so many words, for the recipe. And how he strutted then! Miserable peacock, how he smirked and danced and made it clear to us all that we would get the Bouillabaisse only when he might deign to let us; when and if . . . Disgusting! Mr. Frenchaboy glared at the large man at the end of the table and fumed, quietly. Peskin. A rank amateur, and not a very gifted one at that, before the trip to Africa or wherever the devil it was that he went; then, magically, with that one dish, shooting to the very forefront of the Club, holding them all in thrall, enchanting and tantalizing them and destroying their morale—

Of course, it had occurred instantly to Mr. Frenchaboy that Peskin had resorted to some sort of jiggery-pokery with human flesh; and so—at considerable risk, and with little real hope—he had tried fillets of deceased chauffeur; but it was patently not the answer. No: The secret did not wholly lie in the ingredients, however rare some of them might be: breast of condor, he detected, Alsatian rat tails, et cetera; it lay also in the mixture. And finding this through trial and error was an impossible task. Mr. Frenchaboy knew. He had tried. Simple enough! Peskin had found the *perfect* combination, probably by accident, and had every intention of holding it over their heads indefinitely. And so they would go on being second-raters, for it was true: Nothing could rival (and his mouth began to water as he thought of it) the Bouillabaisse à la Peskin. . . .

"Delicious," a last voice said, insincerely. "My compliments."

The members filed out the door, a disconsolate cortège all but the red-faced fellow, and soon Mr. Frenchaboy was left as alone as a stick of dynamite in an empty warehouse.

He sat down and put his head on his arms.

Dying, he thought: We are dying, thanks to that insufferable ass of a Peskin. Oh—I would do anything to bring back the enthusiasm, the éclat, the downright fizz that were the hallmarks of the club!

He looked up. "Anything?" a small, silent voice inquired.

And Mr. Frenchaboy answered, silently: "Anything."

"Then," inquired the voice, "what are you waiting for?"

Mr. Frenchaboy sighed. "He's too well known. I'd be caught. They'd hang me."

"Not," said the voice, "necessarily."

Mr. Frenchaboy listened. Then he went home and got his wallet and his small .32 revolver and drove to the home of Edmund Peskin.

He knocked.

"Yes?"

"Peskin," Mr. Frenchaboy said, stepping inside, "I will be candid. The Club is not pleased with you."

"Ah?"

"The Club," Mr. Frenchaboy said, more strongly, "is, in fact, not pleased at all."

"I can't imagine what you're talking about."

"Simply this. It has been an unspoken rule with us for twenty years that all recipes are to be shared. Yet you have insisted upon withholding the secret to your Bouillabaisse. Why?"

"That," Edmund Peskin said, "is, I think, my affair. I suggest that you tend to your pots and pans, and I'll tend to mine."

Mr. Frenchaboy turned red. "You refuse to share the secret?"

"Exactly."

"Very well. In that case, I have little choice." Mr. Frenchaboy withdrew a large wallet from his breast pocket. "What is your price?"

The large man looked at the wallet, and drew himself to his full stature. "I am not remotely interested in your crass offer," he said. "There is only one copy of the recipe for Bouillabaisse à la Peskin in existence, and it reposes in my wall safe—where it shall remain. You are wasting your time and mine. Good night."

Peskin turned on his heel and started for the library.

He never reached it.

The report of the revolver sent Mr. Frenchaboy stone deaf for a moment; he trembled; then, ears ringing, he walked over to the still form on the rug, aimed carefully, and pulled the trigger twice more.

The safe proved to be a flimsy affair: relatively little gunpowder was required to blow it apart.

Within, there was a single sheet of paper, folded and tied with a blue ribbon. Mr. Frenchaboy had barely enough time to memorize the contents and burn the paper when the knocking began at the door.

"Come in, gentlemen," he called.

They took him to jail at once, on suspicion of murder. But for all the brutality of his crime, Mr. Frenchaboy was a model prisoner, polite to the guards and uncomplaining of his gray situation. It is true that he fasted, but he made no fuss over it.

Slow days plodded upon slow days. The trial was conducted in a peremptory manner and Mr. Frenchaboy was found guilty as charged and sentenced to hang; yet he bore up with a stolidity and good humor unmatched in the history of the great stone pile. Of him they said: "He's a cool one, all right. Headed for the rope and he still makes jokes. It's eerie!"

Eerie or not, there seemed nothing that could destroy the little man's imperturbability. He whistled loudly, read an astonishing number of cookbooks, and slept like a lamb before the slaughter.

To the members of the Gourmet's Club who visited him, he said only: "Eat well, my friends; the menace is gone!" and "Don't worry. They'll not hang me."

And so it went, for two months, during which time Mr. Frenchaboy ate only fresh bread and drank pure water.

On the third month, third Tuesday night, a group of somber men came into his cell. "Frenchaboy," they said, "it is almost time."

"Quite so," Mr. Frenchaboy said, with a twinkle in his eyes.

"Are you ready?"

"Doesn't that seem a rather pointless question?"

The somber men looked at one another. One of them came forward. "Have you nothing to say?" he asked.

"Nothing," Mr. Frenchaboy said. "And you?"

The man shook his head. "Although it is doubtful that you can have much of an appetite," he intoned, "you are, of course, entitled to your choice of menu for this evening's meal."

Mr. Frenchaboy sat forward. "Indeed?" he said, a sudden glitter to his voice. "Is that quite true? Anything I wish to eat, no matter what?"

"Yes, yes," the man said, as though pained by the discussion. "No matter what."

"Well, then!" Mr. Frenchaboy crossed his legs and leaned backward on his elbows. "For my last meal," he said, "I should like—Bouillabaisse à la Peskin."

There was a moment of silence.

"What was that?"

"Bouillabaisse," Mr. Frenchaboy repeated, "à la Peskin."

"Very well," the man said, and exited.

In a short time he was back.

"The prison chef informs me that there is no such dish," he said.

"The prison chef," Mr. Frenchaboy said, "is mistaken. For verification, I suggest you telephone any member of the Gourmet's Club. They have all had Bouillabaisse à la Peskin at least once."

"In that case," said the man, "perhaps you would care to give me the recipe, which I shall pass along to the chef."

"If only I could!" Mr. Frenchaboy sighed. "I'm afraid it's out of the question, though. I haven't the slightest idea of what goes into it, or in what quantities, you see."

The man paused, opened his mouth, closed it, and went away.

An hour later he returned, looking trapped.

"Mr. Frenchaboy," he said, "it is impossible for us to serve you this Bouillabaisse à la Peskin. The recipe does not exist."

"What a pity," Mr. Frenchaboy said, with deep regret. "I'd so looked forward to it. However, there is a bright side to the picture."

"Eh?"

"I allude to the fact that now the sentence cannot be carried out."

The man blinked. "How is that, sir?"

"Well," Mr. Frenchaboy said, rubbing his thin hands together, "my understanding of the law is—and you have verified it—that a man is entitled to the meal of his choice before he is executed. I have made my request but it has not been granted. Therefore," he smiled, "you can't hang me."

The man looked a trifle panicky for a moment. Then he said, "I'll have to find out about this."

"By all means," Mr. Frenchaboy said. "But I think you'll find that I'm correct."

He listened to the disappearing footsteps, and chuckled.

Unfortunately, they did not find that Mr. Frenchaboy was correct.

They decided to feed him hamburgers and malted milks and hang him anyway.

But when they came to get him just before sunrise the following day, they discovered that the sentence could not be carried out after all. Mr. Frenchaboy was in no condition to be hanged.

He had passed away in the night.

Of acute indigestion.

BLACK COUNTRY

Spoof Collins blew his brains out, all right—right on out through the top of his head. But I don't mean with a gun. I mean with a horn. Every night: slow and easy, eight to one. And that's how he died. Climbing, with that horn, climbing up high. For what? *"Hey, man, Spoof—listen, you picked the tree, now come on down!"* But he couldn't come down, he didn't know how. He just kept climbing, higher and higher. And then he fell. Or jumped. Anyhow, *that's* the way he died.

The bullet didn't kill anything. I'm talking about the one that tore up the top of his mouth. It didn't kill anything that wasn't dead already. Spoof just put in an extra note, that's all.

We planted him out about four miles from town—home is where you drop: residential district, all wood construction. Rain? You know it. Bible type: sky like a month-old bedsheet, wind like a stepped-on cat, cold and dark, those Forty Days, those Forty Nights! But nice and quiet most of the time. Like Spoof: nice and quiet, with a lot underneath that you didn't like to think about.

We planted him and watched and put what was his down into the ground with him. His horn, battered, dented, nicked—right there in his hands, but not just there; I mean in position, so if he wanted to do some more climbing, all right, he could. And his music. We planted that too, because leaving it out would have been like leaving out Spoof's arms or his heart or his guts.

Lux started things off with a chord from his guitar, no particular notes, only a feeling, a sound. A Spoof Collins kind of sound. Jimmy Fritch picked it up with his stick and they talked a while—Lux got a real piano out of that git-box. Then when Jimmy stopped talking and stood there, waiting, Sonny Holmes stepped up and wiped his mouth and took the melody on his shiny new trumpet. It wasn't Spoof, but it came close; and it was still *The Jimjam Man*, the way Spoof wrote it back when he used to write things down. Sonny got off with a high-squealing blast, and no eyes came up—we knew, we remembered. The kid always had it collared. He just never talked about it. And listen to him now! He stood there over Spoof's grave, giving it all back to The Ol' Massuh, giving it back right—*"Broom off, white child, you got four sides!" "I want to learn from you, Mr. Collins. I want to play jazz and you can teach me." "I got things to do, I can't waste no time on a half-hipped young'un." "Please, Mr. Collins." "You got to stop that, you got to stop callin' me 'Mr. Collins,' hear?" "Yes sir, yes sir."*—He put out real sound, like he didn't remember a thing. Like he wasn't playing for that pile of darkmeat in the ground, not at all; but for the great Spoof Collins, for the man Who Knew and the man Who Did, who gave jazz spats and dressed up the blues, who did things with a trumpet that a trumpet couldn't do, and more; for the man who could blow down the walls or make a chicken cry, without half trying—for the mighty Spoof, who'd once walked in music like a boy in river mud, loving it, breathing it, living it.

Then Sonny quit. He wiped his mouth again and stepped back and Mr. "T" took it on his trombone while I beat up the tubs.

Pretty soon we had *The Jimjam Man* rocking the way it used to rock. A little slow, maybe: it needed Bud Meunier on bass and a few trips on the piano. But it moved.

We went through *Take It From Me* and *Night in the Blues* and *Big Gig* and *Only Us Chickens* and *Forty G's*—Sonny's insides came out through the horn on that one, I could tell—and *Slice City Stomp*—you remember: sharp and clean, like sliding down a razor—and *What the Cats Dragged In*—the longs, the shorts, all the great Spoof Collins numbers. We wrapped them up and put them down there with him.

Then it got dark.

And it was time for the last one, the greatest one. . . . Rose-Ann shivered and cleared her throat; the rest of us looked around, for the first time, at all those rows of split-wood grave markers, shining in the rain, and the trees and the coffin, dark, wet. Out by the fence, a couple of farmers stood watching. Just watching.

One—Rose-Ann opens her coat, puts her hands on her hips, wets her lips;

Two—Freddie gets the spit out of his stick, rolls his eyes;
Three—Sonny puts the trumpet to his mouth;
Four—

And we played Spoof's song, his last one, the one he wrote a long way ago, before the music dried out his head, before he turned mean and started climbing: *Black Country*. The song that said just a little of what Spoof wanted to say, and couldn't.

You remember. Spider-slow chords crawling down, soft, easy, and then bottom and silence and, suddenly, the cry of the horn, screaming in one note all the hate and sadness and loneliness, all the want and got-to-have; and then the note dying, quick, and Rose-Ann's voice, a whisper, a groan, a sigh. . . .

> "*Black Country is somewhere, Lord,*
> *That I don't want to go.*
> *Black Country is somewhere*
> *That I never want to go.*
> *Rain-water drippin'*
> *On the bed and on the floor,*
> *Rain-water drippin'*
> *From the ground and through the door . . .*"

We all heard the piano, even though it wasn't there. Fingers moving down those minor chords, those black keys, that black country . . .

> "*Well, in that old Black Country*
> *If you ain't feelin' good,*
> *They let you have an overcoat*
> *That's carved right out of wood.*
> *But way down there*
> *It gets so dark*
> *You never see a friend—*
> *Black Country may not be the Most,*
> *But, Lord! it's sure the End . . .*"

Bitter little laughing words, piling up, now mad, now sad; and then, an ugly blast from the horn and Rose-Ann's voice screaming, crying:

> "*I never want to go there, Lord!*
> *I never want to be,*
> *I never want to lay down*
> *In that Black Country!*"

And quiet, quiet, just the rain, and the wind.

"Let's go, man," Freddie said.

So we turned around and left Spoof there under the ground.

Or, at least, that's what I thought we did.

Sonny took over without saying a word. He didn't have to: just who was about to fuss? He was white, but he didn't play white, not these days; and he learned the hard way—by unlearning. Now he could play gutbucket and he could play blues, stomp and slide, name it, Sonny could play it. Funny as hell to hear, too, because he looked like everything else but a musician. Short and skinny, glasses, nose like a melted candle, head clean as the one-ball, and white? Next to old Hushup, that café sunburn glowed like a flashlight.

"*Man, who skinned you?*"

"*Who dropped you in the flour barrel?*"

But he got closer to Spoof than any of the rest of us did. He knew what to do, and why. Just like a school teacher all the time: "That's good, Lux, that's awful good—now let's play some music." "Get off it, C. T.—what's Lenox Avenue doing in the middle of Lexington?" "Come on, boys, hang on to the sound, hang on to it!" Always using words like "flavor" and "authentic" and "blood," peering over those glasses, pounding his feet right through the floor: STOMP! STOMP! "That's it, we've got it now—oh, listen! It's true, it's clean!" STOMP! STOMP!

Not the easiest to dig him. Nobody broke all the way through.

"How come, boy? What for?" and every time the same answer:

"I want to play jazz."

Like he'd joined the Church and didn't want to argue about it.

Spoof was still Spoof when Sonny started coming around. Not a lot of people with us then, but a few, enough—the longhairs and critics and connoisseurs—and some real ears too—enough to fill a club every night, and who needs more? It was COLLINS AND HIS CREW, tight and neat, never a performance, always a session. Lot of music, lot of fun. And a line-up that some won't forget: Jimmy Fritch on clarinet, Honker Reese on alto-sax, Charles di Lusso on tenor, Spoof on trumpet, Henry Walker on piano, Lux Anderson on banjo and myself—Hushup Paige—on drums. New-mown hay, all right, I know—I remember, I've heard the records we cut—but, the Road was there.

Sonny used to hang around the old Continental Club on State Street in Chicago, every night, listening. Eight o'clock roll 'round, and there he'd be—a little different: younger, skinnier—listening hard, over in a corner all to himself, eyes closed like he was asleep. Once in a while he put in a request—*Darktown Strutter's Ball* was one he liked, and some of Jelly Roll's numbers—but mostly he just sat there, taking it all in. For real.

And it kept up like this for two or three weeks, regular as 2/4.

Now Spoof was mean in those days—don't think he wasn't—but not blood-mean. Even so, the white boy in the corner bugged Ol' Massuh after a while and he got to making dirty cracks with his horn: WAAAAA! *Git your ass out of here.* WAAAAA! *You only* think *you're with it!* WAAAAA! *There's a little white child sittin' in a chair there's a little white child losin' all his hair . . .*

It got to the kid, too, every bit of it. And that made Spoof even madder. But what can you do?

Came Honker's trip to Slice City along about then: our sax-man got a neck all full of the sharpest kind of steel. So we were out one horn. And you could tell: we played a little bit too rough, and the head-arrangements Collins and His Crew grew up to, they needed Honker's grease in the worst way. But we'd been together for five years or more, and a new man just didn't play somehow. We were this one solid thing, like a unit, and somebody had cut off a piece of us and we couldn't grow the piece back so we just tried to get along anyway, bleeding every night, bleeding from that wound.

Then one night it bust. We'd gone through some slow walking

stuff, some tricky stuff and some loud stuff—still covering up—when this kid, this white boy, got up from his chair and ankled over and tapped Spoof on the shoulder. It was break-time and Spoof was brought down about Honker, about how bad we were sounding, sitting there sweating, those pounds of man, black as coaldust soaked in oil—he was the *blackest* man!—and those eyes, beady white and small as agates.

"Excuse me, Mr. Collins, I wonder if I might have a word with you?" He wondered if he might have a word with Mr. Collins!

Spoof swiveled in his chair and clapped a look around the kid. "Hnff?"

"I notice that you don't have a sax man any more."

"You don't mean to tell me?"

"Yes sir. I thought—I mean, I was wondering if—"

"Talk up, boy. I can't hear you."

The kid looked scared. Lord, he looked scared—and he was white to begin with.

"Well sir, I was just wondering if—if you needed a saxophone."

"You know somebody plays sax?"

"Yes sir, I do."

"And who might that be?"

"Me."

"You."

"Yes sir."

Spoof smiled a quick one. Then he shrugged. "Broom off, son," he said. "Broom 'way off."

The kid turned red. He all of a sudden didn't look scared any more. Just mad. Mad as hell. But he didn't say anything. He went on back to his table and then it was end of the ten.

We swung into *Basin Street*, smooth as Charley's tenor could make it, with Lux Anderson talking it out: *Basin Street, man, it is the street, Where the elite, well, they gather 'round, to eat a little* . . . And we fooled around with the slow stuff for a while. Then Spoof lifted his horn and climbed up two-and-a-half and let out his trademark, that short high screech that sounded like something dying that wasn't too happy about it. And we rocked some, Henry taking

it, Jimmy kanoodling the great headwork that only Jimmy knows
how to do, me slamming the skins—and it was nowhere. Without
Honker to keep us all on the ground, we were just making noise.
Good noise, all right, but not music. And Spoof knew it. He broke
his mouth blowing—to prove it.

And we cussed the cat that sliced our man.

Then, right away—nobody could remember when it came in—
suddenly, we had us an alto-sax. Smooth and sure and snaky, that
sound put a knot on each of us and said: Bust loose now, boys, I'll
pull you back down. Like sweet-smelling glue, like oil in a machine,
like—Honker.

We looked around and there was the kid, still sore, blowing like
a madman, and making fine fine music.

Spoof didn't do much. Most of all, he didn't stop the number.
He just let that horn play, listening—and when we slid over all
the rough spots and found us backed up neat as could be, the Ol'
Massuh let out a grin and a nod and a "Keep blowin', young'un!"
and we knew that we were going to be all right.

After it was over, Spoof walked up to the kid. They looked at
each other, sizing it up, taking it in.

Spoof says: "You did good."

And the kid—he was still burned—says: "You mean I did *damn*
good."

And Spoof shakes his head. "No, that ain't what I mean."

And in a second one was laughing while the other one
blushed. Spoof had known all along that the kid was faking, that
he'd just been lucky enough to know our style on *Basin Street*
up-down-and-across.

The Ol' Massuh waited for the kid to turn and start to slink off,
then he said: "Boy, you want to go to work?". . .

Sonny learned so fast it scared you. Spoof never held back; he
turned it all over, everything it had taken us our whole lives to find
out.

And—we had some good years. Charley di Lusso dropped out,
we took on Bud Meunier—the greatest bass man of them all—
and Lux threw away his banjo for an AC-DC git-box and old C. T.
Mr. "T" Green and his trombone joined the Crew. And we kept

growing and getting stronger—no million-copies platter sales or stands at the Paramount—too "special"—but we never ate too far down on the hog, either.

In a few years Sonny Holmes was making that sax stand on its hind legs and jump through hoops that Honker never dreamed about. Spoof let him strictly alone. When he got mad it wasn't ever because Sonny had white skin—Spoof always was too busy to notice things like that—but only because The Ol' Massuh had to get T'd off at each one of us every now and then. He figured it kept us on our toes.

In fact, except right at first, there never was any real blood between Spoof and Sonny until Rose-Ann came along.

Spoof didn't want a vocalist with the band. But the coonshouting days were gone alas, except for Satchmo and Calloway—who had style: none of us had style, man, we just hollered—so when push came to shove, we had to put out the net.

And chickens aplenty came to crow and plenty moved on fast and we were about to give up when a dusky doll of 20-ought stepped up and let loose a hunk of *The Man I Love* and that's all, brothers, end of the search.

Rose-Ann McHugh was a little like Sonny: where she came from, she didn't know a ball of cotton from a piece of popcorn. She'd studied piano for a flock of years with a Pennsylvania longhair, read music whipfast and had been pointed toward the Big Steinway and the O.M.'s, Chopin and Bach and all that jazz. And good—I mean, she could pull some very fancy noise out of those keys. But it wasn't the Road. She'd heard a few records of Muggsy Spanier's, a couple of Jelly Roll's—*New Orleans Bump, Shreveport Stomp*, old *Wolverine Blues*—and she just got took hold of. Like it happens, all the time. She knew.

Spoof hired her after the first song. And we could see things in her eyes for The Ol' Massuh right away, fast. Bad to watch: I mean to say, she was chicken dinner, but what made it ugly was, you could tell she hadn't been in the oven very long.

Anyway, most of us could tell. Sonny, for instance.

But Spoof played tough to begin. He gave her the treatment, all the way. To see if she'd hold up. Because, above everything else, there was the Crew, the Unit, the Group. It was right, it had to stay right.

"*Gal, forget your hands—that's for the cats out front. Leave 'em alone. And pay attention to the music, hear?*"

"*You ain't got a 'voice,' you got an instrument. And you ain't even started to learn how to play on it. Get some sound, bring it on out.*"

"*Stop that throat stuff—you' singin' with the Crew now. From the belly, gal, from the belly. That's where music comes from, hear?*"

And she loved it, like Sonny did. She was with The Ol' Massuh, she knew what he was talking about.

Pretty soon she fit just fine. And when she did, and everybody knew she did, Spoof eased up and waited and watched the old machine click right along, one-two, one-two.

That's when he began to change. Right then, with the Crew growed up and in long pants at last. Like we didn't need him any more to wash our face and comb our hair and switch our behinds for being bad.

Spoof began to change. He beat out time and blew his riffs, but things were different and there wasn't anybody who didn't know that for a fact.

In a hurry, all at once, he wrote down all his great arrangements, quick as he could. One right after the other. And we wondered why—we'd played them a million times.

Then he grabbed up Sonny. "*White Boy, listen. You want to learn how to play trumpet?*"

And the blood started between them. Spoof rode on Sonny's back twenty-four hours, showing him lip, showing him breath. "*This ain't a saxophone, boy, it's a trumpet, a music-horn. Get it right—do it again—that's lousy—do it again—that was nowhere—do it again—do it again!*" All the time.

Sonny worked hard. Anybody else, they would have told The Ol' Massuh where he could put that little old horn. But the kid knew something was being given to him—he didn't know why, nobody did, but for a reason—something that Spoof wouldn't have given anybody else. And he was grateful. So he worked. And he didn't ask any how-comes, either.

Pretty soon he started to handle things right. 'Way down the road from great, but coming along. The sax had given him a hard set of lips and he had plenty of wind; most of all, he had the spirit—the thing that you can beat up your chops about it for two weeks straight and never say what it is, but if it isn't there, buddy-ghee, you may get to be President but you'll never play music.

Lord, Lord, Spoof worked that boy like a two-ton jockey on a ten-ounce horse. *"Do it again—that ain't right—goddamn it, do it again! Now one more time!"*

When Sonny knew enough to sit in with the horn on a few easy ones, Ol' Massuh would tense up and follow the kid with his eyes—I mean it got real crawly. What for? Why was he pushing it like that?

Then it quit. Spoof didn't say anything. He just grunted and quit all of a sudden, like he'd done with us, and Sonny went back on sax and that was that.

Which is when the real blood started.

The Lord says every man has got to love something, some-times, somewhere. First choice is a chick, but there's other choices. Spoof's was a horn. He was married to a piece of brass, just as married as a man can get. Got up with it in the morning, talked with it all day long, loved it at night like no chick I ever heard of got loved. And I don't mean one-two-three: I mean the slow-building kind. He'd kiss it and hold it and watch out for it. Once a cat full of tea tried to put the snatch on Spoof's horn, for laughs: when Spoof caught up with him, that cat gave up laughing for life.

Sonny knew this. It's why he never blew his stack at all the riding. Spoof's teaching him to play trumpet—*the* trumpet—was like as if The Ol' Massuh had said: *"You want to take my wife for a few nights? You do? Then here, let me show you how to do it right. She likes it done right."*

For Rose-Ann, though, it was the worst. Every day she got that look deeper in, and in a while we turned around and, man! *Where* is little Rosie? She was gone. That young half-fried chicken had flew the roost. And in her place was a doll that wasn't dead, a big bunch of curves and skin like a brand-new penny. Overnight, almost. Sonny noticed. Freddie and Lux and even old Mr. "T" noticed. *I* had eyes in my head. But Spoof didn't notice. He was already in love, there wasn't any more room.

Rose-Ann kept snapping the whip, but Ol' Massuh, he wasn't *about* to make the trip. He'd started climbing, then, and he didn't treat her any different than he treated us.

"Get away, gal, broom on off—can't you see I'm busy? Wiggle it elsewhere, hear? Elsewhere. Shoo!"

And she just loved him more for it. Every time he kicked her, she loved him more. Tried to find him and see him and, sometimes, when he'd stop for breath, she'd try to help, because she knew something had crawled inside Spoof, something that was eating from the inside out, that maybe he couldn't get rid of alone.

Finally, one night, at a two-weeker in Dallas, it tumbled.

We'd gone through *Georgia Brown* for the tourists and things were kind of dull, when Spoof started sweating. His eyes began to roll. And he stood up, like a great big animal—like an ape or a bear, big and powerful and mean-looking—and he gave us the two-finger signal.

Sky-High. 'Way before it was due, before either the audience or any of us had got wound up.

Freddie frowned. "You think it's time, Top?"

"Listen," Spoof said, "goddamn it, who says when it's time—you, or me?"

We went into it, cold, but things warmed up pretty fast. The dancers grumbled and moved off the floor and the place filled up with talk.

I took my solo and beat hell out of the skins. Then Spoof swiped at his mouth and let go with a blast and moved it up into that squeal and stopped and started playing. It was all headwork. All new to us.

New to anybody.

I saw Sonny get a look on his face, and we sat still and listened while Spoof made love to that horn.

Now like a scream, now like a laugh—now we're swinging in the trees, now the white men are coming, now we're in the boat and chains are hanging from our ankles and we're rowing, rowing—*Spoof, what is it?*—now we're sawing wood and picking cotton and serving up those cool cool drinks to the Colonel in his chair—*Well, blow, man!*—now we're free, and we're struttin' down

Lenox Avenue and State & Madison and Pirate's Alley, laughing, crying—*Who said free?*—and we want to go back and we don't want to go back—*Play it, Spoof! God, God, tell us all about it! Talk to us!*—and we're sitting in a cellar with a comb wrapped up in paper, with a skin-barrel and a tinklebox—*Don't stop, Spoof! Oh Lord, please don't stop!*—and we're making something, something, what is it? Is it jazz? Why, yes, Lord, it's jazz. Thank you, sir, and thank you, sir, we finally got it, something that is *ours*, something great that belongs to us and to us alone, that we made, and *that's* why it's important, and *that's* what it's all about and—*Spoof! Spoof, you can't stop now*—

But it was over, middle of the trip. And there was Spoof standing there facing us and tears streaming out of those eyes and down over that coaldust face, and his body shaking and shaking. It's the first we ever saw that. It's the first we ever heard him cough, too—like a shotgun going off every two seconds, big raking sounds that tore up from the bottom of his belly and spilled out wet and loud.

The way it tumbled was this. Rose-Ann went over to him and tried to get him to sit down. "Spoof, honey, what's wrong? Come on and sit down. Honey, don't just stand there."

Spoof stopped coughing and jerked his head around. He looked at Rose-Ann for a while and whatever there was in his face, it didn't have a name. The whole room was just as quiet as it could be.

Rose-Ann took his arm. "Come on, honey, Mr. Collins—"

He let out one more cough, then, and drew back his hand—that black-topped, pink-palmed ham of a hand—and laid it, sharp, across the girl's cheek. It sent her staggering. "Git off my back, hear? Damn it, git off! Stay 'way from me!"

She got up crying. Then, you know what she did? She waltzed on back and took his arm and said: "Please."

Spoof was just a lot of crazy-mad on two legs. He shouted out some words and pulled back his hand again. "Can't you never learn? What I got to do, goddamn little—"

Then—Sonny moved. All-the-time quiet and soft and gentle Sonny. He moved quick across the floor and stood in front of Spoof.

"Keep your black hands off her," he said.

Ol' Massuh pushed Rose-Ann aside and planted his legs, his breath rattling fast and loose, like a bull's. And he towered over the kid, Goliath and David, legs far apart on the boards and fingers curled up, bowling balls at the ends of his sleeves.

"You talkin' to me, boy?"

Sonny's face was red, like I hadn't seen it since that first time at the Continental Club, years back. "You've got ears, Collins. Touch her again and I'll kill you."

I don't know exactly what we expected, but I know what we were afraid of. We were afraid Spoof would let go; and if he did . . . well, put another bed in the hospital, men. He stood there, breathing, and Sonny gave it right back—for hours, days and nights, for a month, toe to toe.

Then Spoof relaxed. He pulled back those fat lips, that didn't look like lips any more, they were so tough and leathery, and showed a mouthful of white and gold, and grunted, and turned, and walked away.

We swung into *Twelfth Street Rag* in *such* a hurry!

And it got kicked under the sofa.

But we found out something, then, that nobody even suspected.

Sonny had it for Rose-Ann. He had it bad.

And that ain't good.

Spoof fell to pieces after that. He played day and night, when we were working, when we weren't working. Climbing. Trying to get it said, all of it.

"*Listen, you can't hit Heaven with a slingshot, Daddy-O!*"

"*What you want to do, man—blow Judgment?*"

He never let up. If he ate anything, you tell me when. Sometimes he tied on, straight stuff, quick, medicine type of drinking. But only after he'd been climbing and started to blow flat and ended up in those coughing fits.

And it got worse. Nothing helped, either: foam or booze or tea or even Indoor Sports, and he tried them all. And got worse.

"*Get fixed up, Mr. C, you hear? See a bone-man; you in bad shape . . .*"

"*Get away from me, get on away!*" Hawk! and a big red spot on the handkerchief. "*Broom off! Shoo!*"

And gradually the old horn went sour, ugly and bitter sounding, like Spoof himself. Hoo Lord, the way he rode Sonny then: *"How you like the dark stuff, boy? You like it pretty good? Hey there, don't hold back. Rosie's fine talent—I know. Want me to tell you about it, pave the way, show you how? I taught you everything else, didn't I?"* And Sonny always clamming up, his eyes doing the talking: *"You were a great musician, Collins, and you still are, but that doesn't mean I've got to like you—you won't let me. And you're damn right I'm in love with Rose-Ann! That's the biggest reason why I'm still here—just to be close to her. Otherwise, you wouldn't see me for the dust. But you're too dumb to realize she's in love with you, too dumb and stupid and mean and wrapped up with that lousy horn!"*

What *Sonny* was too dumb to know was, Rose-Ann had cut Spoof out. She was now Public Domain.

Anyway, Spoof got to be the meanest, dirtiest, craziest, low-talkin'est man in the world. And nobody could come in: he had signs out all the time. . . .

The night that he couldn't even get a squeak out of his trumpet and went back to the hotel—alone, always alone—and put the gun in his mouth and pulled the trigger, we found something out.

We found out what it was that had been eating at The Ol' Massuh.

Cancer.

Rose-Ann took it the hardest. She had the dry-weeps for a long time, saying it over and over: "Why didn't he let us know? Why didn't he tell us?"

But, you get over things. Even women do, especially when they've got something to take its place.

We reorganized a little. Sonny cut out the sax—saxes were getting cornball anyway—and took over on trumpet. And we decided against keeping Spoof's name. It was now SONNY HOLMES AND HIS CREW.

And we kept on eating high up. Nobody seemed to miss Spoof—not the cats in front, at least—because Sonny blew as great a horn as anybody could want, smooth and sure, full of excitement and clean as a gnat's behind.

We played across the States and back, and they loved us—thanks to the kid. Called us an "institution" and the disc-jockeys began to pick up our stuff. We were "real," they said—the only authentic jazz left, and who am I to push it? Maybe they were right.

Sonny kept things in low. And then, when he was sure—damn that slow way: it had been a cinch since back when—he started to pay attention to Rose-Ann. She played it cool, the way she knew he wanted it, and let it build up right. Of course, who didn't know she would've married him this minute, now, just say the word? But Sonny was a very conscientious cat indeed.

We did a few stands in France about that time—Listen to them holler!—and a couple in England and Sweden—getting better, too—and after a breather, we cut out across the States again.

It didn't happen fast, but it happened sure. Something was sounding flat all of a sudden like—wrong, in a way:

During an engagement in El Paso we had *What the Cats Dragged In* lined up. You all know *Cats*—the rhythm section still, with the horns yelling for a hundred bars, then that fast and solid beat, that high trip and trumpet solo? Sonny had the ups on a wild riff and was coming on down, when he stopped. Stood still, with the horn to his lips; and we waited.

"Come on, wrap it up—you want a drum now? What's the story, Sonny?"

Then he started to blow. The notes came out the same almost, but not quite the same. They danced out of the horn strop-razor sharp and sliced up high and blasted low and the cats all fell out. "Do it! Go! Go, man! Oooo, I'm out of the boat, don't pull me back! Sing out, man!"

The solo lasted almost seven minutes. When it was time for us to wind it up, we just about forgot.

The crowd went wild. They stomped and screamed and whistled. But they couldn't get Sonny to play any more. He pulled the horn away from his mouth—I mean that's the way it looked, as if he was yanking it away with all his strength—and for a second he looked surprised, like he'd been goosed. Then his lips pulled back into a smile.

It was the *damndest* smile!

Freddie went over to him at the break. "Man, that was the crazi-est. How many tongues you got?"

But Sonny didn't answer him.

Things went along all right for a little. We played a few dances in the cities, some radio stuff, cut a few platters. Easy walking style.

Sonny played Sonny—plenty great enough. And we forget about what happened in El Paso. So what? So he cuts loose once—can't a man do that if he feels the urge? Every jazz man brings that kind of light at least once.

We worked through the sticks and were finally set for a New York opening when Sonny came in and gave us the news.

It was a gasser. Lux got sore. Mr. "T" shook his head.

"Why? How come, Top?"

He had us booked for the corn-belt. The old-time route, exactly, even the old places, back when we were playing razzmatazz and feeling our way.

"You trust me?" Sonny asked. "You trust my judgment?"

"Come off it, Top; you know we do. Just tell us how come. Man, New York's what we been working for—"

"That's just it," Sonny said. "We aren't ready."

That brought us down. How did *we* know—we hadn't even thought about it.

"We need to get back to the real material. When we play in New York, it's not anything anybody's liable to forget in a hurry. And that's why I think we ought to take a refresher course. About five weeks. All right?"

Well, we fussed some and fumed some, but not much, and in the end we agreed to it. Sonny knew his stuff, that's what we figured.

"Then it's settled."

And we lit out.

Played mostly the old stuff dressed up—*Big Gig, Only Us Chickens* and the rest—or head-arrangements with a lot of trumpet. Illinois, Indiana, Kentucky . . .

When we hit Louisiana for a two-nighter at the Tropics, the same thing happened that did back in Texas. Sonny blew wild for eight minutes on a solo that broke the glasses and cracked the ceiling and cleared the dance-floor like a tornado. Nothing off the stem, either—but like it was practice, sort of, or exercise. A solo out of nothing, that didn't even try to hang on to a shred of the melody.

"Man, it's great, but let us know when it's gonna happen, hear!"

About then Sonny turned down the flame on Rose-Ann. He was polite enough and a stranger wouldn't have noticed, but we did, and Rose-Ann did—and it was tough for her to keep it all down under, hidden. All those questions, all those memories and fears.

He stopped going out and took to hanging around his rooms a lot. Once in a while he'd start playing: one time we listened to that horn all night.

Finally—it was still somewhere in Louisiana—when Sonny was reaching with his trumpet so high he didn't get any more sound out of it than a dog-whistle, and the front cats were laughing up a storm, I went over and put it to him flatfooted.

His eyes were big and he looked like he was trying to say something and couldn't. He looked scared.

"Sonny . . . look, boy, what are you after? Tell a friend, man, don't lock it up."

But he didn't answer me. He couldn't.

He was coughing too hard.

Here's the way we doped it: Sonny had worshiped Spoof, like a god or something. Now some of Spoof was rubbing off, and he didn't know it.

Freddie was elected. Freddie talks pretty good most of the time.

"Get off the train, Jack. Ol' Massuh's gone now, dead and buried. Mean, what he was after ain't to be had. Mean, he wanted it all and then some—and all is all, there isn't any more. You play the greatest, Sonny—go on, ask anybody. Just fine. So get off the train. . . ."

And Sonny laughed, and agreed and promised. I mean in words. His eyes played another number, though.

Sometimes he snapped out of it, it looked like, and he was fine then—tired and hungry, but with it. And we'd think, He's okay. Then it would happen all over again—only worse. Every time, worse.

And it got so Sonny even talked like Spoof half the time: "Broom off, man, leave me alone, will you? Can't you see I'm busy, got things to do? Get away!" And walked like Spoof—that slow walk-in-your-sleep shuffle. And did little things—like scratching his belly and leaving his shoes unlaced and rehearsing in his undershirt.

He started to smoke weed in Alabama.

In Tennessee he took the first drink anybody ever saw him take.

And always with that horn—cussing it, yelling at it, getting sore because it wouldn't do what he wanted it to.

We had to leave him alone, finally. "I'll handle it . . . I—understand, I think. . . . Just go away, it'll be all right. . . ."

Nobody could help him. Nobody at all.

Especially not Rose-Ann.

End of the corn-belt route, the way Sonny had it booked, was the Copper Club. We hadn't been back there since the night we planted Spoof—and we didn't feel very good about it.

But a contract isn't anything else.

So we took rooms at the only hotel there ever was in the town. You make a guess which room Sonny took. And we played some cards and bruised our chops and tried to sleep and couldn't. We tossed around in the beds, listening, waiting for the horn to begin. But it didn't. All night long, it didn't.

We found out why, oh yes. . . .

Next day we all walked around just about everywhere except in the direction of the cemetery. Why kick up misery? Why make it any harder?

Sonny stayed in his room until ten before opening, and we began to worry. But he got in under the wire.

The Copper Club was packed. Yokels and farmers and high school stuff, a jazz "connoisseur" here and there—to the beams. Freddie had set up the stands with the music notes all in order, and in a few minutes we had our positions.

Sonny came out wired for sound. He looked—powerful; and that's a hard way for a five-foot four-inch baldheaded white man to look. At any time. Rose-Ann threw me a glance and I threw it back, and collected it from the rest. Something bad. Something real bad. Soon.

Sonny didn't look any which way. He waited for the applause to die down, then he did a quick One-Two-Three-Four and we swung into *The Jimjam Man*, our theme.

I mean to say, that crowd was with us all the way—they smelled something.

Sonny did the thumb-and-little-finger signal and we started *Only Us Chickens*. Bud Meunier did the intro on his bass, then Henry took over on the piano. He played one hand racing the other. The front cats hollered "Go! Go!" and Henry went. His left hand crawled on down over the keys and scrambled and didn't fuzz once or slip once and then walked away, cocky and proud, like a mouse full of cheese from an unsprung trap.

"Hooo-boy! Play, Henry, play!"

Sonny watched and smiled. "Bring it on out," he said, gentle, quiet, pleased. "Keep bringin' it out."

Henry did that counterpoint business that you're not supposed to be able to do unless you have two right arms and four extra fingers, and he got that boiler puffing, and he got it shaking, and he screamed his Henry Walker "WoooooOOOOO!" and he finished. I came in on the tubs and beat them up till I couldn't see for the sweat, hit the cymbal and waited.

Mr. "T," Lux and Jimmy fiddlefaddled like a coop of capons talking about their operation for a while. Rose-Ann chanted: "Only us chickens in the hen-house, Daddy, Only us chickens here, Only us chickens in the hen-house, Daddy, Ooo-bab-a-roo, Ooo-bob-a-roo . . ."

Then it was horn time. Time for the big solo.

Sonny lifted the trumpet—One! Two!—He got it into sight—Three!

We all stopped dead. I mean we stopped.

That wasn't Sonny's horn. This one was dented-in and beat-up and the tip-end was nicked. It didn't shine, not a bit.

Lux leaned over—you could have fit a coffee cup into his mouth. "Jesus God," he said. "Am I seeing right?"

I looked close and said: "Man, I hope not."

But why kid? We'd seen that trumpet a million times.

It was Spoof's.

Rose-Ann was trembling. Just like me, she remembered how we'd buried the horn with Spoof. And she remembered how quiet it had been in Sonny's room last night. . . .

I started to think real hophead thoughts, like—where did Sonny get hold of a shovel that late? and how could he expect a horn to play that's been under the ground for two years? and—

That blast got into our ears like long knives.

Spoof's own trademark!

Sonny looked caught, like he didn't know what to do at first, like he was hypnotized, scared, almighty scared. But as the sound came out, rolling out, sharp and clean and clear—new-trumpet sound—his expression changed. His eyes changed: they danced a little and opened wide.

Then he closed them, and blew that horn. Lord God of the Fishes, how he blew it! How he loved it and caressed it and pushed it up, higher and higher and higher. High C? Bottom of the barrel. He took off, and he walked all over the rules and stamped them flat.

The melody got lost, first off. Everything got lost, then, while that horn flew. It wasn't only jazz; it was the heart of jazz, and the insides, pulled out with the roots and held up for everybody to see; it was blues that told the story of all the lonely cats and all the ugly whores who ever lived, blues that spoke up for the loser lamping sunshine out of iron-gray bars and every hophead hooked and gone, for the bindlestiffs and the city slicers, for the country boys in Georgia shacks and the High Yellow hipsters in Chicago slums and the bootblacks on the corners and the fruits in New Orleans, a blues that spoke for all the lonely, sad and anxious downers who could never speak themselves. . . .

And then, when it had said all this, it stopped and there was a quiet so quiet that Sonny could have shouted:

"It's okay, Spoof. It's all right now. You'll get it said, all of it—I'll help you. God, Spoof, you showed me how, you planned it—I'll do my best!"

And he laid back his head and fastened the horn and pulled in air and blew some more. Not sad, now, not blues—but not anything else you could call by a name. Except . . . jazz. It was jazz.

Hate blew out of that horn, then. Hate and fury and mad and fight, like screams and snarls, like little razors shooting at you, millions of them, cutting, cutting deep. . . .

And Sonny only stopping to wipe his lip and whisper in the silent room full of people: "You're saying it, Spoof! You are!"

God Almighty Himself must have heard that trumpet, then; slapping and hitting and hurting with notes that don't exist and never existed. Man! Life took a real beating! Life got groined and sliced and belly-punched and the horn, it didn't stop until everything had all spilled out, every bit of the hate and mad that's built up in a man's heart.

Rose-Ann walked over to me and dug her nails into my hand as she listened to Sonny. . . .

"Come on now, Spoof! Come on! We can do it! Let's play the rest and play it right. You know it's got to be said, you know it does. Come on, you and me together!"

And the horn took off with a big yellow blast and started to laugh. I mean it laughed! Hooted and hollered and jumped around, dancing, singing, strutting through those notes that never were there. Happy music? Joyful music? It was chicken dinner and an empty stomach; it was big-butted women and big white beds; it was country walking and windy days and fresh-born crying and—Oh, there just doesn't happen to be any happiness that didn't come out of that horn.

Sonny hit the last high note—the Spoof blast—but so high you could just barely hear it.

Then Sonny dropped the horn. It fell onto the floor and bounced and lay still.

And nobody breathed. For a long, long time.

Rose-Ann let go of my hand, at last. She walked across the platform, slowly, and picked up the trumpet and handed it to Sonny.

He knew what she meant.

We all did. It was over now, over and done. . . .

Lux plucked out the intro. Jimmy Fritch picked it up and kept the melody.

Then we all joined in, slow and quiet, quiet as we could. With Sonny—I'm talking about *Sonny*—putting out the kind of sound he'd always wanted to.

And Rose-Ann sang it, clear as a mountain wind—not just from her heart, but from her belly and her guts and every living part of her.

For The Ol' Massuh, just for him. Spoof's own song:

Black Country.

ALSO AVAILABLE FROM VALANCOURT BOOKS